T0343666

BEN LADOUCEUR
I REMEMBER LIGHTS

Book*hug Press
TORONTO 2025

FIRST EDITION
© 2025 by Ben Ladouceur

Library and Archives Canada Cataloguing in Publication

Title: I remember lights / Ben Ladouceur.
Names: Ladouceur, Ben, 1987– author.
Identifiers: Canadiana (print) 20240524357 | Canadiana (ebook) 2024052652x
    ISBN 9781771669351(softcover) | ISBN 9781771669368 (EPUB)
Subjects: LCGFT: Gay fiction. | LCGFT: Novels.
Classification: LCC PS8623.A35577 12 2025 | DDC C813/.6—dc23

The production of this book was made possible through the generous assistance of
the Canada Council for the Arts and the Ontario Arts Council. Book*hug Press
also acknowledges the support of the Government of Canada through the Canada
Book Fund and the Government of Ontario through the Ontario Book Publishing
Tax Credit and the Ontario Book Fund.

Book*hug Press acknowledges that the land on which we operate is the traditional
territory of many nations, including the Mississaugas of the Credit, the
Anishnabeg, the Chippewa, the Haudenosaunee, and the Wendat peoples. We
recognize the enduring presence of many diverse First Nations, Inuit, and Métis
peoples, and are grateful for the opportunity to meet and work on this territory.

This is dedicated to the one I love.

Part One

YOU ARE YOUNG

X X

I headed to the bathhouse nearest to my home, hoping to find some good company. In case I couldn't, I brought a book, though once I took my place in the empty sauna, it sat unopened in my lap. I leaned back and felt sweat develop on my forehead. It was late in the autumn, which in Montreal meant that the air outside was always cold, even on days of bright sun. The heat of the sauna was novel and welcome.

Another man came in a few minutes after I did. He carried a paper cup and took a seat on the lower row, beside my feet. From behind, I looked at his shoulders and the back of his neck, and the little drops of sweat instantly blooming from his skin. Though I couldn't see his face, I knew he was very young, maybe twenty; his body had that easy beauty, unearned and unwitting. After a few seconds, he held the cup up and poured water over his head. In a frisky voice, he went, "Aah." The water darkened and flattened his shaggy blond hair. "Feels great in a hot room," he said without turning around.

I wanted to put my hand in his hair, and my mouth over the little divot between his collarbone and neck, before the water collecting there lost all of its cold. "I'll try that sometime," I said.

He leapt from his seat and out the door, returning moments later with a big grin and his cup once again full of water. "Close your eyes," he said, dumping the water on my head. He asked if I liked the feeling. I said I did, and I offered my name. "I'm John," he replied.

John remained standing as we talked about Scandinavia, where the people often ran out of their saunas, over and over, to roll in the snow. Neither of us had ever travelled as far as that, and he, in fact, had never left the country, not even to visit the States. He was on a work trip from Ottawa. His job, like mine, was too boring to bother explaining.

So much of him was on display—like me, he wore only a towel—but I still wanted more information, about the most remote details of his body. What his face and breathing were like when he was coming, what his cum exactly smelled like, what white thing from nature its colour most closely resembled. How close he was to falling asleep when he closed his eyes while lying still, on a soft surface, in a dark place. He knocked on the book that sat in my lap. *Knock, knock.* Then he read the title out loud.

"*The Death of the Heart.* The pages will warp in here, you know."

"That's all right. I'm not really enjoying it."

He kept his hand in a fist and rested it against the book, putting his weight into it. The paper cup was in that fist, all crumpled up. "What's the story?" he asked.

"An old friend wrote me about it. It was hard to find. He told me the title was *Broken Hearts.* He'd read it in French, but it's an English book, and I guess when they translated it, that's what they called it. *Broken Hearts.* Anyway, eventually I found it."

"The *story,*" he said, laughing. "What happens in the book? That's what I meant."

4

"Oh. Hard to explain."

Before I could say more, the lights turned off, then turned back on, over and over for a few seconds. John made a confused face.

"That's on purpose," I said. "They're telling us that cops have come to a different bathhouse. Not this one. But it's still a good idea to leave now."

I could hear in my own voice a fleck of panic. This warning had happened weeks earlier, at this same bathhouse, and at that time I had felt a strong rush of gratitude that I was not at the wrong one, followed by an equally strong rush of terror, because I could have been. John did not look scared—only annoyed about having to leave. In the humid air between our faces, I could feel the breaking apart of our sexual charge.

"I live nearby," I said hopefully. "Come over for a beer. I have a dog. She loves guests."

I could hear, on the other side of the door, men scurrying out of the other rooms.

"Dachshund," I added. "Short-haired. Very sweet. Name is Dorothy."

"Let's go dancing somewhere first," said John.

In the locker room, I took much longer to dress than John, who slid into a burgundy jumpsuit without donning any underwear, cinched a thick yellow belt around his waist, and was done. "See you outside," he said. He glided through the crowd of men who were quickly getting their clothes on. He was an odd duck in that room. No one else spoke, or made eye contact, or moved without urgency. I had worn to the bathhouse my usual daily outfit—a suit, this one light blue and windowpane-plaid, with a thin tie, also blue. Now I kept the tie off, and the top shirt button undone.

5

When I met him by the entrance, John said Truxx—his favourite dancing spot in Montreal—would be our destination. "With two *x*'s," he said. "Not like the vehicle."

I couldn't remember if I had been there before. Years had passed since I had last kept track of which bars had what vibrations, which were for dancing and which were for chatting, which had a true mix of patrons and which had informal policies to keep out women and straights.

"I have to warn you, I'm not much for dancing," I said.

"I have a cash stipend all weekend," he said, smiling cheekily. "I'll buy our beers and loosen you up. Tax dollars at work."

"So long as you don't pour any over my head."

Once we were moving, the cause of his odd-duck behaviour occurred to me easily. All I had to do was watch him walk beside me, in his stylish tight clothes, with his long, gorgeous hair, in his confident strut. He wasn't dumb, he wasn't newly out, he wasn't pretentious or especially arrogant. He was simply young—*truly* young—and aware that the world was his. His to possess, his to squander. His to make a strong impression on. He was going to share it with me that night—he was going to share all his possessions, the dark streets and the cool air, the promise of dancing and booze, as well as the promise of his own bright and slender body. Knowing that a single layer of fabric concealed it, I was preoccupied by this last promise—I who had moments before enjoyed a complete, prolonged view.

"Do raids happen a lot?" he asked.

"They started last year with the bathhouses. Sometimes the bars. It began just before the Olympics, but it didn't stop when the games ended. One more thing to hate about the games. It was all such a shambles. They were just trying to recapture the glory, if you ask me."

"The glory of Expo 67, you mean."

I nodded.

"My family came for a weekend," he said. "I don't remember a whole lot, but I remember that I felt sad when we left, because we had so much left to see."

"You would have felt that way no matter how long you stayed."

I felt something on my hand—it was his hand, grabbing mine and giving it a big squeeze. The part of his world that was most generous of him to share, and the part I enjoyed most acutely, was the lack of concern about our safety. Cars and pedestrians passed us, apartment windows faced us. But in his opinion, we could still hold hands. We'd head from one queer establishment to another, a bar called Truxx, spelled with two *x*'s, and possibly to more spots after that. Under his direction, we were unassailable. Instead of being safe in some places and genuine in others, we'd be both these things at once, everywhere we went, all night long. I squeezed his hand back, and then we both laughed, because holding hands at length was something couples did. We weren't one of those. We were just two men, spending a moment together, and probably a few more after this one. I didn't let go.

"The Spider," said John, grinning. "I remember the Spider." He was still talking about Expo; the Spider was an amusement ride for children. I pictured a child version of him, holding his mother's or father's hand in the lineup. I had gone to Expo many times, and he and I might have visited at the same time. But back then, I was a young man, about the age that John was now. And he was a little child.

We stood at an intersection, waiting for our light. Our hands remained entwined. "Spider," I said, without much thought. I considered kissing John, but maybe that would be too brave, even for his liking. Brave in terms of our surroundings, brave in terms of our connection. It occurred to me that he might not have been certain whether to sleep with me, and that he might only decide once he had seen me dance.

1

I first arrived in Montreal when I was nineteen years old. Still a child in many ways, though I didn't feel that way then. Some classmates back home in New Brunswick had already become engaged or even married. If they hadn't, two options were left: for the clever, school, and for the others, including myself, the tobacco fields, in which a living could be made no matter a person's brains or physical strength. All he needed was tolerance regarding the stench of the plants, the heat of the sun, the slow but discernible yellowing of his own hands. I had these qualities. By the end of summer, my arms were gold, all the way up to the elbows.

I had a friend named Lucy. When we were still in school, we usually walked home together, and I often ate supper at her parents' house. We would listen to records together too. Dionne Warwick, Dusty Springfield, Barbra Streisand. For a time, we were made fun of. It was said that this was how total squares lost their virginity: they found other squares to do it with. But before long, Lucy and I disappeared into the classroom and the schoolyard, unnoticed. When high school was finished, we kept up the walks. She apprenticed at the drugstore, to eventually become a pharmacist. She took correspondence courses and bought devices and tool sets that looked fun until their purposes, unfailingly bland, were explained.

We were happy together. She kept me from feeling the bottomlessness of my own insides, a feeling that was strongest on alone nights of television watching or radio listening. But we never kissed or even touched, except when she grabbed my hips while teaching me cartwheels one afternoon, or when together we lifted an empty nest back into the branch from which it had fallen in a gust, before our eyes.

When Lucy finished her courses in the fall, her parents encouraged her to travel somewhere. Exams would take place next, and her adult life might then come together quickly. There would be no time for trips. Her parents offered to cover her travel costs. I had just enough money to accompany her, and her parents were okay with this. Lucy and I determined that Montreal was an exciting destination, though it made her parents a little nervous, because whenever the news mentioned Montreal, it was about terrorist attacks by the FLQ, who planted homemade bombs throughout the city in support of some cause that to me seemed convoluted and somewhat boring. I didn't know what the letters FLQ stood for. Lucy's parents asked her to call every day, but there was no doubt that she was going to do that anyway.

I had a feeling that they expected something of me, and I eventually figured out what it was. They expected that Lucy and I would return as an engaged couple. And I thought: *Maybe they're right*. I had a feeling that change was coming. Something consequential, something healthy and painful, some task that I was putting off so thoroughly, I was even putting off identifying it exactly. I just knew it was inevitable, this thing I was going to have to do, now that school was long over and a different kind of ordinary was taking shape. Perhaps the thing was proposing. Perhaps these were the feelings that always preceded that life step, in the chests of all young men. Without thinking too hard about it, I pocketed the ring that my dead mother had received from my father when they became engaged. It was an emerald, and my stepmother had made clear before my father's proposal that she disliked it. As a young boy, I sometimes unearthed it from the kitchen cupboard in which it was kept, to slip onto my thumb, confident that placing it on any other finger would be an affront to my mother's dignity, and to my own masculinity, but that thumbs were different. Thumbs were fine. My half-sisters, when they came along, agreed with their mother, dubious of the emerald's value and ignorant of its beauty. Nobody would notice its absence from the drawer. Shoving the ring in my pocket, I felt that my own absence too would go unnoticed.

At the train station, the specialness of travel occurred to me in earnest. The only people I knew who had travelled at all were rich people, or men who had gone to war before I was born. Lucy and I were two young people travelling for pleasure, and this made us laugh giddily, though Lucy's levity degraded into tears when she said goodbye to her parents. As we took our seats, she called herself ridiculous and cleaned the tears off her face with her fingers. During the ride, she read a book, and I did nothing in particular, except feel the ring pulse in my pocket. After lights out, I slept poorly in my seat, while Lucy got a good night's rest.

"It reminds me of childhood," she said in the morning, as our train pulled into Montreal's gigantic Central Station. "You fall asleep on the couch, or in the car, and when you wake up, you've been taken somewhere else."

This idea didn't resonate with me. Where I fell asleep and where I awoke had always been the same.

I FELT CONFIDENT THAT I WOULD KNOW TO REVEAL THE ring upon the arrival of a sudden shimmering need, sent from the same part of the brain that told my hand to cover my mouth at the sight of something shocking. Proposing would suddenly become my only option; I wouldn't even realize it had happened until it already had. But throughout the vacation, Lucy complained about a garbage-like smell I didn't notice, and about the steep incline of the streets, and about the impossibility of true silence, even with the windows of our hotel room closed. Cars honked, buses braked, voices shouted and obnoxiously laughed. She said a few times that we should have travelled in the other direction and stayed somewhere blue-skied in the Maritimes. The urge to propose never passed through me.

One evening, we found a bar with a martini sign outside and music coming through the door. Two men came out as we tried to enter, one young and lean, one old and gruff, each with a cigarette behind his ear. The four of us almost collided, and the young man rested his hand on my waist as he passed us, as though that was necessary to do to keep himself upright, and to keep me upright too. I found it odd that such different-looking men, from two different generations, were friends.

"*Pas de filles,*" the older man said abruptly, before Lucy and I entered.

"Sorry," I said. "What does that mean?"

He lit his cigarette, then lit the other man's. "No girls," he said, and grinned at me, the smoke leaking out from behind his teeth. As there was no breeze, the smoke stayed near his face, all white and thick.

In solidarity, the young one nodded. He wore a bright blue tank top. It seemed like a strange colour for an undergarment, and so perhaps it wasn't an undergarment. Perhaps this was his outfit, and his arms were on display because he wanted people to regard them. I regarded them. They were lean and covered in fine, peach-fuzz hair, even lighter than the blond hair on his head. I wondered if his arms were cold to the touch, or warm, or if their temperature was nothing notable, like the temperature of the air.

"You can come," the young one said to me. "She cannot."

He re-established eye contact and kept it. I felt a dryness sloshing between my teeth and tongue. I couldn't imagine this being the only moment of its kind in my life. I wanted to look at other men for long stretches of time, often, and to be looked at right back. Men would learn, from my gaze, and its length, all about me, and we could provide each other with company. We could wear clothes with our arms and shoulders on display, because we were beautiful and because we knew this about each other.

This was the frantic sensation I had been awaiting. But instead of compelling my hand toward the ring in my pocket, it compelled my entire body toward the younger man. It was not my first time feeling attracted to a man. However, it was the first time that I understood that such a feeling could be reciprocal.

Something got in the way of my introducing myself to the two men: a powerful, pesky awareness of what I could get away with and what I couldn't. Without speaking, I kept walking. Lucy walked beside me. I felt incredibly proud of myself for resisting the urge to enter the doorway that I could enter and she could not.

"What's wrong with you?" she asked, in a hollow voice that I had never heard her use. "They were horrible to me and you said nothing."

THAT NIGHT WE LAY IN OUR SEPARATE HOTEL BEDS, AS WE had the previous nights. Light from a street lamp came through the crack between the hotel curtains. I tried to sleep and couldn't. I was too busy thinking of Lucy, over in her bed, beneath the covers. I could sense her eyes remaining open, as mine were, and her brain buzzing with the same preoccupations. I needed to prove to her that I wouldn't disappoint her any further. After a while, I gathered the nerve to get out of my bed. I would go and kiss her, and place the ring on her finger.

When I sat on her bed, she jumped in surprise. I had woken her up, she who I assumed had been kept awake, like me, by thoughts of our relationship. I was wrong, she had fallen asleep fine.

"What's happening?" she asked.

"Can't sleep," I said, and she sat up, giving me an empathetic look.

"Homesick?"

"Strange bed."

She rubbed her eyes and suggested we go down to the recreation room, to find a boring book for me to read the first chapter of. There were a few hardcovers on a shelf, but they were all French. Instead we found a jigsaw puzzle. The cover read *The Lady and the Unicorn*. We emptied the box, saying we'd just do the border, but we wound up completing the whole thing, only ever speaking on the topic of the puzzle. "Have you found a dog's face?" "Does this piece not fit, or am I going crazy?" Once, when I started crying, Lucy left and returned with a handkerchief from her luggage. She let me put the last piece in and said it was the most satisfying puzzle she had ever done. Not too easy, not too hard. Then we broke it up and poured the pieces back into the box.

"Everything's fine," Lucy said unprompted, as soon as we entered our beds, while the room around us went pink with morning light.

When I woke up in the afternoon, her bed was made and her luggage gone, and I was truly alone, though I felt less alone than when she had been there. Less alone than I had ever felt before.

X X

Though John and I let go of each other's hands as we walked down the Metro stairs, I still felt him pulling me in specific directions, down the deep stairways and tiled corridors. The night was his gift to me, and I was happy to receive it, and to hear more from him about how much fun we would have at Truxx. As we waited for our train, he listed the songs he hoped they might play. "Dreamer." "Raised on Robbery." "Go Your Own Way." His favourite songs to dance to. But after we boarded our train, he lost his liveliness, becoming nervous and shy instead. I thought for the first time about the direction of the train; we were heading away from downtown.

"Are we heading the right way?" I asked, smirking. He did not smirk back. In a way, I felt honoured to be a person in front of whom this young man was capable of embarrassment. More badly than before, I wanted to go somewhere private and quiet with him. In a more intimate context, would his face retain its performative charm or would he forget the world around him and allow it to go slack and plain? Would he look at my eyes, or at my body, or away, or would he first make sure the room was too dark for reading faces?

"I get mixed up all the time," I said. "Miss my stop, or get off early, or go in the wrong direction."

We got off at the next stop and walked up and down stairways, to the other side.

"You really still get mixed up on the Metro?" he asked. "After ten years?"

"I moved here ten years ago, but I haven't been here that whole time. I've moved around. England. France. Vancouver for a bit. I just always end up back here."

He regained some liveliness. There was nobody else on our side of the platform, nor on the side we had just come from; I took his hand, kissed the knuckles, and gave it back. I wanted for him never to feel embarrassed. The train arrived and we boarded.

"What brought you to England?" he asked a few stops in. We were now headed downtown, toward Mile End.

"A guy," I said.

His mouth shot open, then formed a grin. "A *guy*. Did you fall for him because of the accent? Or does it work the other way around, where they find our voices sexy, like we find theirs?"

"It was all a bit deeper than that," I said.

He nodded knowingly. But, considering his age and disposition, I doubted he actually knew much about love. I might have even known that from the first seconds we'd spent in each other's presence, when he sprung up from his seat to get some water to pour on my head. What kind of person would do that, who had never before gone through a love affair, and the end of one? It was impossible to imagine.

He talked about his own desire to visit England. He had come close to getting a work trip there once, but then it fell through. He had wanted to go ever since he started watching James Bond movies as a young boy. He had seen all of them, many times at the matinee. "Which one is your favourite?" he asked me.

"Hmm. *You Only Live Twice.*"

"For me, it's *On Her Majesty's Secret Service.* That's the one where he gets married at the end."

"He gets married?"

"Yes, but his wife is gunned down right after the wedding. Bond cries when it happens. People booed in the theatre, but I didn't boo. I thought it was a beautiful movie. I kept going over and over, even when the screenings were moved to the worst times, and the theatre was totally empty except me."

At the next stop, a few people got into our car. John scooted closer to me and lowered his voice.

"I want to know if it was hard to go," he said, with sudden intensity.

I knew that we were back on the subject of my moves. "Which time?" I asked.

"Every time. Every new place."

"It was always easy," I said to him. "Once you've done it just once—gone anywhere new, even once—you learn how quick the fun part is. The fun part *is* very fun. But then it's over, and you have a routine all over again. A favourite laundromat and all that. At some point you realize that all your best memories of this new place, well, they're from that exciting beginning. Your life is just a normal one again. So you might as well go somewhere else now."

He went quiet and unexpressive. I knew I had said too much and had revealed a truth that was unwelcome. I knew also why he had been so embarrassed about his mix-up. He wanted to be a worldly person and to use this city's Metro as smoothly as a Montrealer would. He wanted to belong. I put my hand in his hair and kept it there. His body loosened, expression returned to his face. "Still damp?" he asked.

"Still damp," I said. I brought my hand to my nose and inhaled the smell of sweet, cheap shampoo from the dispensers at the bathhouse. We spoke no further as the car took us in the direction of Truxx.

2

I had some experience sleeping outside; back home, if I had spent the evening on an aimless wander and didn't want to get flack for coming home so late and waking up the whole house by opening the front door, I'd sleep on the swinging bench on the front lawn. So I saved some money by cancelling the rest of my hotel stay, and I spent a few nights on park benches, using my backpack as a pillow. Sometimes people walked down a nearby street, and their conversation would wake me up, but this charmed me more than it annoyed me. City dwellers thought of the nighttime as something they had a right to fill, with the sound of themselves—a stark difference from the countryside, where the quiet was so absolute that people didn't interrupt it, even on long accompanied walks down the borders of giant swishing fields. Each time Montrealers disturbed my sleep, I fell back asleep quite easily, thinking soon I'd be one of them, heading toward a home of my own, with someone beside me to talk to, beneath a night sky that was not so venerable as to merit silence, because I would be venerable too: an occupant, a citizen.

During the days, I explored the city. There were French neighbourhoods and English neighbourhoods, places where people lived and places where people mostly worked. Almost everywhere, there was a view of Mount Royal, which every day seemed to develop another patch of uncooperative yellow and orange trees among the green ones. It was getting later in the autumn, and colder every day.

One afternoon, in a neighbourhood full of giant trees and tall, old-looking houses fitted close together, I watched a woman on a café patio pick up her purse and abandon a muffin, with only one bite taken from it. I went and snatched it. Eating as I walked, I eventually came to a lookout in a small, wooded area and scored a clear view of the entire downtown, including the construction project in the middle of the river. I knew so little about Expo—just that the city had recently made two islands from scratch, and now they were constructing a bunch of buildings called pavilions, one for every country on the planet, to celebrate Canada's hundredth anniversary. People on the radio said it would provide a *vision of the future*, and tourists would be coming from all over the country, and all over the world, to visit it.

As I studied the work-in-progress from my lookout, it became clear how unusual the buildings would look when complete. They sported impractical shapes and ghastly bright colours. The most easily distinguished building was a delicate unfinished dome, hollow and half-open, like a palm waiting for something to be placed in it. I thought of how, if I stayed in Montreal and looked at the island every day, the view would keep changing. And then, at some point, the work would finish, and nothing there would make anyone think particularly of open palms or incompletion. A new component to the skyline would simply exist. I thought also of how the site was best at embodying a vision of the future *right now*, while unfinished. In its state of incompletion, it belonged to the future, so firmly that it gave me the desire to go to the future myself and see the final product with my own eyes. To help the site succeed at its *vision of the future* mission, I figured, the builders would do best to stop there and keep the island's onlookers in that yearning, dissatisfied state. The future would feel real, and the unfinished buildings would be responsible for that feeling.

But the builders wouldn't stop. They'd finish their efforts and give the site to the present. It was their job, even their passion. Sometime after completion, and after the celebrations, the buildings would no longer seem new, and the brightest elements of their facades would fade because of constant sunlight, at which point they would belong to the past. Then, later still, the distant past.

I felt a sudden surge of sadness and nausea, intertwined. Hoping I only needed to get out of the sun, I headed into the shade of the woods. But even in the cooler air, my jaw got that sloshing pre-vomit sensation, and I dropped to my knees to barf muffin into the dirt. As soon as I got it out, I felt all better and knew I would stay in Montreal for a long time, at least long enough to see Expo for myself. I felt like the construction site. I was a project still ongoing; I didn't exist right now, but soon I would.

IN THE DARK THE NEXT MORNING, I STOOD ON A STREET corner in Little Portugal, the pickup spot for the only job listed in the newspaper that required neither French nor previous experience of any kind. The van pulled up; the passenger door was thrown open. The driver was a man my father's age. His thick French accent made each of his questions sound flat and statement-like.

"*Étudiant*," he began.

"What?"

"Student. Are you a student."

"No," I replied, to this question and the questions that followed: "Married. Girlfriend. Fisher. Hunter. Music." The last one he asked with the most disdain: "Causes."

I didn't understand and said so.

"Stop the Vietnam, women are working, *libération* for Quebec. *Causes.*"

"Oh. No, none."

There were no more questions. He threw a big grey jumpsuit into my arms and told me his name, Michel. We drove from door to door throughout the fancy neighbourhood I had discovered the previous day, which was called Westmount, as the sun arrived and turned the city purple, then pink, then unremarkably bright with proper morning light. It was diaper delivery. My job was to pick up bags full of soiled cloth diapers from the vestibules of houses and replace them with bags of clean ones. In the driver's seat, Michel chain-smoked and spoke occasionally about how difficult it was to hire help.

"Nobody likes the hours," he said. "Young man, it is good for me that you are...unattached. And for you—this is good." He had had to search hard for the word *unattached*, but once he found it, he used it over and over all morning. Once, he asked me to run into a depanneur to buy him cigarettes, and I bought a pack for myself as well, my first. At the end of the six-hour shift, he paid me in cash and said to wait at the same corner the next day.

I WALKED UP SAINT URBAIN STREET THAT AFTERNOON, UNTIL Mount Royal was beside me instead of ahead. Eventually I took a side street, and in the door window of a small row house, I noticed a sign for a room for rent. I rang the bell. A short old woman welcomed me in and offered me a seat at her kitchen table. She placed a glass bottle of Coke in front of me. I saw she was in the middle of cutting a raw chicken into pieces, and her apron was covered in blood and sticky chicken pulp. Like Michel, she had a thick accent, but Portuguese, not French. Her name was Maria.

As did Michel, she asked me several questions. She liked that I was English-speaking, so that I could help her to improve her own English. She wanted to be able to talk to her six-year-old grandson, a boy named Tomas, who knew no Portuguese. I would sleep on a couch in the TV room, which was separated from her bedroom by a beaded curtain.

"Sounds fine," I said.

"Good, good," she replied, getting up to put my empty bottle in the sink, then going further, to remove the *For Rent* sign from the window of the door. I felt sudden relief: I had a place to live.

My pay for the day only covered half of first and last weeks' rent. "I'll give you the rest tomorrow," I said.

The television was blaring a soap opera while she showed me around the apartment. "Red is *cold*," she said, indicating the two knobs of the kitchen faucet. "Blue is *hot*. I know: wrong. Now you know." During her tour, when someone on the television yelled or a loud music cue sounded, she would halt and watch to see what happened. She asked me to explain words she didn't understand. It wasn't until the end of the tour that I noticed a little boy lying on the couch, fast asleep under two thick blankets, despite the blaring television.

"His mother works the day," said Maria. "In night, he goes home, and it is you who is under the blanket."

I HAD A JOB, I HAD A BED. I HAD A HEADACHE FROM INTERpreting so much imperfect English. I had a pack of cigarettes in my back pocket, and a book of matches too. But I didn't have a strong sense that my new life had begun yet. While Maria sat on her couch—my bed—watching more soap operas, with her grandson's head in her lap, I went for a walk. The word *unattached* was caught in my head like a song. I lit a cigarette and headed in no particular direction. My lack of a destination gave me a feeling of celebrity, as though strangers on patios and in windows took notice of me and wondered or even discussed what my plans for the day might entail.

I hoped to come across the martini sign I had found before, and to enter the bar this time, and meet some men there. But I couldn't find it, even though I searched into the evening. I feared that the world of men who admired each other was too hidden away for me to find it again. Perhaps my chance had come and gone. I took a drag off my cigarette, watching for the bright unfocused flare of orange in front of my nose. I could hear, beyond the traffic sounds, the rush of water. I had led myself downhill, close to the river. I entered a thick patch of bushes, to follow the sound of the water to its source; I decided that the greenery, and for that matter the night itself, was something I could enter from any angle. The city featured built paths through certain places, but a man only had to understand that other paths existed too, unsanctioned and invisible, and shining with promise, and patient for feet.

I stepped into the dark, and onto many branches that cracked beneath my shoes. Through the trees I could see a source of light

I hadn't noticed before. It was the construction site, over at the man-made islands. Though I couldn't hear their work, there must have been men there, or else the floodlights wouldn't be on. The water, more audible now, brought to mind that I had to pee, so I opened my fly and did so, facing the distant bright light, then turned to head back. I saw a man entering the same way I had come. The whites of his eyes caught some of the light, and his hand went over, or possibly down, the front of his pants. As I headed toward him, he offered enough leeway for me to get back on the path, but kept his body open toward mine. It struck me that I wasn't in his way. Coming close to me had been his whole idea.

I had two impulses at once. The first was to move along and politely say, "Excuse me," an expression I was certain he would repeat back to me, so we could both pass this off as an ordinary encounter. The second impulse—to place my hand on his waist, just as the man outside the martini bar had placed his hand on mine—was the impulse I chose, because I felt that the world was mine, and the man with white light in his eyes was part of the world.

His hand lifted off his crotch and onto mine. *"Tabernak,"* he said, more to himself than to me, and I moved my own hand onto his penis, which like mine had grown hard. As I began to introduce myself, he spoke again—*"Pas de noms."* He kissed me passionately. We both went down to the ground, and he climbed over my body. Beneath me, leaves and twigs and slabs of bark crunched and fell apart, and over me he took giant desperate breaths. Past our heads, the rush of the water kept a frantic pace. We both had lace-up shoes, and our pants and underwear wrapped at our ankles in unmanageable clumps, preventing us from opening our legs. Neither man wanted to turn his body away from the other; impatient with the logistics, we started jerking each other off. Within moments, his cum shot across my T-shirt, and then mine did as well. He kissed me on the eye, mumbled something in French, and was gone. I lay there alone, shocked and ecstatic, laughing and panting in damp dirt. The world was mine, and I was its. I fitted into the earth perfectly, like a stone yielding to the suck of the mud it has landed in.

X X

Truxx was dark and crowded and loud with music, but there was no apparent dance floor. Just men at the bar and at tables, drinking in clusters and pairs.

"I swear this was a dance hall," John said.

"Were you thinking of Cabaret PJ's? Or that place, Les Ponts?" I listed other bars I could remember, uncertain if each was even still around.

John shook his head and gave a phony smile, embarrassed all over again. He said he'd find us a table. I ordered the beers. He had promised to pay on our walk from the bathhouse, but I didn't mind. I was eager to get him home, or to go to his hotel, but I wasn't against the idea of a few beers first.

I found him at the other end of the bar, thanks to the bright yellow of his belt. On the tiny table he had found for us, there was barely room for our two glasses and the book I was still carrying. Though he was hard to see, I could tell his spirits were down. He had been given another reminder that he didn't know the city as well as he thought. And he had wanted to dance.

As though to cut the silence that formed between us, he sang along to the music that was playing—"You make me feel like dancing!" His falsetto cracked charmingly on the last word. It surprised me, and the men around us, who turned to see the singing man. Then they registered him as harmless and rustled back into their French conversations.

Laughing, I said, "You are *so* young."

"You know, I'm sick of hearing that," he said. "My boss, my dad, my sister. *You're young, you're young.* Sure I am. But I'm smart too. Smart about the world."

I wanted to tell him that I was sorry, and hadn't meant it the way he thought I had. But in truth, I had meant it that way exactly, so I couldn't think of anything to say.

"How many times did you go to *Star Wars*?" he asked.

"One."

"Last week was my twenty-second time," he said. "There was a little boy there, sitting in front of me. I heard the mother tell another woman that it was his very first time at the movies. His first movie—*Star Wars!* Can you imagine?"

I was almost done my beer, and his was still totally full. I picked it up and handed it to him, and he took it from me automatically and drank a big gulp.

"That kid is going to think that every movie is as amazing as that. I mean, it isn't even a *movie*—I really think you need a whole new word for it. But for that kid, that's what a movie is. I love that that's what he thinks. I guess it's…the opposite of smart."

"Naive."

"Sure. Naive. But that's the feeling that young people have. And when *I* feel that way about movies, about the world, or anything—when I feel like it's *amazing*, like it should always be *amazing*—that's when I feel the smartest." He took more gulps and finished the glass. "My turn to buy."

Watching John head toward the bar with our empty glasses in his hands, I tried to remember a single thing about *Star Wars*. I never really watched movies at the theatre; at the Pigalle Theatre, I typically bought tickets for the late and unpopular shows, not to watch, but to cruise. The night I went to *Star Wars*, I found someone almost as soon as the movie began—vaguely I could recall gigantic yellow words flying across a night sky—and after we had made each other cum, I left.

John returned from the bar.

"The sauna might've messed with my head," he said, placing down fresh glasses. "First my mix-up with the Metro. And now I'm just talking and talking."

"Not at all, John," I said. "Look: you're actually a very smart man. I can tell." Hearing myself, I wondered if I meant it. I certainly found him beautiful. Compelling as well. I liked to hear his thoughts and to know that I was his only addressee. But maybe I was only telling him what I knew he wanted to hear.

He leaned across the table and surprised me by kissing me, first on the cheek in a cautious peck, then on the mouth for much longer. It gave me another dose of that feeling he had previously provided. We were unassailable, everything was ours.

The music moved on to a tune I knew very well. "Words of Love." I hadn't heard the song in years, perhaps not since the death of Mama Cass, which somehow changed the way it sounded. Before, whenever I heard her sing, I'd thought that hers was surely the best singing voice in the world. Now, I just thought of her lying dead in the bed of a friend's apartment, on a night that should have been like any other in her life.

Pulling away, I said, "This song is divine. Let's dance like you wanted."

I shoved my hand down my pants to adjust my erection, not especially discreetly. John laughed and did the same, moving his hand over his jumpsuit. Though it wasn't exactly a slow song, we danced slow, and close. I sang along in a whisper, about worn-out phrases and longing gazes. If others looked our way, I didn't notice. I only wanted to give John something he really wanted, in return for all he had given to me.

Though my eyes were closed, I noticed sudden bright light. The main lights had turned back on. Then the music ended abruptly, and so did all the conversations around us. I looked beyond John and saw cops, all with bulletproof jackets on their chests and guns on their hips. Some carried machine guns. I thought that an error had been made. I turned to John with a smirk, finding this somewhat funny. There was no reason for cops to be there. John smirked back.

Some men sprang from their seats and rushed for the exit, and I found that funny too. All that had to happen was for someone to explain to the police officers that this was just a bar.

The officers began blocking the ways of men who were trying to leave; that was when it became clear that they knew where they were and what they were doing. I was already aware of the raids taking place in Montreal, but I hadn't thought that they involved guns, or such large numbers of cops, or that they could happen as quickly as a light switch being flicked on.

The men being blocked spoke to the officers in English and French.

"Que faites vous, câlisse?"

"Who do you think you are? Let me leave."

"C'est quoi ton problème?"

Then more officers walked through the door, all armed, and the men trying to exit slowed. An empty space opened up around the officers.

John and I were still and silent, the smirks gone from our faces. I could tell that he understood perfectly—as I did too—that we were both connected now, in a bad way instead of a good way. This night would never fade into the greater context of our vigorous lives. It would stick out forever, a horrible critical juncture.

The yelling men were the first to be pressed against the walls and to have their wallets taken. Then the officers waved us over, man by man. It was my turn to go before it was John's. I moved obediently, because I didn't want to die. An officer led me to the wall and told me to place my hands above my head and against the bricks. I did this without protest. He kept one hand on his gun. My fear—my desire not to die—moved like ice through my brain, and through all my body's veins.

The cop reached into my blazer pocket and took my wallet. "Stay," he shouted at me, in a voice that I associated with commands given to dogs. Indeed I couldn't believe I was both his addressee and a human. I was more confident about the first of those two conditions. My life was his to control, if I had one at all.

3

Quickly each day took on the same consistency: morning diaper runs, afternoon soap operas, evening walks to spy on the progress of the islands, and, in the nights, men—twigs snapping beneath the small of my back, street lights shining in my face from the uncovered windows of bedrooms I would never again occupy. Sometimes I met them in the woods near the water, or the woods of Mount Royal, and sometimes in one of the gay bars I had gotten wise to, including a place called the Peel Pub.

The bartender there, an American named Davey, knew how to make every cocktail I could name. He could even make gimlets, a drink I'd discovered while watching *As the World Turns* with my landlady, Maria. On that show, a woman in long gloves nursed a gimlet alone at a bar, preoccupied by some point of tension in her fascinating life. To me, nothing looked as cosmopolitan as someone leaning against a bar all alone and sipping a cloudy drink called a gimlet from a tulip-shaped glass. Davey played Motown records: "Stop! In the Name of Love," "She Blew a Good Thing," "You Keep Me Hangin' On." This too, I felt, was cosmopolitan.

One night, I noticed a man looking me up and down from his seat at the bar. He wore a big gold watch and a sharp brown suit. Most men at the Peel Pub wore paisley, which I wore that night, or somehow otherwise went in for the beatnik look, so he stood out. I thought for some reason that I recognized him. I took a seat beside him and asked Davey for a gimlet. The man said in a French accent, "Make two of them."

"Have I seen you here before?" I asked.

"No," he said. He didn't add "of course not," but he could have, the way he said the *no* so emphatically. I suspected that he had no plans of making any friends. He wanted someone to take home, efficiently. I wondered if I recognized him from a hookup in the woods—if he had, in fact, been the first man, the one who had shared with me the practice of not providing names.

"Can you tell me what it means when a man says *tabernak*?" I asked him.

He laughed at my question and took one sip of the drink, the sourness of which was a clear shock. "It is like a swear word. Like *fuck, cocksucker, shit*. But it seems an innocent word. The what-you-say—the *dirtiness*—is because it is a word of God. In another sentence, this word is not dirty. But all alone, it is worse than *fuck*. *Câlice* is another you have maybe heard."

"*Câlice*," I said.

He downed the rest of his drink in one gulp and motioned for more. I downed mine too.

"You—you are very new to Quebec, if you do not know this," he said. "When did you hear a man say *tabernak*?"

Davey brought two additional gimlets, and this time we clinked them in *cheers*.

"It was by the water," I said. "I didn't see his face well. The light was very dim."

"Moonlight."

"No. From the construction site, over on the islands."

He laughed at this, and as we drank our second drinks, he explained that he knew men who were involved in the Expo construction project. It didn't surprise him that they had to use floodlights and work throughout the night. He explained that the entire operation was held together with tickertape. The buildings were shoddy, the job was rushed. I listened with my hand on my cheek, shaking my head indulgently. I liked the notion that this enormous event was a failure in the making. It was an exciting secret to be in on. I told the man my name. He shared his, Honoré.

"Will You Still Love Me Tomorrow" was playing. The first few times I'd heard this song, I thought it was simple and happy. Then once, when the bar was quiet, I paid attention to the words and understood that I was wrong. When Honoré wasn't speaking, his breath was lined faintly with the timbre of his voice: *"Nnnn, nnnn."* It made me want to hear his breath, and only his breath, with no music or din in its way, in a room that was warm and safe and ours. Drunk on gin, I felt bold and placed my hand on his, which rested on the stem of his third gimlet. He flinched, then laughed. *"Câlice,"* he said, laughing more, and I laughed too. I still didn't know if he was the man from before, nor did I care if I ever found out.

"We can't go where I live," I said.

"You have a family."

"No. But the room where I sleep has no door."

He laughed. Then, seeing that I was not joking, he flared his eyebrows. "Me, I am in Westmount," he said.

"I know Westmount," I said. "I thought Westmount was where English speakers live."

"Mais non, mon ami," he said cheekily. Hearing him speak French was very satisfying, as though his voice had been poured smoothly into its proper container. He went on, "It is not the English live in Westmount. It is the *rich* live in Westmount. Really, it is not too far—we can take a cab."

This was fine by me. He was footing the bill. Plus, I had nerves to numb. This man lived in a well-off neighbourhood, wore a nice suit, and evidently couldn't even imagine that the world had people who slept in doorless half-rooms, on musty couches, with their landladies snoring on the other side of a beaded curtain. I felt that I measured up poorly and that it was only a matter of time before he caught on. So we both kept drinking, until our cocktails pushed the night away from us, into a filthy fog, until it was something shared so intimately, not even our future selves had access to the whole thing. Later I would recall only faint traces. A cab ride. Getting escorted aggressively into the elevator and down his hall. Becoming aggressive myself. When we got through his door, he told me I looked like James Dean. I tried to reply but I was too drunk to form words; instead, I smiled big. I thought: *I'm disgusting, I can't even speak. How is this man finding me attractive enough to continue to kiss me?* But he did continue. Next we lay somewhere. Next his shirt was unbuttoned and my shirt was thrown onto the floor, its arms open. Next we formed a fort out of the bedclothes around us without meaning to. He kissed the crease of my thigh and made me flinch, all ticklish. We babbled like babies, trying our best to form language, and failing, and laughing at the failing, and laughing from the tickling. At some point I managed the word *please*, and it was like I reminded him of that word. He repeated it back, over and over. *Please, please.* It was now the only word we knew. We came into each other's begging, laughing mouths.

I WOKE UP IN THE DARK BENEATH LUSH, WARM BEDCLOTHES, wearing just my briefs, beside Honoré, who wore only his gold watch. He remained asleep. Gently, I held his wrist up to read the time. It wasn't too late to check in with Michel about a shift. I slipped out of the bed to find a telephone.

The main room of the apartment was large but very spare—just a sofa facing a television, a bookshelf that was mostly empty, a dining table with two chairs. I found the phone in the kitchen and confirmed with Michel that he could use my help that morning.

"I can meet you at the nunnery," I said, and was surprised to feel a hand on my back. Honoré, still nude, moved his hand down my stomach and into my underwear. He pressed his mouth against my neck in giant, sloppy kisses, close to the receiver.

"Bring a matchbook please," said Michel. "Mine is low."

"Little one," whispered Honoré groggily, close to both my ear and the receiver, a stale lime juice odour on his breath.

"Will do, see you soon," I said to Michel quickly, and hung up the phone, laughing out of irritation and excitement. "That was work. I should go."

"It's Sunday," said Honoré. "Day of rest. Skip it. Stay with me."

At this I laughed—I had worked through all kinds of weather, and once through a bad head cold. Skipping work based on the day of the week was a ludicrous thought. Ignoring my laughter, Honoré kept kissing my neck and the back of my head. I decided

I had a bit of time before I had to go. I was already in West-mount, I could walk to the pickup spot. We staggered to the bedroom again.

My sobriety made everything clearer. I noticed that Honoré was long-limbed and a few years older than me, perhaps in his mid-twenties. I noticed his assertiveness as well. He might not have had experience going to gay bars, but he knew what he wanted in bed too precisely to be new to sex with men. When I began to take off my underwear, he told me not to, fishing my penis out of the leg opening with his hand; when he got on his back and pulled his knees up to his chest, he cupped his palm and held it near my face.

"You spit," he whispered. "I want it to be your spit."

I spat, he wiped himself, I offered fingers first and he declined. As I entered him, he said thank you, and kept saying it, manic and earnest: "Thank you, thank you."

I had already lost track of how many men I had been with. Following my first encounter near the water, I had gone about things greedily. I also felt a strong need to take codes of conduct to heart, until the counterintuitive rules of homosexual life seemed familiar and uninteresting. For instance, I had put together that, when two men woke up together, they weren't supposed to like each other anymore. They were supposed to feel and look and act embarrassed by the sight of each other, and equally embarrassed about being seen. Ideally they didn't even wake up together; ideally they were apart before sleep. Honoré hadn't felt that way that morning, and he had even expressed hope I would stay. Now we were sharing our bodies for the second time, and in the arriving daylight, he studied mine closely, regarding with astonishment my nipples, the paltry hair around them, and the middle of my chest, where the ribs sank most. Maybe, like me, he cared little for the protocol of lives like ours—maybe his freedom, and his gratitude, were grounded in love, or an openness toward it.

MICHEL WAS WAITING IN HIS CAR WHEN I ARRIVED AT THE nunnery. He had a cigarette in his mouth, unlit. "Where's your jumpsuit?"

"Forgot. There's a spare in the back, right? And I did remember these," I said, taking out the matchbook and lighting his cigarette for him.

Halfway through our shift, we passed the apartment building I had come from. I wanted badly to get out of the car and go join Honoré's world again, warm and cozy and spare. He had given me a key and told me to return whenever my workday was done, though he hadn't asked when that would be.

I helped myself to a cigarette from Michel's pack. "Does it ever bother you that we work on Sundays?" I asked him.

"No," he said, then took a long drag and exhaled it slowly. "The wife minds. Right now, she is leaving church with her mother, I think. I get it from them both, in fact. Why I have to work the Sundays, why-why-why."

"What do you tell them?"

"Nobody cares about Sunday for *these* jobs," he said. "Dirty jobs. People want dirty jobs done every day."

"Not even God cares?" I asked.

We came to a red light, and Michel looked right at me. "I thought you were a good one," he said. "Don't get wise now. Too many your age get wise."

"Sorry."

"*Sacrement.* I pray every night. And when I do this, you know, I pray for you."

"I didn't mean to upset you."

The light turned green. He threw his finished cigarette out his window, then grabbed mine from my hand and threw it too, though half was left. "You take but you do not ask," he said. "Young man, you don't know me, I don't know you. We like this that way."

He gave me a long and meaningful look; he knew that I was gay. He had heard Honoré's voice on the phone, calling me *little one*—or he hadn't but had somehow put it together.

We had already collected lots of diapers, and I could suddenly smell the putrid greenness of baby shit in the hatch behind us. I had rushed to the nunnery without washing, and my penis remained tinged with my own dried spit, and possibly with some of Honoré's shit. I had dressed in the dark. I wondered if my crotch gave off a smell that Michel could differentiate from the cargo, and strangely I hoped that it did.

"I don't want you to pray for me," I said to him. "I'm doing fine."

He stopped the car again and gave me another look, this one of sincere disgust. Not even at the sight of a leaking soiled bag had I seen him make such a face. Then he looked beyond me and nodded briefly. We were at another customer's front door, and I had bags to swap. When I came back to the car, he didn't look at me at all. I lit myself another cigarette, and this time he didn't stop me. I had a feeling that, at the end of this shift, he might fire me. It turned out to be the correct feeling.

DROPPED OFF IN LITTLE PORTUGAL, I HEADED TO MY ROOM-rent. Tomas once again lay on the couch that I used as a bed.

After I washed and changed, he slithered into a sitting position to make room for me. *Thunderbirds* played on the television.

"Where's your *vo-vo*?" I asked.

"She went to the store," he said, without looking away from the screen. "You have to stay here with me because I'm just a boy."

"Will do," I said. I leafed through the newspapers on the coffee table and found the job listings. The only job that looked remotely feasible was at a clothes factory in Hochelaga. When the show cut to commercials, Tomas shook me with his feet.

"Did you drive in your truck today?"

"All day long, chief."

Tomas made an amazed face. He loved construction sites and big vehicles; because I spent my workday in a truck with a specially designed back compartment, I was as impressive as an astronaut. I didn't tell him I had just lost the job.

Maria came home shortly, and at the sight of me she said accusingly, "Mouse *co-co* in the kitchen. Yesterday night. The traps, I set myself."

Setting mousetraps fell under my expected duties, along with taking out the garbage and calling repair people.

"I'll take care of the body once it's caught," I said.

"Already done!" she replied. "Caught just by the snout. *Squee-squee-squee*. Needing to strangle in a bucket of water. You think I had fun doing this?"

I would have told her that animals don't get *strangled* in water, they *drown*—but she was too hotheaded to be receptive to that kind of correction. She didn't mind my coming home late, but she got upset if I wasn't there in the morning when she woke; though she didn't say so, she worried about me.

"And now you read my papers," she said, flicking the paper in my lap. "This is not free."

"I'm only looking for a better job," I told her. "I might see about this one." I pointed out the factory listing.

"No, no, no," she said, reading it over. "Do not work in a factory: *ka-boom*."

"Right," I replied, though in truth I paid almost no attention to the news stories about the FLQ and the bombs they planted, and felt barely sure that this was even what she was referring to. Maria changed the television channel to her soap opera and sat on the couch on the other side of Tomas. I wanted nothing but to return to Honoré. I packed a few of my clothes from the shelf, and a comic book that Tomas wanted me to borrow. On the cover, above the heads of the costumed men fighting for their lives, the sky gave off a shade of blue I had never seen the real sky achieve, beamingly bright and almost green. When I said "Goodbye," Tomas said it back, but Maria just kept watching television and said nothing.

ARRIVING AT HONORÉ'S APARTMENT, I USED THE KEY HE had given me on the street entrance door. But inside, his unit was locked, and I didn't have the key for that door. There was no answer when I knocked. I went back outside and was relieved to see him at the end of the street, heading my way with a lit cigarette in one hand and a freshly opened pack in the other.

Once we were in his apartment, he covered my mouth with his own and felt with his tongue the back of my front teeth. "I'm glad you're here," he said, taking a last drag off his cigarette and throwing it in the kitchen sink. "I'll make dinner."

I put my bag of clothes and my comic book on the counter, and leaned there while Honoré took dishes out of drawers.

"Do you know how to build a bomb?" I asked.

He laughed. "What are we building a bomb for?"

"To explode a factory, let's say."

"Ah." He turned on the radio and the oven, and filled a kettle. "If you are the FLQ, you don't *build* a bomb. You *steal* your bomb. There are many places in this city for a person who would like dynamite, you know. The Expo, the Metro. If you are the FLQ, you don't care who owns it. You don't care about anything."

"They must care about something," I said. "What's the idea?"

"They think they can stop the world," he said sharply. From what, he didn't say. But he spoke with a distinct irritation, and I felt the discussion was now over. He opened his fridge and removed two plastic-wrapped bricks. He placed them in a casserole dish and slid it into the oven.

"Should be about half an hour," he said. "Wine?"

He opened his fridge again, and I came up next to him to look inside: a few bottles of wine, a few greasy Chinese takeout boxes, and many more plastic-wrapped bricks. These weren't the pre-made meals available in the frozen section of the grocery store. They were homemade. When I opened the icebox, I saw more of them.

"Me, I am hopeless in the kitchen," he said, pouring wine for us both. "I promise it will be very tasty. Chicken à la King, I believe. I never check. I like the surprise."

"Who made the meals?"

"*Maman*," he said, with no embarrassment. I now understood why he seemed to live beyond time, with no appointments

43

or obligations ahead of him. His family was rich, he didn't have a job, he didn't need one.

As we ate, an American radio station was working its way up the Hot 100. Currently an Elvis-y crooner tune played, maybe the Righteous Brothers or Paul Anka—a rich, slogging song that reminded me of church mixers back home and watching the other teens slow dance in their stiff suits and dresses. I told Honoré I had gotten fired that day.

"What was the job?"

"Diaper delivery service. Tomorrow I might go see about a job at a factory in Hochelaga."

He laughed. "Diapers? Factory? These are silly jobs for a beautiful boy like you. Let's see if we can find you work at the Reine Elizabeth."

"The hotel?"

"My father—well, he doesn't *own* it, but it's as *though* he does—he has what he calls, you know, a *portfolio*. And this hotel is part of this. Leave it with me. Do not go to any factory."

I laughed, ecstatic, and thanked him over and over, joyous that my nagging sense of insecurity had disappeared so instantly. The religious-sounding song on the radio ended in a crash of strings and two men's voices, harmonized. They sang about how God is sad to see the way we live, but that he'll nonetheless forgive us.

"How did you get fired?"

I explained about Michel's condescending talk, and how he seemed to piece together that I was gay, and how he prayed for me. "I said I didn't need his prayers. I think that's when I lost him."

Honoré licked his teeth and seemed to consider saying something, then thought not to. Cheerfully he said, "I like to lick my plate. It is bad manners, but I think you will not mind."

"I'll lick mine too."

We held up our plates and licked them clean, and when our plates were down again, we smiled at each other.

"I do not know your age," he said. "I suppose already I should have asked."

"I'm nineteen," I said.

"A beautiful age."

I suddenly became nervous. Out of my pocket, I pulled my mother's emerald ring and played with it. I couldn't help but do something fidgety like this, when I had nerves to calm.

"Nice ring," he said. "You could ask for a woman's hand with a ring like that."

"I almost did. A girl from home. But then I changed my mind."

He held out his hand, to see the ring for himself. Instead of handing it over, I put it back in my pocket and asked, "What do you mean, that nineteen is a beautiful age?"

"I mean there's so much left," he said. "To see, to learn. A beautiful, innocent age. You don't know all the ways that life is lived. There is much you will have to do wrong first, and then you will know."

For the first time it occurred to me that, at the start of that day, Honoré and I should have gone about things ordinarily after all. I should have dressed and left, he should have stayed in bed, we should have remained ignorant of each other's names and lives. When men spent too long together after sex, it was only a matter of time before they would displease each other in some way. One would say to the other something damaging, as Honoré had just said to me. He had been wrong to ignore this protocol, kissing my neck while I spoke on his phone. And I had been just as wrong to take his defiance as an opportunity to flout the rules myself.

I collected our plates and placed them in the sink; Honoré remained sitting. "What would you have said?" I asked.

"Hmm? When?"

"If someone told you that they pray for you every night. How would you feel?"

He waited for a time, and took a very deliberate breath. Then he said, sincerely and certainly, "Grateful."

Taken aback, I lit myself a cigarette.

Honoré went on: "You have heard of therapy."

"Sure. I've never done it, and I don't know anyone who has, but—"

"Yes, you do," Honoré said, speaking with certainty again. "You know men who see doctors, and you have slept with such men. Only they don't mention this."

I said nothing.

"*I* am such a man. I have been since I was a boy much younger than you." He came to the counter and stood next to me.

"Do they electrocute you?" I asked.

He laughed a little and lifted the cigarette out from between my fingers, to light his own. "No. I talk with a doctor, a few times a week. Just talk."

"Will you tell your doctor that you went to a gay bar last night?" I asked. "And you brought a man home, and you shared your mother's cooking with him?"

He gave me a tempering look, like a parent compelling a child not to act out.

"I like my doctor. Much more than the others I have had before. This doctor understands: good things take time. And we speak about bigger things than *this*," he said, gesturing at me. "I do not tell him about men, and I will not tell him about you. But I do not tell him about women either."

"You date women?"

"Yes. I'm a young man, with plenty of life. I want love one day, sure." He retrieved the wine from the fridge and filled both our glasses back up.

"Well, I want both," I said. "I want men and I want love. I want both."

"*Gay liberation,*" he said knowingly. "This is very anglophone, I must say. But I really love it. You think you can change everything."

He tapped at the comic book that Tomas had lent me, with the impossible blue sky.

"You want to be a *hero*. This is an attractive thing in a man, and when you are older, you will find the"—he searched for the words—"the way to use it best. This quality."

I had not heard of *gay liberation*. I had just shared thoughts that were my own. Now Honoré came close to me and with winey breath kissed my neck, my cheek, my nose.

He spoke in a whisper. "Listen. What I want more than anything—more than *anything*, little one—is to lose my legs between our chests, right now. You to fold me into nothing. This is what I want."

When he pulled away and looked at me, I was taken aback by the sight of tears in his eyes. I felt dizzy, from the cigarette and from the many emotions—I remembered, seconds ago, a feeling of advantage. Through this man I would have new work, and all the wine I could drink, and dinners, prepared in advance and out of sight, warmed in baths of boiled water. I had the compulsion to kiss his eyes, and when I did this, I liked that they were slippery and warm. I brought him to the couch and removed his clothes. I laid him down on his back and did as he requested: I folded and entered his body. I kept my own clothes on and my pants around one ankle, with the ring in their pocket, where it would stay for months. Having it there to play with, harmless and costly, hidden and gorgeous, gave me the energy I needed to get through certain moments, and certain days.

X X

With my chest and cheek against the wall of Truxx, I felt a sudden strong need for something familiar. My situation was intolerably unreal; seeing a friendly face, one that saw me back, would confirm my own existence to me. I searched the corner of the bar that fell in my limited field of vision. I looked for John and couldn't find him. I made eye contact with the man to my right, who was pressed against the wall as well, by an officer of his own. In his face, I saw no trace of panic—only disbelief. He shook his head at me and rolled his eyes. It helped my anxiety subside, to focus on the ridiculousness of the situation. We had all been drinking beers and listening to music. We did not deserve walls against our faces. I looked forward to the end of this whole exercise, so we could all buy more beers and debrief. I let out one curt laugh—then felt a sharp jab on my shoulder blade.

"Qu'est-ce qu'il y a de si drôle?" asked the officer, considering himself the subject of the laughter.

A different cop shouted, "This way for the paddy wagons, ladies," and I understood that I wouldn't be returning to my table or buying another beer. That I had been foolish to think of that, even for a moment. Previous raids had resulted in small numbers of arrests, but this one had a different magnitude. I was being arrested, same as everyone else there.

My cop held both my hands behind me, peeled me off the wall, and led me through the exit. The cop behind us walked more quickly, and as he passed, the man in his grip looked into my eyes and said sharply, "Do you see?" He was speaking to me in particular.

"Honoré," I said, recognizing him more by his voice than his face. He had grown a beard since our last encounter. As he was shoved forward, he turned his head to keep my gaze. His face was intense with scorn.

There were several paddy wagons parked outside the bar, one of them already full of men; Honoré's cop shoved him into that vehicle and chained him to the bench in a swift motion. Honoré looked at me again, but this time his face conveyed terror. The door slammed shut; the wagon drove off.

Usually, when Honoré and I saw each other, at some bar or bathhouse, we would pretend not to see each other and not even say hello—though every several months, we scrapped this unratified agreement and spent a whole evening speaking. He had broken the agreement now, to share some unkind words. *Do you see,* he had said. I knew what he meant by this: *Do you see what it leads to? The open life, the free life. Sitting in places like this. Do you see what we do to ourselves? What we've done to ourselves already, by deigning to forget, for even a moment, our station?*

But it hadn't mattered to me, in that moment, that his words were unkind. I derived comfort from them. A man had spoken three words to me—to me in particular—so I knew that I existed.

4

At the Reine Elizabeth, I manned a windowless, closet-sized room within the kitchen, with a dumbwaiter and a shelf with a few recipe books, all French. My job was to make drinks for the people who didn't want to leave their rooms. When I had no drinks to make, I was supposed to wash the dishes that accumulated in the sink outside the little room.

After a few shifts, I noticed that sometimes the other dish boys were pulled to the bar if things were getting busy and the boys had proper clothes on. I decided I'd start to wear a good shirt to work, and I'd hope for the same opportunity. Just one shift at the bar would mean I would share in the tip money that got pooled that night.

I had a nice white shirt at the room-rent in Little Portugal, so I took a walk there one afternoon. By this time, I had been sleeping at Honoré's practically every night. Tomas's mother, Gloria, sat alone on the couch reading a magazine when I arrived. "Tomas is in my mother's bed, sick. He puked on the sidewalk after the movies this afternoon. His *vo-vo* is out shopping right now."

"I'm not staying," I said. "I'm just getting some clothes."

"Sit with me. There's coffee."

I poured myself up. She put aside her magazine and bit her lip before speaking. "You know, I think my mother isn't very happy with this arrangement. She wants to replace you actually, but she'll never say that to you. You know she doesn't want *just* the income. She wants English practice, help around the house. That was the idea."

I nodded.

"Not that there's anything wrong with you. You're young, you're having fun, and that's what you should be doing. You don't need to watch cartoons with a six-year-old all day. I'll bet you have so many friends. Maybe a girl." She gave a discreet, indulgent look. Hearing our chatter, Tomas came out of the bedroom, wrapped in a blanket.

"I hear you're sick today, chief," I said.

He didn't speak. He just crawled onto the couch and put his head on my lap and his feet in Gloria's lap.

Maria arrived next, coming through the main door with arms full of paper bags.

"I'm leaving," I said to her. "I can pay for the week and get my stuff out today."

"Yes," she said. "Okay."

She and her daughter headed to the kitchen to unload the groceries.

Tomas looked up at me. "I knew," he whispered.

"What did you know?"

"I knew the popcorn makes me vomit. At the matinee. It's the butter. It's happened before."

"Then why did you eat it?"

"Because I love it a lot," he said, tearing up. "It's my favourite." He stifled a big sob.

"I understand," I told him. "It's really tough." I wiped his tears away and kissed him on the forehead, and once I knew he was asleep again, I carefully removed myself from below his head. Maria came back in, with some of the boxes she kept behind the sink skirt in the kitchen. We fit all my stuff into just one box though, and she and I shared a light moment, laughing about how little I had to pack. Some pairs of jeans, a turtleneck, a few tank tops—and my one nice-collared shirt, still clean and bright white.

Maria offered to help me get a cab outside.

"I'll take the Metro," I said.

She yelped: "No! You cannot!" I knew already that she was suspicious, even frightened, of the new underground system. I tried to reason with her, but she put the cash for the cab between the flaps of my box. I mentioned nothing about having taken the Metro around town many times already. Then she kissed my cheek. I wanted to tell Tomas goodbye but didn't want to wake him.

Maria said, "Wait now." She looked behind her to make sure Gloria was not near, and then she looked down at her hands, which played with the apron strings tied over her stomach. "I do not know this person you have. But I know, there is person, and I know he is…"

She jutted her shoulders forward, uncomfortable saying more here. "He" was all she needed to say to establish her point.

"I know it that you will…smarten up. Smart boy here. But listen to me. You must do *quick*. You will be a husband soon. And your wife cannot know."

At this point she looked into my eyes instead of into her own palms.

"That will be the worst thing for the woman. But you take longer, you go further. And further. It will all be harder to...to *put away*. So please. Smarten up."

She cleared her throat. Then she spoke jokingly, as though nothing she had said was all that serious. "Smarten up, young man!" she said, all jovial. She gave me a fake smack on the head and we both laughed nervously. I said goodbye and left.

On my walk to the Metro, it hit me how Maria had deduced things: underwear. Honoré's pairs were bigger than mine, but I sometimes wore them instead of my own, because they were also much higher quality, silky instead of papery. I likely left pairs in my clothes bin, on my increasingly rare visits to the room-rent. She would have seen them and wondered why I shopped in two different sizes. Then it would have fallen into place for her. In that moment, she'd made a decision to convey something to me, some time before we spoke for the last time. She'd waited until the last minute. People do that with the tasks they find unpleasant.

I had been quiet about my private life, to her and to others. It was an issue of vocabulary. Honoré was not simply a *friend*, but he would never have considered us boyfriends, husbands, or lovers either, and I could not have described him that way. On the nights I spent at the room-rent, he sometimes went on dates with girls, arranged by his mother and father. But that word, *date*, didn't capture the time he and I spent together. No word did, or none that was at hand. Other men at the Peel Pub used certain terms during stories.

I met a paramour at the swimming club.
A sweetheart, a gentleman, a darling.
Met eyes with a young thing. A beauty. A fruit.

But there was a sheen of irony to these terms, as though they stood in for different, more sincere language. I had yet to learn those other, accurate words; I had begun to doubt they existed at all. Riding the train with my box of clothes in my lap, I felt the earth all around me, clumpy and stable, unseen and unfathomably heavy. The excavated earth had been used to make the islands for Expo. There in the ground, where there should have been only earth, there were people like me, flung from place to place, in vehicles that moved through the dark. And where there should have been only water, over in the river, there were islands and ridiculous buildings. The water, once calm, now rushed like rapids on either side of the islands. Things were becoming possible that hadn't been possible previously. The past was the wrong place to look for a proper understanding of the world. I felt this very strongly and clutched my cardboard box tightly.

As the train approached my stop, I resolved to be more careful about things like the underwear. More discreet. I never wanted to be spoken to again the way Maria had spoken to me, playing with her apron strings, telling me what my future would be, thinking that she knew better, or that she knew me at all. There was going to be so much love in my life—real love. It was coming for me soon; it would cover me like mud. All I had to do was wait, and a future would arrive that was limitless.

I ENTERED HONORÉ'S BUILDING WITH MY BOX OF CLOTHES in my arms. I still didn't have a key to the deadbolt of his unit. When I knocked, he wasn't home. Sometimes when this happened, I would wait in the diner down the street for his return. This time, I just sat in the doorway, with my box in my lap, feeling nauseous from the Metro ride. The radio had once said that, in New York, everyone was nauseous at first when they got their underground system, and then everyone got used to it. Same with Paris. I decided this would happen for me also. Things only felt sickening at first, and then they became routine.

Honoré got home after an hour or so. I stood up from the floor and said, "You need to make me a key."

He didn't reply. I could tell from the blankness of his face that a game was taking place. He opened the door, squeezed in, and closed it behind him, leaving me in the hallway, the deadbolt locked.

"Honoré, please," I said. "Open it now. I have to pee."

I heard him fussing around in the apartment, first in the main room, then in the bathroom; I slumped back down to the ground. There was no question that he had just spent time with his parents, probably eating at some expensive restaurant. It was the only explanation for the severity of his mood, the singularity of his focus. He was probably drunk too.

I heard the bolt unlatch, and when I passed through, I saw that he was standing in his bedroom doorway wearing nothing, his arms folded across his chest, his genitals a pale pink focal point beneath an unkempt patch of pubes. He did not look at me and did not speak.

"I really do have to pee," I said, heading to the bathroom, where his clothes were on the floor and his douche was sitting in the sink, freshly used and freshly cleaned. The douche was a recent development, the product of a therapy session. Honoré rarely spoke much about his sessions, but as I understood it, having clean sex with men was seen as a meaningful step in his greater retreat from having sex with men at all. When I came back out, he was gone from the doorway. In the dim lamplight of the bedroom, I found him sitting with his legs folded beneath him, how a spoiled domestic animal would sit on a tasselled pillow, awaiting something pleasing, food or affection. Now he did give me eye contact.

"I lost my place," I said. "I'll need to stay here, for a few nights at least."

He did not indicate that he had heard me. He didn't have the patience for us to talk. I stripped down to my underwear and sat beside him. I kissed his shoulder, which seemed like the most enticing part of his body, olive dark and all alone, and he moaned. As we progressed, I almost felt embarrassed by his theatricality; he was a crazed, outrageous version of himself.

"I'm yours," he said. "You can have me, I am yours." He looked at me with desperate eyes, like he couldn't accept that our time together was limited. I came inside of him, and seconds later his cum landed across his own stomach. He smeared it into his skin and licked his hands, and licked the parts of my chest where some of it had landed. Then he held me tightly, and once we were both soft, he left to use the bathroom and the douche.

When he emerged, he was clothed, and once again unaffectionate. He turned on the television and sat on the couch. A hockey game played. "You can't stay here tomorrow night," he said.

"I lost my place," I said, putting on a fresh pair of underwear—my own, not his.

"Yes, you said. But you can't stay here tomorrow."

"Look," I said, taking a seat beside him. "I'm working on it. I found my nice clothes, and I'm going to make tips soon at the hotel. Then I'll get a place of my own—not your bed, not anyone's couch. But I don't have enough bread for that, not quite yet."

"Tomorrow night just won't work," he said. He kept quiet for a moment, pretending to be absorbed by the television, even though it was commercials.

"You have a date."

He responded with a curt nod. Now I understood: his parents had, at some point that day, informed him that he would be taking a girl out on a date, some daughter of some family friend. He wasn't going to sleep with her, but he would be expected to have her over for a drink after dinner, and to impress upon her his sanity, his cordiality, his unsuspicious heterosexuality. She would report back to her parents, who would report back to Honoré's. This kind of thing had taken place before.

"I won't come home until really late," I said. "I promise. Please. I need a place."

He grunted, finally obliging me, then looked my unclothed body up and down. He licked his pointer finger and pressed it through a strip of my thigh hair, where a small bead of cum had remained. He scraped his finger across his bottom front teeth, and with his eyes closed swallowed. He breathed audibly: *"Nnnn."* On the television, beautiful white hands swooped through the air. The word *residue* appeared on the screen, but the hands dislodged it, and then the word dissolved into nothing.

X X

I was brought to one of the paddy wagons. My hands were cuffed, and the chain of the cuffs was attached to a larger chain, connecting me to the other men on the bench. The larger chain felt incredibly heavy in my lap.

I was the last man in. The door closed, and when we began to move, the man beside me gave a brief scream with the sudden jerk of motion. In the dark, I couldn't tell if John was in this vehicle. I said his name out loud as we gained speed. When nobody answered, I said it again. Through the walls of the wagon, I did not hear any traffic sounds; it was too late in the night. We moved on the road all alone.

"Are you in here, John?"

Still nobody spoke. For a spare moment, I wondered whether John existed at all, or if he was something other than a person. A harmless spirit, a faulty memory. Someone I had invented, so I wouldn't have to deal with the idea that I had gone to that bar by myself. That I had made myself so vulnerable, with such a thoughtless decision.

"They can't fucking do this," said one man. His voice was not John's. Nobody responded to this man either.

I suddenly had a panicked thought about my dog, Dorothy, who would not know what to make of my long absence tonight. I knew she would carry all my shoes to the blanket she slept on, as she did whenever I was gone for too long. If I didn't come home all night, she would give up hope for the last walk and pee on the apartment door. Picturing this, I started to cry. The tears annoyed me, because my chained hands could not reach my face to wipe my eyes. To stop, I told myself that Dorothy was just an animal, whose moods were fickle and unimportant. I decided her anxiety didn't matter, and regained myself that way.

When we arrived and were unbuckled and shoved out of the wagon, I studied every face and still could not find John. Inside the station, we were told to wait in a line, which moved in stops and starts, as more wagons came and unloaded. The cops surrounding us no longer carried machine guns, but they all still had handguns in their holsters, and bulletproof pads on their backs and chests. We found-ins stood unspeaking, until one man broke the silence when a cop passed by very close to him: "We aren't criminals," he said in French. Little coppery rings hung from both his earlobes, and his fingernails had chipped black nail polish.

"You'll see the judge soon," the cop replied in the same language.

"I'm not a criminal. We are not criminals. We want to know the charges."

The cop continued walking.

"Tell us the fucking charges!" the man yelled. "You can't do this!"

"Bawdy house," said the cop, without slowing down or turning around. "Spending time in an indecent establishment."

"This is not fucking acceptable!" he yelled.

The cop kept walking, and the other cops surrounding us pretended to be deaf to the exchange.

The man on my other side asked in English what the cop had said, and I couldn't bring myself to translate. It seemed like a waste of energy. His face bore an anxiety that, like Dorothy's, didn't matter to me anymore. I had problems of my own. I needed to use the bathroom, and became fixated on the idea that nobody would let me do this, and that I would shit myself.

The man found himself a different translator, and after hearing the story, he yelled: "*This* is the criminal behaviour. Taking us here is criminal!" Others yelled as well, in English and in French, but for every clearly angry man, there were many others who were quiet and morose. Nobody was angrier, or at least louder, than the man with chipped black nails. The cops continued to feign deafness, and eventually the yelling died off and silence overtook us again. I just wanted to go wherever we were going and to find a bathroom there.

The line moved forward. We were led down a hall, into a very large cell. There were many of us, perhaps over one hundred men. I decided that, once the last man had been added to the cell, I'd try to count everyone and determine the number. Doing that would take my mind off things, until we were freed.

As men came in, the man with black nails told everyone, in both languages, not to plead guilty. "When they release us, they'll ask how you want to plead, and you can't plead guilty. If you do, then you can't appeal later. We all have to appeal."

Some men nodded and others ignored him completely, or seemed not to register what he was saying. I ignored him too. One man shook his head at the suggestion of pleading not guilty.

"C'mon," said the man with black nails. "Have a sense of fraternity."

"I am an immigrant," whispered the man, in a thick Slavic accent. "Not guilty, they ask questions. Guilty, they ask for money and I go. I am an immigrant; I am guilty."

At this, the man with black nails stopped his campaigning. He took a few deep breaths and leaned against the bars. I thought he might next slump down and crouch or sit on the ground, as other men had done. Instead, he kicked the bar in front of him, which gave off a jarring *ping*.

I noticed a toilet at the back of the cell. I walked quickly in its direction, and when I reached it I pulled down my pants and defecated. The men around me turned to face away. The toilet paper was rough and translucently thin, like the pages of a Bible.

At the front of the cell, men asked cops on the other side when we would be released. The cops kept pretending not to hear. Still sitting, I remembered that my wallet had been taken, and touched my blazer pocket, just to make sure it was gone. If they had taken my wallet, I knew they would take my name as well, off a piece of ID. Eventually, I imagined, I would get the wallet back. My name, however, would never be returned to me.

5

A lot of snow fell, wet and blustering. I walked through the wind wearing Honoré's warmest jacket over my newly retrieved white shirt. Arriving at the hotel, I saw that there were almost no customers at the restaurant, and that the manager, Rémi, had sent home every waiter except one, a man named Étienne. "He might need extra help," said Rémi, "so make drinks up front tonight."

I was pleased that the shirt had worked already, and that I would get a share of tips, even if business would be measly on such a quiet evening. I made the odd drink, deep-cleaned the basin and fridge, and watched Étienne tend to his tables at a leisurely pace. He was very handsome, with a charming asymmetrical smirk. His shining, slicked-back hair jutted out from a pronounced widow's peak, and when he came close, he gave off a super-clean, almost chemical smell.

I wasn't certain if he and I had ever had a conversation. Some nights after work, after the last of the customers had left, the restaurant staff would stick around drinking wine. Some of us were English, some were French; some were Protestant, some were Catholic, some were neither. Out of necessity, we all mingled.

That way, the boys had plenty of girls to pick from, and the girls had plenty of boys. For the most part, I found those developments boring. I stuck to my drinks and to managing the record player. Nina Simone, the Supremes, the Temptations, or Dionne Warwick to begin. Later in the night, when we all got in the mood to really move, the Troggs, the Rolling Stones, and the Beatles. Étienne never stayed around for drinks. He said his girlfriend worked days, in an office, and they only ever got to see each other in the late evenings. I was privately excited to get so much time one-on-one with him for a whole shift.

There was hardly any noise that night, and I could hear every conversation taking place in the restaurant. I noticed that, at every table, a man would ask Étienne the same question. *"D'où venez-vous?"* This phrase I knew. *Where are you from?*

He supplied the same ready made response each time, asking them to guess. Their guesses were always the same.

"D'Afrique?"

Étienne responded with a wink, or by putting his thumb in his cheek and giving a big plosive pop. Then a rapid conversation would take place and would conclude with Étienne walking off, saying, *"Merci, merci,"* all flattered. To my ear, his accent clearly wasn't Québécois, but I suspected it wasn't African either, in spite of the customers' guesses.

In a brief moment when we had no customers at all, he came to the bar and asked me to fix him a sidecar. I knew this drink without looking it up: lemon juice, Cointreau, and lots of cognac, mixed and poured into a martini glass, with an orange rind for garnish. The only orange within arm's reach had already been halved and juiced for a screwdriver. Étienne watched as I carved some of the rind off the floppy hollow half orange.

"How could you!" he whispered, horrified. He gave me a look like I was insane, then shook his head grinning and went *tsk-tsk-tsk*. "It is not good, what you have done," he said.

"Why not?"

"*Why not?* You crazy kid. You do not see this done. You have made me a drink out of garbage." He gave me a smirk that felt specially made, like it was a look he'd always had in him and I had finally been the one to earn it. But I knew that men existed who imparted such looks all day, to everyone they met, and Étienne was one such man. When I handed him the drink, he gave it a few sarcastic sniffs before taking a sip. Then he sat on a bar stool and drank the rest, reading from a paperback he kept beneath the bar, a book called *Un autre pays*.

Reading his book, he let his face go slack-jawed. His mouth hung open a little, and he looked plainer than before. He and I were the only people in the room; he wasn't putting any focus on the impression he made on anyone who saw him. I scrubbed the walls of the fridge. When I finished and shut the fridge door, Étienne looked my way, spooked by the sound, remembering now that he wasn't alone. His face went back to handsome.

"Enjoying that book?" I said.

"*Enjoy* is not a good word for this. I do not know the correct word and maybe there is none. The author lived in Paris when I was a boy, you know. And actually, this is a translated book—he wrote in English." He peeled back the flap so I could see the author's photo. A young-looking black man, staring just above the camera with indifference in his face.

"So you're from Paris," I said. "You were lying to the customers."

"*C'est vrai*," he said, smirking. Then he spoke slyly, as though he didn't want us to be overheard. "But I do not lie to trick them. I lie to make them happy. If I say *France*, they are embarrassed, and they don't like me. I say *oui, Afrique*, and they do not get upset. The tip is better this way, you know. You should thank me."

He issued another smirk, and I did thank him. "Did you ever meet him?" I asked, gesturing at the book.

He laughed. "Paris is big. And we don't all know each other."

I didn't know if "we" meant Parisians or black men. Embarrassed, I stuttered apologies before I could even think of the right words. Étienne raised his hand to shut me up and made a friendly face.

"I was there twenty-five years," he said, "and there are many parts that are to me the same as the moon. The back of it, the part with no light."

A couple came in and sat down; he set the book on the bar.

"Paris is big," he said. "And so is the world, and this is a very unfair thing actually. You could travel all your life, and always somewhere new, and still the parts you see will be much, much, *much* closer to nothing than to everything. Terrific sidecar, except the garnish. Crazy kid." He left the glass there for me to empty and clean, approaching the new arrivals with a big smile.

Rémi came in from the lobby and noticed Étienne's paperback on the counter beside me. "Are you reading?" he asked me sternly.

"It's mine, it's mine," said Étienne, rushing over.

Rémi turned to me and pointed his thumb in Étienne's direction. "This man, he asks for a helper tonight, but he still has time to read a book."

The two of them then spoke in French too quickly for me to understand. At the end of the conversation, Rémi said in English that Étienne could manage alone, and told me to head home. I didn't mention that I had no home to go to that night— Honoré had a girl over on a date. I needed to buy time until late, and it was too cold out to simply wander. As I slipped on my coat, Étienne registered the nervousness in my face and handed me all the tip money collected that night so far.

"Is my fault you are leaving," he said, placing the cash right into my jacket pocket. "I will earn more. The night is young."

Exiting the hotel, I popped into a depanneur to buy cigarettes and determined that I was dressed up enough for the movies, in my good white shirt. At the Pigalle Theatre, I came in halfway through a crowded screening of *Fantastic Voyage*. Onscreen, a submarine navigated a web of translucent neon tubing. I scarfed my popcorn down. Tomas had been right: it tasted so, so good. I cobbled together the film's plot. Scientists had shrunk the submarine and injected it into a man's veins, and the crew's mission was to find and destroy a rogue blood clot. The inside of a body, according to this movie, looked garish and plastic, its fibres covered in jam-like pulp and hot condensation. At the end of the film, the crew exited the man through his tears and grew back to normal size. But their submarine remained small, abandoned in the man's body forever and unmentioned by the scientists.

THOUGH THE FILM WAS OVER, I STILL HAD TIME TO KILL. I liked the idea of a drink at the Peel Pub, and maybe even a night spent in new company.

Davey got started on my usual drink at the sight of me. I had not been to that bar for a while, and already my clothes had fallen out of sync with the popular look of wider pant flares, louder patterns, and longer collars. Necklines plunged low enough for chest hair to show. I subtly undid the top two buttons of my shirt, wrapped my hand around my gimlet, and stared without focus into the jewel tones before me, as men in pairs shouted to hear each other over the Motown that Davey blasted.

He had just put on a new record, and as soon as the needle landed I knew it was *James Brown Live at the Apollo*, which he played often. He had once told me that he was at the Apollo during the recording. That he had lived in New York City and visited the Apollo all the time—that his voice was one of the cheers you heard on the record between songs. He said that when James Brown came onstage, it was instantly clear that this person could only fully be *himself* while onstage, with a giant cheering crowd before him. The record began with a man introducing the band: "So now, ladies and gentlemen, it is *star time*." Then the man listed off Brown's best-known singles, as a way of exciting the audience. Between each song title, the horn section blared an ascending note, and the crowd went madder and madder.

"'I'll Go Crazy.'

"'Try Me.'

"'You've Got the Power.'

"'Think.'

"'If You Want Me.'

"'I Don't Mind.'

"'Bewildered.'

"Million-dollar seller, 'Lost Someone.'

"The very latest release, 'Night Train.'"

I saw Étienne's face at the other end of the bar and recognized him at once. I felt the blood in my face go hot. I mustn't be seen by him there, because I knew him from work. I turned around and found a vantage point, behind other men, from which to watch him more discreetly. He wore a red tank top, tight and neon-bright, nothing like the crisp shirt he had been wearing a few hours before. He was acting shifty, looking everywhere, his arms crossed. Had he not realized what kind of bar this was, and was he too polite to leave right away? He looked in every direction but mine, and it hit me that he was doing what I was doing, avoiding acknowledgement. Maintaining deniability. He knew exactly what kind of bar he was in, and he had seen me before I had seen him.

I decided we were both being ridiculous. I went up to him and said, "Aha!" all friendly. We laughed and had a long hand-shake, and I bought two gimlets with some of the money he had placed in my pocket earlier that evening. We snagged a couch beside the dance floor. I had so many questions for him. My first was whether this was his first time at the Peel Pub.

"Yes," he said.

"Have you gone to bars like this a lot?"

"Yes-yes-yes," he said. "At home there were such bars. I lived in *la banlieue*, but I would go into the city, one hour on bike. I bike fast. This was good exercise."

"Do you really have a girlfriend?"

"No," he said. "She is lies."

"I never would have guessed," I said.

At this he smiled proudly. "With you," he said, "I would have guessed. You here is not a surprise."

Then he inhaled and made a sincere sorry face, as though what he had just let himself say would potentially upset me.

"My advice is, just say there is a girl," Étienne continued. "Then there is no problem. People do not have imaginations. When you tell people something, to the people it is true."

"I don't know," I said, unable to specify what the thing was that I didn't know, even to myself. I didn't want to dwell on unhappy things with this burgeoning new friend—but I had already tolerated so much from Honoré, and I couldn't face the notion of a second person in my life with whom there were things I could discuss and things I could not. I asked, "What would be so bad if people could tell, if people could guess about me?"

Étienne did not respond to the question. He was pretending not to understand, or pretending not to have heard the question over the loud music. I let it pass and got us onto other topics, asking why he moved to Montreal.

"*En fait,* I came for school. I was in law school for two years *à l'Université de Montréal.* I did not finish. I needed money, and *voilà,* a job at the Reine."

"Do you miss Paris?"

"I miss the cheese."

"What about your friends and family?"

"It is more simple to be here." He took a big swig from his gimlet. "Biking to the gay bar in Paris, this was very difficult each time. I had to tell stories. *I am going to the library; I will sleep at a friend's home.* I told these stories to my family and my friends. More stories, more stories. This becomes impossible. But here it is easy. I do what I want to do, and nobody is caring."

"But you tell stories here. You lie at the hotel about having a girlfriend."

"Yes—and this is what is perfect about new friends. They come knowing nothing, because you are new too. Any lie will work. I will say it again to you: people do not have imaginations." He downed the last of his drink.

"And what would your loved ones back home think about you if they knew?" I asked.

He responded first with a volatile look, like he couldn't believe the question. "Do *your* family and friends know you are here?" he asked. "Not your now-friends. Your before-friends."

"I didn't have any friends before," I said. "And I don't talk to my family."

Étienne tilted his head and squinted his eyes at me the tiniest bit, like I had suddenly fascinated him. "Then *this* life is very easy for you," he said, gesturing again at the place and people around us.

Now I understood that he had been addressing my first question this whole time after all, in a deeply considered way, the question I thought he had pretended not to process. Again, I did not know whether to feel insulted. And again, I felt a dread-laden preference not to let the conversation get too heavy. We listened to the music together and without interest watched the small group of men who danced. Eventually I asked, "Did you ever take the Metro in Paris?"

"*Oui.*"

"And it never made you feel sick?"

He laughed emphatically and expressed that Montreal had a much newer, nicer, less rickety system. He was certain I would get used to it before long. "It will be nice when Expo begins," he said. "The whole city will be full of people, using the Metro, using the Expo Express. This town will come alive."

I wanted to ask why he called Montreal a town, not a city. But he spoke before me.

"You are finished," he said, tapping at the empty glass in my hand. "I am finished mine too. I don't want to spend more money—but this is nice. Talking. At home, I have whisky, and we can go to drink it. But listen, crazy kid. Nothing funny."

"Nothing funny," I said.

He held his finger in my face and furrowed his brow. "Talking and whisky," he said firmly.

HIS APARTMENT WAS PERMEATED WITH HIS DISTINCT CHEMical smell. We sat on his bed with our shoes off and glasses of whisky in our hands. He didn't have any ice, so we took the drinks at room temperature. I could barely tell where the whisky ended and my tongue and gums began. I stared at the bushy dots of Étienne's chest hair, showing at his neckline, and thought about how their texture might feel against the pads of my fingers. At some point, I grabbed his feet and placed them in my lap, and at some other point he pushed my hair out of my face and behind my ear. But despite these tiny moves we made on each other, the bed didn't feel loaded with potential, the way beds did when I had sat on them drinking with other men. It felt like just a place to sit. I was more interested in friendship. That would have been the more unusual outcome of a night like this, and the more valuable outcome.

When our bottle was almost finished, we had the idea to water it down at the bathroom sink (there was no other sink, and no real kitchen area) so we could be sure we'd consumed every drop. By this time, it was really late. He asked if I was in good enough shape to walk home.

"I don't really have a home," I said. He poured me a glass of water, told me to drink the whole thing, and then told me to lie down. I fell asleep over his covers with my shirt and pants still on, and had no sense of his state of dress, below the covers, on the other side of the bed.

I WOKE UP IN THE MORNING TO THE SOUND OF TWO VOICES fighting in French. Étienne was at the sink, shaving his face. He wore a pair of boxer shorts, with a black cloth wrapped around his head, tucked neatly behind his ears. The fighting took place above our heads. I stared upward, at a hairline crack in the ceiling's foundation.

"Every morning they fight," he said when he saw, through the mirror, that my eyes were now open. "Did you have dreams?"

"I don't think so. You?"

"Always I have dreams," he said, "and always I forget them."

"What's with the turban?"

He froze on the spot. Again it was as though he had forgotten that I counted as a person and now was embarrassed to be seen in this state. "My hair will go messy," he said self-consciously. "It is to keep the style. My hair is not naturally so straight. But if I let it get kinky, I am sure that Rémi would not like this. Or any employer in this city, I believe."

Upstairs something ceramic or glass shattered, and the yelling paused. It was morning, and Étienne and I had not kissed, or even much touched. I was incredibly glad to have woken up in his room, in his company. Above the ceiling, the bickering resumed. I clutched my forehead, in need of more sleep.

"Some mornings, I think I should find a new place," he said, scrubbing his face, then his armpits, with his dripping wet cloth.

When he looked my way again, he asked, "Why are you smiling like this?"

Part Two

FANTASTIC VOYAGE

6

Étienne and I found an apartment in Mile End, on the third floor of a triplex. It was a *deux et démi*, with a steep and wiry staircase that bent at every step. To Étienne's delight, there was nobody above us to make any sounds, and our street was quiet too. We had a bay window that faced the street, showing the endless row of homes just like our own, on the other side of the street.

I learned that I sang sometimes. Étienne would ask, "What is that song?" while I made our dinner or our drinks, and I would realize I had been singing. I liked "California Dreamin'" by the Mamas & the Papas and "No Milk Today" by Herman's Hermits. I liked "The Times They Are a-Changin'" by Bob Dylan, and anything from the Beatles, but my very favourite of theirs was "Ticket to Ride." I liked a lively, melancholy song called "Some Things Just Stick in Your Mind" by a high-voiced female singer whose name I never gathered.

In the thick of the winter, the hotel failed to attract many visitors. This meant empty tables at the restaurant, and fewer shifts, and worse tips. One day, quite joyously, Étienne quit. He had found work at the French Pavilion at Expo, which would open in the spring. Orientation was already underway.

Étienne slept on the bed in the second room, and I took the couch. The Expo staff worked him hard ahead of the opening; literature about the French Pavilion littered our coffee table, which was two milk crates pushed together. We intended to restructure our sleeping arrangement somehow, as soon as I was making real money, but for now it was Étienne who needed the better night's rest. He taught me French some mornings, knowing that French would help me get more shifts at the hotel and to find better work elsewhere. He tried to teach me France-French instead of Québécois French, but he wasn't a natural teacher, and usually I wound up frustrated.

"No-no-no-no-no," he said one morning, early in the lessons, as he walked me through the word for hope, *espérer*. My mouth could not differentiate its vowel sounds. "Shape your mouth like mine."

Flustered and laughing, I shouted, "You don't move your mouth at all!"

"Please. Try."

"J'espère que ton journée est bon," I said laboriously, trying at once many words he had recently taught me. *I hope that your day is good.*

"No-no-no, *bonne* for *journée*. Day is a feminine thing. *Que ta journée est bonne.* But this is too much. *Bonne journée* is right. *Bonne journée.*" Then he left for a day of work, and my morning and afternoon took on the same foggy lightness as they usually did. By evening, I always knew what things I had done, but could not recall the order. Groceries had been purchased, the next few dinners planned out. Potential new employers were cold-called. I often spent some time in the bay window, reading *Fantastic Four* comics or thinking about how day is a feminine thing. And at some point every day, I had a nap in the bed, after removing my underwear and making myself cum into it.

Étienne kept pornography beside the bed. About half his magazines were, ostensibly, fitness magazines, filled with muscular male figures in thongs, striking rugged, showy poses. These magazines featured short articles detailing dietary and exercise advice, and some encouraged readers to submit their own photographs. I knew that Étienne didn't go in for the health advice stuff, and I was skeptical that many readers did. The other half of Étienne's magazines featured explicit photography of sexual acts between men. These ones had no mailing addresses and not much text at all, and they were printed on crummier paper.

All these magazines got stacked beside the bed, not beneath it—Étienne didn't hide them away. When we moved in together, one of the first things he clarified was that he enjoyed spending time with his porn collection. "Now I will masturbate," he said plainly as he retreated to the bedroom on our first night. He had told me to help myself to it if I wanted, and I liked doing this, though I ignored the fitness rags, opting instead for the explicit ones. It calmed and encouraged me, how all these men had gotten together and allowed other men to photograph them, and then more men assembled and distributed the images, for men like Étienne and me. The existence of such a system was somehow reassuring as I sat alone in my apartment, day after unvaried day.

IN THE EARLY SPRING, I ASKED RÉMI IF HE HAD A MOMENT to talk.

"Now is okay," he said.

I took a deep breath, as Étienne had advised, and shared the arguments he and I had developed together. "The hotel is getting busy again, and I know you need help at the front of house, especially with Étienne gone. I've been at the dumbwaiter for a few months, and I think I'm ready for more time up front. I could really use the extra hours."

Rémi asked, *"Parles-tu français?"*

"Un peu," I said.

Then he spoke more French very quickly, and I had no idea what had been said.

"Pardonnez-moi," I said, smirking cheekily.

Rémi looked immediately annoyed.

"I have just ordered a drink," he said. "You come here, and you decide you will stay in the big city with the pretty lights, but you don't even want to learn the language. *Incroyable.* You know, I was not smart when I hired you. Where can you go? The dumbwaiter, that's all." Then he made a brushing gesture with his hand to mark the end of the conversation.

If Étienne had asked for a promotion in the tone I had used, he would have gotten away with it; he had that sort of charm. Coming from me, the request sounded pesky and selfish. A couple of hours into my shift, Rémi poked his head into the dumbwaiter station and told me I was done for the night.

"So quiet," he said. "We will close the dumbwaiter station door—it is a waste of heat. Front of house can make drinks for the rooms."

"When do you want me coming in next?"

He shrugged. "We'll see," he said, then made the brushing gesture again.

I headed home, dreading the moment when Étienne would ask how the conversation went.

Indeed, Étienne asked this as soon as he got home from orientation that evening. I was by the stove, frying liver and onions for our dinner.

"I think I got fired. When I asked about my next shift, Rémi said, 'We'll see.'"

"Oh, you crazy kid. Yes, you got fired."

He put down a paper bag full of beers and searched for something he could use to open the cans. Having combined our possessions, there were some things we had two of—combs, pomade canisters, those tiny bottles of Angostura Bitters with the labels too tall—and plenty of things we didn't have at all, like a clock, a broom, or, evidently, a can opener. Eventually he gave up on the search, and we went with whisky instead. While dinner simmered, I made old-fashioneds, using maraschino cherry syrup instead of sugar water. Jars of maraschino cherries were another thing we had two of.

"This all seemed easier when I first arrived in town," I said. "I didn't know how good I had it, driving diapers around with Michel. I thought there'd be more and more for me, after that first job. More and more, better and better." I stabbed at the onions with my big wooden spoon.

"Call Michel," said Étienne. "Ask for this job back. Tell him you are sorry for the fight, and tell him also there's a girlfriend now. You want to make money to take her on dates." He read the protest on my face. "This will make him comfortable, that is all."

"I'm not going to lie like that. But I can call him tomorrow, sure."

I served us up, and as we ate, we poured over a pile of pictures that Étienne had brought home from work. For the first time, I saw the buildings of Expo from closer up than the other side of the river. I realized that distance hadn't rendered the buildings weird-looking; they truly were very strange buildings. The one that featured most prominently in the photographs was a colossal round dome.

"Hideous," I said, pointing at it.

"No-no-no," said Étienne. "It's a hearty shape. The ultimate shape. The American Pavilion. Very resilient, good for all weather. The future of the house is such domes, it is said."

He walked me through the rest of the pavilions, including the one where he would work, which looked like a radiator. Then he held up a pamphlet saying, *"C'est moi."*

There was a photograph on the inset of the team of French Pavilion attendants in their funny space-age uniforms. The group of young men formed a long row of equally tall, handsome, clean-shaven men, behind a row of young women who had long pale necks and scrawny arms—all white, aside from Étienne. "I should not be in this photograph," he said. "The men with the cameras told me, 'You go at the end. Far-far-far.' But I knew this was because they wanted it all white, all nice, all the same, and later they would cut me out. My friend *here*," he said, pointing to one of the identical men, "he says, 'Étienne goes in the middle.' So it is thanks to him that I am in this photograph."

With this photo, we played a game that Étienne devised. We went across the row and tried to determine potential homosexuals. Étienne did most of the talking, illustrating certain tells: the cheeks, the eyes. "Pansy," he said about one of the men. "True blue cocksucker," about another. He made these comments quietly, and grinning, studying the faces closely, resting the rim of his glass against his chin.

When we reached the man who had helped him stay in the photo, I took a guess. "Pansy," I said.

"No-no-no," went Étienne. "I would know if he was. Please believe me. I would be very happy if he was, in fact."

Until then, I had never heard Étienne admit to any crushes. Now I knew for certain that he liked men most and was most comfortable discussing their beauty when they were only images.

"You never know," I said encouragingly.

"No," he said with a condescending firmness. "I fear he is a truly good man."

I laughed. "You can be both. Gay and good. Whatever *good* is."

He clicked his tongue in his mouth, as though to end the conversation. "I am a perpetual student of English," he said. "What I meant and what I said were different—*quel dommage.*"

I knew he was fibbing. He had captured, in his second language, concepts much more intricate than this. But the phone rang before I could protest. I answered it as always; most of the people who had our number were potential employers. This time, the voice on the other end spoke French. I heard the word *Étienne* and handed the phone over.

Étienne spoke too quickly for me to understand, but I could tell that the conversation made him childishly giddy. "*À bientôt,*" he said to the caller, and hung up the phone. He unravelled the wrap on his head and gave his reflection in the bay window a close look. Then he looked over to me grinning and said, "Feel like a party?"

I rolled my eyes because he knew the answer. *"Allons-y,"* I said, with intentionally terrible pronunciation, so he could roll his eyes at something too.

I WORE A BROWN TURTLENECK THAT BELONGED TO ÉTIENNE, who wore a crisp shirt the same deep, sharp shade of red as the apocalyptic sky on the cover of one of my *Fantastic Four* comic books. We took a cab downtown, then rode on a new train system called the Expo Express, to the edge of a remote peninsula that had no attractions except a mammoth-like building made of jumbled-up concrete cubes, called Habitat. It was not yet fully constructed; cranes remained at the far end, floodlit and abandoned for the evening. Étienne explained to me that construction had fallen behind, but they planned to claim that it was unfinished on purpose, to showcase the process of construction. I was nervous about a party where I wouldn't know anyone, but also thrilled to enter a building so widely discussed and brand new. We headed up walled and unwalled staircases, and through long half-covered corridors, the rushing water to our side, invisible but audible. It didn't feel like we were indoors or outdoors; it felt like some third condition.

One of the building's units, off in the distance, served as a source of light and commotion. We made our way toward it and eventually came into a space filled with smoke, music, and many people. A Beatles record played, *Revolver*; we entered during "Taxman." A staircase led to a second floor, beyond which we could see a crowded balcony, with its enormous doors thrown open, and conversations taking place through the partition. Some people wore Expo uniforms, just like in the pamphlet. Others wore paisley, or denim, or shaggy leather jackets. All the girls had miniskirts, and one had a diagonal checkerboard dress with sleeves that went past the tips of her fingers.

Étienne gave me a look of glee, like all this imagery was a meal we were about to divide and tuck into. Then someone waved to him from the upstairs, and he scurried off. My own attention got caught by a beautiful crystal punch bowl, with lime slices and flower petals floating inside. I took a glass teacup full of punch toward the music, where no conversation was taking place. Only listening. I parked on a couch; a joint made the rounds and I had some. I felt on friendly terms with those who were in the same little zone as me, and in the same mild haze as well, scattered on floor pillows and ottomans, and under blankets. The checkerboard woman was among us, often cupping her mouth to speak into the ear of the man she was with. Beside her, two girls played with each other's hands.

A man in a Fair Isle sweater clutched a glass cup just like mine. Beneath the sweater he wore a collared shirt and a tie, but he didn't look out of place at a party like this. In fact, he looked like he belonged so much that he could dress however he liked and his belonging would remain unaffected. His hair was thick, black, and combed back. Noticing me, he raised his glass and mouthed, "Cheers." Then he went back to watching the interesting people in their interesting outfits. I watched along too.

When the first side of the Beatles record finished, a man nearby got up to change it. But the checkerboard woman stood and stopped him. He tried to coax her back down, but she insisted, *"Maintenant, maintenant!"* She signalled to a few of the people around us, emphatically making *get moving* gestures. Someone pulled a guitar out from behind the couch, and someone else cleared the drinks off the fallboard of a bright pink piano, which I had at first thought was just a shelf. The checker-board woman grabbed a tambourine off the piano and handed it to the man who had been shushing her. People would make music now, and not on a stage. Just from where they sat. I thought I should probably get up and go, but then they started, and it felt most polite to stay where I was, and to pretend I was enjoying myself. They played a French song I did not know. Everyone sang, some very seriously and others half-heartedly. Everyone, that is, except for me and the man wearing the Fair Isle sweater, who seemed as surprised as I was by the sudden music-making. Another joint went around, and I helped myself.

After a few songs, all French and unfamiliar, I wasn't pretending to enjoy myself. I really did enjoy the music. One song I even recognized as a track from a Ginette Reno record that Honoré and I had liked to play, on the nights we got along.

I hadn't thought of him much since leaving his apartment. When I did think of him, the thought was always followed by other specific thoughts: how little I thought of him and how strange it felt to think of him so little. Now, as I listened to the checkerboard woman hit the same notes as Ginette Reno, though not as capably, I realized I did not need Honoré. He was, for a moment, a source of information for me—information on what my life might look like. But it was the wrong information, and now I just had to try again, and find a new and better template.

The man in the Fair Isle sweater got up, came over, and took my cup from its spot on the floor by my feet. It was empty, same as his. He went to the punch bowl and filled them both, and when he brought mine back, he sat with me. Unspeaking, we listened to the singers together. He put his arm behind my shoulder on the couch, stretching out. Sometimes people did this—stretching out felt comfortable. If a man's arm fell over another man's shoulder in the process of stretching, there was nothing affectionate about it, not necessarily. Even to think so was silly. I pretended not to notice his arm at all.

On one of the floor pillows, a man unbuttoned his flannel all the way and started to pull on his own long chest hairs, like drawstrings. He slid onto the ground and lay before a couch. Everyone on the couch shoved their bare feet beneath his body, to keep warm. The flannel man stared up into the ceiling transfixed, like he could see the night sky through it. I listened closely as the singers moved on to "California Dreamin'." Across the room I saw a window. It was dark out, but I could clearly see the brightly lit window of a different building, like a square floating in the night. The window was filled with people, also young and glamorous. They could have been part of this same gathering. Then I realized that, indeed, the window belonged to this same building; the building jutted in and out, facing the world and itself. In the window, I spotted Étienne, in his apocalyptic red shirt. We had gotten so distant from each other. He had spotted me too, and from his little floating square, he gave me a look like *Can you believe it?* I returned the same look, shrugging and grinning. I wasn't sure what it was we couldn't believe. But when I shook my head in amazement, I really meant it, I was amazed. The thing we exchanged looks about was unbelievable, and also unidentifiable. It existed around and beyond us, and brought us a positive feeling.

When the song ended, the man with his arm around my shoulder asked me, "Not a singer?" It came across as strange to me, for a man to care if another man could sing or not.

"No," I said. "I'm terrible."

"I'm sure that's not true," he said. "I bet you sing great." This too felt off-centre. I found his smile endearing, and his accent sounded like none I had heard before, silly and stringy. He asked me which pavilion I worked at.

"No pavilion. I'm here with a friend."

"You must find this all quite cloying."

"No. I think I'm in love with Expo. I have a great feeling... about the whole future."

"The whole future!" he parroted, laughing.

I laughed too. I knew I wasn't being as articulate as I wanted to be, but I kept trying. "Not the *future*. Just the summer. The present. Like nothing bad is going to happen for a long time now. We're all going to stay right here, in this moment. Nothing hurting us. Just a fantastic party, all summer long."

He laughed more, nodding brightly. I gave up trying to talk like this. Instead I placed my right foot between his two feet, anchoring us together. He didn't mind, and made this known by pinning my foot down with his big toe. This was far more exciting than any prospect of sex or affection I had ever encountered in the Peel Pub. The arm around my shoulder, the toe over my toe—they felt like additional intoxicants to the punch and the joint. These things were happening for me, at a party I had happened to come along to, same as they happened for ordinary people.

"What about you, which pavilion?" I asked, but then the next song got going, loud from the start. He conceded to the music, holding up a finger: *We'll talk more soon.*

Everyone sang a ubiquitous tune from the radio about Expo. *Ca-na-da*. For the first time, I sang along, as did the man who was with me. The performance was tongue in cheek, with everyone rolling their eyes at lyrics about the anniversary of Confederation, and bouncing with exaggeration to the rhythm. When the song finished, it proved to be the lighthearted note the evening's music would end on. Everyone dispersed. In my stomach, I felt sudden churning.

"Australian Pavilion," he said, when I looked up at him. "That's where I'm from. I'm just here for the summer."

"Vomit," I said. "I think I have to vomit."

He pulled me off the couch, grabbed my arm, and led me toward the bathroom, but there was a long lineup at the door. He took me out of that apartment and through the outdoor hall; he tried a different unit, but the door didn't open, so he brought me to the concrete railing overlooking the water and looked down quickly to make sure nothing that mattered was below.

"Chunder," he said, and though it was a brand-new word to me, I knew that it was a command, and how to heed it. I leaned over, releasing punch-coloured vomit into the air. He stood right beside me, expressing no disgust. "Let it all out," he said. "Chunder till you're done." He clapped my back and put the other hand on my forehead, steadying me as I emptied out.

"I'm sorry," I said, without picking up my head, and then I vomited more. He kept his hands exactly where they were. I was crying—because of the embarrassment of the situation, because of the physical strain of retching, and because of the kindness of his company and gestures. We stood together, listening to the din from the party inside. We could also hear the water, constant and urgent and sloshing.

After a moment, my eyes adjusted to the dark. By the faint light of the building, we could see an eddy in the river: a triangle with giant warbling edges. It kept its place very tidily, in the middle of the river. Somewhere in the dark beyond the eddy sat the islands, but I could not find the silhouettes of any of their buildings. With his hand, the Australian man wiped my chin, which must have had some vomit on it. He wasn't disgusted at all. It was like he was cleaning the face of his own child.

"It must be very late," he said, releasing my forehead. "Lights out for everyone."

"We're not facing the city," I said. "We're facing Expo."

"This building faces the city," he said.

"It faces both. It's a weird building."

He laughed at himself. "I never know which way I'm looking here. The city light blocks out the stars."

I didn't understand the relationship between these two sentences and said so.

"When I was a boy," he said, "I used the constellations to find my way home. But actually, it was different stars there, on a different hemisphere. The stars here are no use to me."

"I didn't know about that," I said.

"Yes," he replied, "of course. There are many differences between the top and bottom halves of the planet, you know. On this half, the south sides of the mountains get all the sun, and that's where you find all the vegetation. On my half, it's the north sides that are greener. The steeper the slope of the mountain, the more this is the case. Where the sun is means everything," he said. "You just have to eat two pieces of fruit from the same tree. The fruit on the sunnier side tastes twice as sweet."

"No," I said, astounded.

"Yes," he said, "and there'll be differences of sweetness even between the two sides of that piece of fruit."

This information made me aware of the planet I stood on, and the reaches of outer space that I was being shoved through, along with the rest of the Earth, around and around the sun. I felt the dizzying presence of all these mountains and oranges, there upon the surface, keeping me and the other humans company as we looked up and found stars, stars in which some humans found images of animals, as well as ways home. I was really stoned. I leaned again over the railing, mistaking my astonishment for nausea.

He put his hand back on my forehead. "Why do you think you're sick?" he asked.

"Not enough love," I said immediately. I said this because I thought his question was about my attraction to men. This attraction was front of mind for me, aimed as it was specifically toward him. I had so few faculties with me, trying not to look as disgusting as I felt, so I spoke unfiltered. I had shared my theory thoughtlessly.

He gave me a reprimanding squint, like I was hitting on him with a terrible cheesy line. He thought I was asking him for the love I didn't have enough of. I was glad he was mistaken. That was less embarrassing than what I had really meant.

To give a proper answer to his question, I told him about the whisky drinks I had consumed before the party. "I think it makes me sick," I added, "to think too hard about where I am."

"That's a possibility," he said.

We shared a little staring moment, filled by the sound of water scrambling over water. He put his hand around my bicep, squeezed, and raised one eyebrow.

"I thought you were in shape," he said, "but now I think maybe you're just young."

"Nineteen."

"You should start taking care of yourself *now*. It's all about good habits." Then he took a few steps back, crouched, and placed his hands on the concrete ground. He pounced into a handstand that he maintained for a long time, first with his legs bent and eventually with them fully extended.

"Calisthenics," he said, his voice only a little strained. "Your body weight is all you need. And gravity, which is in good supply."

He folded down and came to me, and it was clear that I was meant to attempt the same thing.

"You won't barf," he said, and I believed him.

I took the emerald ring out of my pocket. "Take this," I said.

"Beautiful rock." He put it on his pinky and made a fist.

I placed my hands on the ground and launched my body up easily. Staying up was the tough part. He grabbed my ankles and kept me straight. Blood filled my head, dark and warm and spiralling. I felt the Earth more than ever, its size and invisible influence. We were people on a planet, going fast through space, staying still on land. I also felt his firm grip on my ankles. Slowly my turtleneck rolled down from my waist and fell around my head.

"I used to catch eyefuls of classmates this way," he said.

"Boy classmates?" I asked through the fabric of my sweater.

"It was all boys."

"You were flirting. Before I barfed."

"Yeah, maybe."

"Maybe still. A little."

"Well, sure. We should stop."

I rolled my body down. Coming back up to standing position, I understood that the thing he wanted to stop was not the handstand, but the flirting. "We're just having fun," I said.

He took my chin again. There wasn't any vomit left; he was just holding my face. He did not look at me with the same warmth as when he'd put his arm around me, or first helped me vomit. I had lost him in some way.

He gave me back my ring. "When I go home after this summer," he said, "there's a girl I'll probably marry."

"You like girls the way you like boys?"

"Well enough."

"But boys more."

"Maybe. But I'm marrying this one."

I looked into the stars. I looked for animals. I thought of Honoré, and my landlady Maria, and all the sentiment I had ever heard about gay life being a youthful thing, a thing you put aside one day. I resented the fact that, even here, at this limitless party of glowing windows and lost edges, such irritating notions could come up in discussion.

"Do you have to?" I pleaded.

He laughed, and it felt incorrect to join him in his laughter, which had a quality of solitude, like someone reading a funny book.

"Do *you* have to stay fixed on the ground?" he said, imitating my tone a little. "Why don't you flap your arms and fly over to that island?"

I didn't know what to do with this comment. His laughter stopped. I pictured myself flapping my arms, and now I was the one who laughed alone. At a delay, he laughed once again. I flapped my arms for real, and together we laughed harder. I pretended to lift off.

"I want to give you my phone number," I said. "Let's meet again."

He said, "Okay," gesturing for us to head back inside together. A handful of conversations were gathered here and there, but the party had thinned out.

"I didn't get your name before," I said.

"Noah," he said.

"And you work at the Australian Pavilion?" I asked.

"Yeah," he said. I wrote my name and my and Étienne's phone number. He took the paper and kissed me on the cheek. Then he left the party, and after one last glass of punch, I left too.

I walked home in a giddy haze. When I got up the stairs of my place and through the door, a new enormous pair of shoes sat by the entrance. I lay on the couch and heard whispering in the bedroom. Étienne had somebody in there, some man from the party. I didn't know who. Maybe the man he had found beautiful in the pamphlet. I slept through their soft chatter and dreamt I was standing with my new friend, Noah, at a distance from an enormous hole in the ground. The ground was sort of earth and sort of seawater. All around us, leaves rustled. We were arguing in a friendly way. My argument was that the hole, over there, had a bottom we couldn't see from our vantage point. His was that there was no bottom, that bottomless holes existed and this was one of them.

7

Noah did not call the next day, nor the day following that. This was fine, even a relief. It would happen on the third day—that was what people did, they waited for the third day. I didn't leave the house unless Étienne was home, and I annoyed Étienne by asking if the phone had rung every time I came home from an errand. With the start of Expo just days away, he was very busy, and I wasn't fun to be around, all jittery and obsessive. The third day passed, then the fourth and fifth.

After a week or so, our phone did ring. It was Michel. I had left him a message as Étienne advised. Michel told me he had found new work for himself, something better than driving diapers. He had become a repairman. He enjoyed it because he got to work regular hours, instead of starting in the dark of early morning. Plus it didn't stink. He needed an assistant, someone who could work on weekend days, as well as the odd afternoon during the week. When he said this, I replied the same way I had replied to the rest of the conversation so far: "That's great, Michel." Then I clued in that he was actually offering me a job. I accepted immediately and felt a happy thrill. But when the call ended, I was mostly just relieved that the telephone line was open again. I had spent the conversation preoccupied by the possibility that Noah might call and find the line unavailable.

When Étienne came home that day, I told him I had found work, and I would start in a few days. "Then you can cover rent soon," he said. He added a congratulations and told me about a party taking place on the first day of Expo. He was working that day but suggested I go without him, as there would be some of the same people as the Habitat party. He didn't mention Noah, but we both knew I was still thinking desperately about him.

The party took place in an apartment in Old Montreal. Though the air had some chill that day, everyone in the apartment stood around in summertime clothes, tank tops and jersey shorts, tube tops and miniskirts. Feeling overdressed, I quickly unbuttoned and removed my shirt, beneath which I wore a faded yellow tank. I stuffed the shirt into the bottom of the closet. It had been Honoré's, and I didn't care if I ever saw it again.

I introduced myself to a foursome in the kitchen. Once their conversation resumed all around me, I noted that none of them were native speakers of English. I asked where everyone was from. France, Japan, Germany, India. The apartment, I learned, was being rented out to the German woman and two of her girl-friends, who worked at Expo. We talked a bit about the previous day's opening ceremonies, which some had seen in person and others had watched on television. We all shared a laugh at the shocking volume of the aviation show. I didn't mention that I had been sleeping in the afternoon and the jets had woken me up.

During a lull, the Japanese woman asked, "What is your blood type? Each of you."

We all shrugged. I asked her, "Why do you want to know?"

"It tells me... who you are," she said with difficulty. Then she grew flustered and waved it off apologetically, like it didn't matter. All the conversations had stilted moments like this, in the seating area beyond the kitchen, and on the balcony beyond that. At the Habitat party, loud music and narcotics had prevented people from having to speak to each other at any length; we had all been limited to waves hello, meaningful looks, group songs. Here, silence filled the room, palpable as the deep orange of the afternoon sun. Nonetheless, I had no desire to leave. People were trickling in, and it was always possible that the next person would be Noah.

I didn't want to be standing around when he arrived, looking like I had nothing to do. I discovered a tiny bar cart on the balcony, with a few random half-full bottles of liquor, and made a start on drinks, pouring everything into little juice glasses from the kitchen with worn-out cartoon apples on their sides. I played up the theatrical elements of bartending, shattering ice cubes in my palm with the back of a large spoon and holding the shaker over my shoulder when using it, the way lumberjacks hold their axes. There was gin and there was Campari, so I made negronis, using white wine in place of vermouth and peeling the rind off an orange with a kitchen knife. When the rind was gone and the orange was all white pith, I picked it up instinctively while finishing the tenth or eleventh drink, before realizing the fruit was no longer useful.

"All done," said one of the women watching.

"Sure is!" I said animatedly, and I threw the naked orange over my shoulder and off the balcony. People gasped; we all laughed. I began pouring drinks into mugs and cereal bowls that were brought to me, so quickly had we moved through the juice glasses.

When someone new came through the front door, I flinched to look—but instead of Noah, it was a young-looking man with long, wavy red hair that fell almost halfway down his back. He wore a white Mickey Mouse T-shirt with the sleeves rolled up to his shoulders. He looked too young for the scene, but his gestures and voice gave away his not being a teenager. I wondered briefly if he knew everyone here, so readily did he engage with them. In truth, he was simply one of those very outgoing people, his energy undampened by the sluggishness of others, his self-appointed job to get people to have fun.

I saw and heard him over in the kitchen, making jokes, in a boomingly loud voice, that others blushed at. The glass door between us was half-closed, and I couldn't make out the words, not until he was speaking to the Japanese woman, and I heard him shout, in a singsongy accent, "O negative, darling! That's the universal kind. I could give my blood to anyone and it would do the trick."

Shortly after his arrival, the general conversation turned to when we would be heading to the island. But the German girl, who had been to Expo earlier in the day, chimed in that the crowds were ridiculous and it had felt almost impossible to fight through them. People expressed hesitation. What really did it was a second bit of information from the German girl: there were Vietnam protesters at Expo, quite a few of them.

"It is a wrong war," someone said. Others added: "Yes." "I think so too." "Very wrong."

So after a while the group determined that we wouldn't head over there after all, in a vague gesture of solidarity with the protesters' cause. We would all gather again and go the next day instead. I was surprised that everyone had such roomy availability. I myself had a shift the following morning, with Michel and the TV repair truck.

"I'm sure it's like a play at the theatre," said the redheaded man reassuringly, once the group reached its decision. "We'll give them a good day or two, to work out the kinks and get better."

Someone asked, "What will we do instead?" and everyone turned to the redhead, our ringleader.

"Games!" he said. Then he went about the room very busily, preparing things. With the German girl's help, he gathered twine and scissors and cardstock; he made a little card with holes and pushed the strings through them, then got others involved in making more, like a kindergarten class. His next destination was my station on the balcony, where he introduced himself as Tristan and asked me what I fixed up. I told him I was out of gin and out of drinking vessels too.

"Never fear," he said, grabbing the bright red bottle of Campari, giving the label a quick, uninterested look, and flicking the cap with his pointer finger, to make it spin off and land on the balcony floor. He took a sip of the room-temperature Campari, making a face like he loved it.

He told us all to write down the name of someone famous on our card, without letting anyone see. Then we switched cards with our neighbours and tied them onto our foreheads. Now we had to ask each other questions to try to guess what each of our cards read. Many had written the names of American actors— Jane Fonda, Ursula Andress, John Wayne. Others were Queen Elizabeth, Elvis Presley, Jesus Christ. Only a few people couldn't guess theirs at all, like the Filipina woman who had become

Yves Saint Laurent, and me. I was Pierre Trudeau, a man I had never heard of. When I was the last person left and I had to give up, everyone said I shouldn't feel too bad. He was a politician, the minister of justice, and they only knew who he was because many of them had met him briefly during one of the orientation days at Expo.

"He made quite the impression," said Tristan. The Campari bottle sat by his feet untouched. He had been Nancy Sinatra and had guessed correctly.

"Trudeau was very handsome," said one girl.

"No, he was not," the girl beside her said emphatically. They discussed this between themselves in Italian, then came to an agreement, sharing their consensus with the rest of the group: "He is ugly *and* he is handsome."

At this everyone nodded.

"Canadians know Trudeau, only Canadians," said Ye, the petite Chinese woman seated next to me, to make me feel better about my defeat.

"I *am* Canadian actually," I said, and the room burst into laughter. In the kitchen I had said I was from New Brunswick, and others had taken this to be a place in England. We did a show of hands, and it came out that I was the only Canadian there.

"But not a very *exemplary* Canadian," said Tristan, initiating more laughs. Someone put on a Bob Dylan record. We played charades, which got all the shyer people more comfortable socializing, and spoons, which was easy to keep up while drinking and chatting. When Tristan replaced Dylan with a Herman's Hermits record, it got people dancing. At some point, a loud bang from outside interrupted the fun. We saw that it was fireworks, over at the island. The balcony was small, so we had to take turns standing outside to watch them, two by two. My counterpart was Tristan, who said as we watched, "What a story they tell."

A woman from Russia didn't enjoy the fireworks. She said she thought at first that perhaps it was the wrong kind of explosions.

"Bombs," said Ye knowingly. As the only Canadian there, I was asked to explain the issue with the FLQ. I tried to remember what I had learned, from the radio and from Honoré. But it had all melted out of my head.

"I don't know anything about it," I said sincerely. Again, there were lighthearted accusations that I wasn't a real Canadian. When everyone laughed, I perhaps laughed hardest. The teasing felt like affection. There was a big dumb smile on my face, and I felt it grow.

When a woman from Mexico produced a joint, I removed myself from the group. I wanted to keep drinking, and adding grass to the mix had gone poorly at Habitat. I needed to stay functional in case Noah arrived. Tristan came to the kitchen and sat with me.

"Are you British?" I asked.

"Welsh," he said, "but no one here knows the difference. The whole United Kingdom is simply one place to most people."

Behind Tristan's head, Ye had started singing for everyone. She could sing opera, and her voice sounded too big to come from such a small person. Tristan and I shared impressed looks. I found a bottle of liquor in the pantry. It had a deer on it, and the label read *Jägermeister*. I gave it a sniff. The text was all German.

"That will get you absolutely bashed," Tristan whispered over the opera song.

"What do I mix it with?" I asked, whispering too.

He made a flicking motion with his hand and threw his head back: take it as a shot. I rinsed out a couple of used teacups and poured us each a finger. Tristan muttered something in Welsh, a charm or toast, before we threw it into our mouths. It burned going down, and immediately I wanted more.

"How do you like Canada so far?" I asked, coming closer to him so we wouldn't have to talk too loud while Ye sang.

"Well," he said, "there are a thousand little differences that are driving me crazy. For instance, at home, you *have* a good time. In Canada, it seems that people can *be* a good time. As in, *that fellow's a good time*. To my ear, it makes no sense."

I poured us each another.

"I also can't just sit in a pub and order a Coca-Cola," he said. "On the motherland, that's nothing special. When I tried it here, I was made to feel rather too fancy."

"You could get away with that at a bar in a hotel," I said.

He gave me a look like *Good thinking*.

"Does Wales have its own pavilion?"

"No. Once again, we are thrown in with the Brits."

I made a motion to fill his teacup a third time, and he put his hand out, politely refusing. I refilled my own.

"So if you're not working for Expo," Tristan asked, "who brought you here?"

"He didn't end up coming. His name is Étienne, my roommate."

"I believe I know him," said Tristan. "Dark skin, fantastic little accent, amazing hair with a vicious widow's peak?"

"That's him."

"You're roommates, eh," he said, his singsong voice muddying the sentence's identity as a question or a statement. Perhaps deliberately.

"Yes," I said, "Roommates and that's all."

Things felt a little tricky now. *That's all.* What more would it be, with two men living together? But I wasn't especially nervous, because I suspected that Tristan was himself a homosexual.

"And do you and Étienne know my friend Dorothy?" he asked.

"Maybe Étienne knows her. I don't really know anyone."

He started laughing to himself, quite a bit.

"What's funny?" I asked.

He sighed, slumping his shoulders. And he looked me up and down. "I'll tell you," he said, defeated by something. "I don't want you to find me rude for laughing. I'm a queer, you see. Surely not the first one you've met. And another way of saying that you're queer is to say that you're a *friend of Dorothy.* It's how we manage to find each other. You're two men, you're roommates, my mind wandered. Apologies for giggling like a fool. Please take no offense."

I grinned.

"So," he said, "I've let you in on something. Do with this information what you will."

"I'm a queer too," I said. His face lit up, relieved. "And so is Étienne," I added, "though we *are* just roommates, like I said. I didn't know about Dorothy."

"Well, there you have it," he said, more to himself than to me. "Maybe in Canada it's a different woman you say you're friends with."

"It probably isn't," I said. "There's a lot I don't know."

"So we're all learning," he said, smiling slyly. "You don't know Dorothy, you don't know Trudeau, and you don't know anyone at this party. Who the hell *do* you know?"

I pretended to throw my drink in his face (the cup was empty now). He flinched, then smiled. I found with him, as I had often found with other redheads, that when his emotions were strongest and simplest, his face gave a glimpse of exactly what he looked like when he was a little boy. He was gleeful once he saw that I was joking, that we were joking together, and in his glee, he looked impossibly young.

"Why Dorothy?" I asked.

"Judy Garland plays Dorothy in *The Wizard of Oz.*"

"I loved that movie."

"Exactly."

He pretended to throw his drink into my face, but I knew the cup was empty and didn't flinch. Again I got a juvenile smile from him. "I must admit," he said, "I'm surprised to hear this about Étienne. I wouldn't have guessed, except perhaps hopefully."

"I think that's a point of pride for him. The way you wouldn't guess."

"Ah. Yes. Well, *there's* a good example of someone who is *not* a good time."

"That's unkind," I said, uncertain of my allegiance.

"No, no. Sometimes it's good when someone is not a good time. You can have a very good time spending time with someone who is not a good time. You get to *be* the good time, and then you feel like even more of a good time than you really are."

I couldn't tell if this was a compliment or an insult to Étienne. I watched Ye, intensely and seriously, as though Tristan and I had agreed that this was what we were doing now. Listening. He turned around and leaned against the counter.

"Such beauties," he said, studying Ye's captivated audience. I reviewed them newly, as they circulated their joints while transfixed by Ye, who had watery eyes from the exertion, or the emotion, of her song. Maybe from both. She was attractive, a brittle white sculpture; they were all attractive as they stared. Even now, with the focus of the room thrown elsewhere, it was like they were pausing to get photographed. They lived their lives that way, the way Étienne lived too, remaining beautiful until nobody important was watching. Ye's singing reached a crescendo, then became a screech, but a pleasant one. It was a lively but sad song. A love song, I assumed. Most songs were love songs. She took on a pose like a warrior, as though she wanted to convince all these people to come and join her in some meaningful battle they could all die young in.

TOGETHER THE THREE OF US WALKED THE SAME WAY HOME at three in the morning—me, Tristan, and Ye. We happened to live in the same direction.

Tristan asked Ye what the song she had sung was about. She did her best to summarize the plot, but most of the words were out of reach for her. All we knew for sure was that a mountain was involved, and that the mountain looked scary, but after a spell of rain, it looked somehow welcoming instead. The story, as she told it, was awkward and difficult to understand. Then she petered out, exhausted by talking in English, and the three of us fell quiet, with just the sound of the odd car piercing our silence.

"I'm sorry if I was unfair about your friend," Tristan said to me, a block or two further on. "I do like the fellow. I was probably being too cheeky by half."

"Don't feel bad. In fact, Étienne and I are getting on each other's nerves lately. But it's my fault, not his. There's a phone call I'm anticipating, and it's making me a nervous wreck."

"You can tell us all about it, if you please. We have a fair bit of walking before my place. Let's spend the time problem-solving. I love that."

Many blocks of our uphill walk got consumed with my story about Habitat and Noah, whose name I never provided. Ye's thoughts on homosexuality were difficult to guess at, and I avoided mentioning even once that Noah was a man. So did Tristan as he responded to my telling. "This person and I really clicked," "This person worked at Expo," "How sweet of this person to hold your forehead while you vomited." Stepping around so many pronouns, we probably sounded like idiots. Ye pretended to find the buildings we passed really fascinating.

"I just find it hard to get my head around," I concluded. "I think I usually get a good read on people. I really thought that we connected, and that this person is supposed to be around now. And now it's almost like the person has vanished instead."

"Well, maybe that's exactly what happened," said Tristan.

"That's grim," I said.

"I don't mean dying," he said. "I just wonder if it has occurred to you that this person didn't vanish exactly, but rather, wasn't really a person?"

I looked over to him with a grin on my face, thinking he was joking. But his face was perfectly straight.

Ye murmured an agreeing sound: *"Mmmm."*

"Like a ghost?"

"*Ghost* is a strong word," said Tristan, "but sure, something like that. Some harmless spirit."

"*Mmmm*," went Ye, nodding her head emphatically.

"They come and go. They sometimes help. It sounds like nobody else saw you interact. This person was very helpful, very kind to you. Maybe you needed that then."

"Yes," said Ye, "a person you needed."

"You both must be joking."

Mount Royal was right beside us now, a big void of silence and darkness, like an unbanistered space a person could fall into. Tristan took a big breath. "When I was a boy," he said, "a girl named Dorrie lived across the street for a time. A snotty brat—but secretly I wanted to be exactly like her. To be particular, like she was. We all had to carry pencil cases to school, and she just *hated* doing this for some reason, so she shoved her pencils up her sleeves. You couldn't carry them loose or the nuns would slap your hands, but if you weren't carrying a case at all, nobody noticed. Anyway, *years* after all that, when I was in high school and it was auditions day for the school play, I decided I wanted to look my best. Feel my best. My pencil case suddenly struck me as the ugliest thing, so I shoved my pencils up my sleeves just like Dorrie would. The day was the kind where you don't need your pencils all day, and it wasn't until I got home that I took off my school clothes and saw the pencils, not only up my sleeves, but up my skin."

"Oof," said Ye.

"I know. My parents *forbade* me from being in the play, and, in fact, the school forbade it too. After my tetanus shot, my parents asked where I had gotten the sleeve idea, and I said, 'Dorrie. Remember Dorrie?' And they *didn't*. Nobody did. There was no Dorrie. I had just gotten the idea, and it saved me from something."

"Didn't you want to be in the play?" I asked.

"Yes, but it was all for the best," he said. "I'm not saying you were talking with a ghost at Habitat. But maybe the whole conversation never happened, and the memory is there anyways."

It was an interesting theory, but I didn't go in for ghost stories. I kept quiet out of politeness. Then Tristan approached a doorway. We had made it to his building. "I'll see you, pet," he said, kissing my cheek. He kissed Ye's too, then passed through the door. Ye and I continued on, untalkative without Tristan. When we reached her apartment, a couple of blocks further up, she headed right up without saying goodbye. I felt now that she would have preferred to walk home by herself.

I also felt that, if her home had come first instead of Tristan's on the walk, then Tristan and I might have quite naturally entered his doorway together and slept together. It would have been convenient, even expected. A doorway to enter, and nobody watching. But his was the first door, not the second, so nothing like that happened.

After my long walk home, the couch looked especially uncomfortable. I was achy and short of breath. I went into the bedroom, where Étienne was sleeping alone, and found just enough space for myself beside him. I closed my eyes and thought of Tristan, who had outed himself so fearlessly and dispensed advice so readily. I could not remember ever meeting such an exciting person.

"No calls," whispered Étienne, who I had thought was asleep.

"What? Oh," I said. "I don't care. I'm sorry I've been such a gnat about that. It was like a fever, and it's broken now."

"You're a romantic," said Étienne, so many moments later that I was surprised to hear him speak. He put his arm around me. "Beyond hope."

"Were you ever a romantic?"

I could sense him formulating an answer. "Everyone was," he said eventually. "It is hard to stay this way, however. Look. The sun."

I opened my eyes. Indeed, the faintest light was coming in through the window. I closed my eyes again, and pressed my back against Étienne's chest. If I didn't fall asleep now, it would only get harder to do; it would only get brighter, and quickly.

8

I n the morning, Michel called to say his truck was out of commission for a little while. I winced at the news; I wanted the
money. But as I boiled eggs for my and Étienne's breakfast, I
realized that it freed me up to join the previous day's partygoers
on the rescheduled trip to Expo.

At the German girls' apartment, all the same people were
there as the previous day, except for Ye. Tristan wore his long
hair in a ponytail that fell down his left shoulder, and his left
hand played with it as he checked in with the room, making
sure everyone had fare for the Expo Express.

As we walked to the stop, Tristan did what he could to keep
us all together. I walked beside the two Italian women who had
determined the previous day that Pierre Trudeau was both ugly
and handsome.

"Adesso?" asked one to the other, who shook her head. She
asked this several times—*Adesso? Adesso?*—and whatever that
meant, the answer stayed "no" the whole walk. Once we reached
the Expo Express, the one who had been shaking her head said,
at last, *"Adesso!"* She produced two folded-up pieces of waxed
paper from her purse. Within the waxed papers were many

squares, like little postage stamps. She put one square on her tongue and one on her friend's tongue, laughing. Others helped themselves. When the waxed paper made its way to Tristan, he turned it down, using the same soft cupped hand he had used when I'd offered to refill his Jägermeister the previous night. I followed his lead and turned it down too.

Our train passed Habitat and went further than I had ever gone before, right to the islands. Immediately we transferred to a Minirail car that had no windows, only open air. The cool of the wind made the skin on my shoulders prick. We emerged from a tunnel and were suddenly suspended high above the ground. Behind Tristan's head, I saw all the buildings I had seen for so long from a distance. Instead of a gradual approach, we were instantly flying through the middle of the festivities.

The buildings formed a geometric mess all around us, with a distinct lack of borders—every element was only sort of what it was. Transparent windows became, at a different angle, vibrantly neon and wholly opaque; staircases erupted from the ground, a great deal wider than the buildings they led to; people sat on the stairs, treating them like benches, smoking their cigarettes, eating their ice cream, fixing their children's collars. The buildings were certainly unlike others I had seen, but I couldn't determine if they were really beautiful. They were clearly very costly, as were the Minirail tracks and cars, the fountains and pathways, the statues and playgrounds. The islands they were built on too. Reflecting on this expensiveness, I decided that all of this had to be beautiful, because people didn't let ugly ideas get this far.

One building outdid the others in its differentness, absolutely colossal and perfectly spherical. This was the American Pavilion, the dome that Étienne had called the future of living.

As I wondered what its insides might look like, the Minirail brought us right through the dome, with some from our group gasping at the sudden change. Visitors covered the ground floor, and escalators and footbridges, also full of people, jutted unpredictably through the open space. Guitars, bicycles, paintings tall as houses, and fake plastic lips big as loveseats were fixed to the walls. Then, just as easily as we had entered, we exited through the other side, and all the calamity inside the dome was once again hidden. Across the water, on the other island, a gigantic rectangular building, with the letters USSR/URSS across its front, seemed to float above the ground. We chugged toward more giant shapes, more bustling crowds. The two Italian women spoke closely to each other. Others stared out the window with their mouths open and their eyes manic.

The Minirail stopped at a giant upside-down pyramid. As we debarked, Tristan said, "This is the Canadian Pavilion." He addressed me specifically, I assumed, because I wasn't high. Everyone else's glazed condition put us at a distance from them. They filtered over to the pyramid slowly, unbothered by the lineup, embracing each other's hands and bits of fabric from each other's clothes. I was turned off by the idea of waiting around in lines, and I asked Tristan if he felt like wandering instead. He beamed and said, "I'd love nothing more."

We fought through the current of the crowds, losing sight of our group, firmly becoming a twosome for the day. "Why didn't you take acid?" I asked.

"Like any other lonely little faggot with a surplus of emotions stuck in the middle of nowhere his whole childhood," he said, "I have given hallucinogens a go. I remember trying to eat a clementine, and I had to ask my mate—how can anyone be expected to do this without at least one towel? A real bore. I never tried a second time."

Every building we came across had a lineup. Tristan and I had fun trying to guess at the countries of origin of all the buildings. Some seemed unclear, and others obvious, like the British Pavilion, which wore a bursting three-dimensional Union Jack on its top, like a Christmas tree with a big chunky star. Tristan didn't want to go near it; he'd be working there the following day and for many days after that. He wanted to see everything else instead.

We could smell a fish-piss funk from the water around us, which hung heavily in the air, occasionally mixed with—but never overtaken by—the other smells of the island. A popcorn stand's bubbling oil; the botanical smells of a garden we walked through; perfume, cologne, and body odour from the people we squeezed past. I feared that the buildings might topple because the workers had erected them so fast. I feared too that the ground might fall apart and swallow things up, under the weight of these bulking structures and unfathomable crowds. Beneath our shoes was concrete, and beneath the concrete, land, but the land did not belong there, nor the concrete, nor the people. The land had come from the earth, deep inside, and had been brought here over time by trucks and men with plans and budgets. Now other people were here too, reaching their heads behind the corners of pillars. They pointed at walls and went, "My!"—bringing each other's attention to finials, buttresses, windowsills, fountains, every inch and moment. I agreed with them. Everything had a fascinating quality. But I had to admit to myself that it all seemed really, really goofy too, like the set of a hokey variety show. As Tristan and I walked through the paths, I felt sad on behalf of the whole event. It was meant to feel significant, but maybe all that money, work, and dirt had indeed been put toward something very silly, a bad idea that had gotten out of hand.

Walking beside me, Tristan peered all around, absolutely beaming, his face looking how it must have looked during his childhood's happiest moments. "Don't you love how *too much* it all is?" he asked. "It's just *so* excessive. In fact, it's bloody madcap. I don't think I quite *got it* before. Now that it's alive, with mankind moving through it, I do."

"I don't know if it's trying to be *too much*," I said.

"Of course it isn't!" He sighed in admiration, playing with his long ponytail. "And that's why it's so great. None of this would be any fun if it had any idea just how camp it is."

As we headed to another corner of the island, we noticed many children, everywhere we went. Running through the crowds, riding miserable elephants and shivering camels, splashing each other with fountain water, cotton candy stuck on their faces, hard candy falling from their hands to the ground and exploding there. Children having tantrums and laughing fits. Supervised and unsupervised children. Watching three of them play a game of tag on a staircase, I felt embarrassed for myself and Tristan. We were two adults who had come to this enormous playground by themselves.

In the late afternoon, we came to a building that was like a gigantic trapezoid, its longest end at the top. A lineup was coiled around it. At the sight of its sign, I froze up: *Australian Pavilion*. Tristan grabbed my arm and brought me with him in the building's direction. He had also noticed the sign.

"The only lineup I'm willing to tolerate," he said gamely. "Let's find your mysterious man."

"I don't know if I care anymore."

"Don't you though? Even just to *see* him. You can resume the seduction the next time. This time is just to prove that he's real."

When we got in, there were all kinds of maps and models, and bulging tables surrounded by uncomfortable-looking chairs. An indoor enclosure housed several kangaroos, looking weak-spirited and sleepy. Most had lain down, with gumballs and wrappers at their feet. Children around us threw them yet more treats to ignore, and none of the attendants, in their bright orange outfits, did much to stop this.

Tristan approached one of the attendants and said, in a convincing Australian accent, "My mate Noah should be working here, as an attendant, just like you. We came up together back at home. I've no clue where to find him exactly. Wondering, could you help?"

"Noah?" the woman said. "No, no attendant by that name."

"You're certain?"

"There's just a handful of us. Yeah."

"Maybe in the offices?"

The woman consulted with a different attendant, who confirmed that nobody named Noah worked there.

"Thanks kindly, from one Aussie to another," said Tristan, and we left.

When we came outside, he seemed irrepressibly delighted by something.

"There you have it then," he said. He had taken this development as actual proof of the previous night's hypothesis. He truly believed that Noah was a ghost of some kind.

His conviction amazed me. "I'm trying to imagine that you're right," I said, "and I just can't. It's too far out for me. It's easier to believe that he just told me a fake name. Maybe the water near us made him think of floods."

"To each their own," Tristan said with polite indifference.

We walked to a plasticky footbridge, over an inconsistently sputtering little stream. We stopped in the middle of the bridge and saw a ramp in the distance, in the middle of the river, from which small yellow powerboats launched into the air. We leaned against the railing and watched the water, though really I just stared out, focusing on nothing.

It was getting overcast quickly. People around us headed to lineups, anticipating rain. Tristan stared into the water. "What's on your mind?" he asked.

"Mountains," I said. "Oranges. How we're moving through space all quick, all together, around and around every year."

"Oh, that," he said, nodding solemnly.

"When you told your ghost story," I said, "about Dorrie with the pencils, why was that a positive story, instead of a sad one?"

"I certainly didn't think of it as positive at the time, missing out on the play. I had a gift for the stage, more than anyone else in my little town. I spent weeks in utter agony, thinking of how perfect it would have been. To be part of the rehearsals, part of the show. I was so, *so* blue about it. Then, the morning of opening night, I shat myself during maths class."

He looked at me directly, confirming with his terse gaze that I had not misheard him.

"I have fits," he said firmly. "Fits without a fix. They visit me in times of stress. Sometimes they visit just because. The flailing on the floor, the shaking like a fool. That first one was the only time I completely lost bowel control, though I do piss myself about half the time. Prohibitive for a life on the stage. Prohibitive for a great number of lives."

He chuckled to himself. Then I chuckled too.

"Had I been permitted to play the role, it would have been the best idea to drop out. But I wouldn't have done that. Instead, I would have pressed on, and eventually, some night, in front of my parish or some neighbouring one, I would have had the greatest humiliation of my life, or of any life I've ever known. Not just in maths. In front of *everyone*. I truly believe that that's what Dorrie saved me from. The humiliation of attempting any life onstage. Those horrid days, I might have been one humiliation away from—well. From doing the thing you can't undo, to be honest."

Again, a terse and certain look from him.

"Difficult years," he said, shrugging. "Even before the maths incident. In any event, I value the girl's judgment and intervention a great deal."

"How did you think of doing it?" I asked.

"I liked the idea of rocks in the pockets," he said, "and perhaps my paperback of Virginia Woolf's *Orlando* would be shoved in there too, just so everyone might understand that I was wise to the reference—and that, if I was being derivative, at least I knew that about myself. But the trouble with all the bodies of water I could walk to was that none were quite as deep as I am tall."

We both laughed. I noticed an eddy, far beyond the ramp. First I thought, *That chunk of water is the same shape as the one I saw from Habitat, when vomiting.* Then I thought, *It's the same water, the same eddy, seen now from lower down, and from the other side.*

"It's been a few months since the epilepsy has graced me with its company," he said. "The fits are actually a very funny thing. How they come and go as they please. My hope is that they've taken the summer off. I certainly didn't tell the folks here to expect my little soft-shoe, and, in fact, I told a lie by omission during the screening process. But I know the fits are out there, or rather, in here"—he pointed at his temple—"gearing up for a return. It's my job not to tempt them, nor deny them. My job, really, is the same as any man's. It's to remember my lot."

I noticed a branch in the water, lost from some tree, approaching and meeting the eddy, which swallowed it down with no effort.

"Why didn't the ghost take away your seizures?" I asked. "Cure you, instead of just giving you a certain idea."

"A question I've wondered many times," he said gingerly. "Especially at the theatre, watching all those glorious people participate in magic-making. *Why can't it be me up there?* What I've concluded is that you can't do much about human bodies. They have wills of their own. Otherwise, I would have so much redone with this one. I would make myself stuffed full after one side salad with maybe a bit of good cheese. I would want women and not men—how much simpler that would be. But I can't do much about these matters, nor can anyone or anything. Not even the doctors you read about now, trying to take one man's heart and place it in another's chest. Waste of time. That's what I think."

He put his hand on my back, all friendly, and held his other hand out, palm up, to see if he could feel any rainfall.

"This is Welsh weather. It seems to be about to rain, but any moment the sun will come back after all. When I left home, I lived in youth hostels; young boys can hitch rides and arrive saying, *My father knows I'm here.* I did that plenty, even though my father didn't know a thing. I saw the whole countryside, and many grey skies. When the weather is like this, it feels like something I brought along with me."

We left the bridge and wandered again. We bought a bag of doughnuts to share and arrived at a tiny, elevated ice rink, with a little awning over it, and a man and two women skating there, doing what they could in the space they had. All three wore pinstripes and bow ties, the man with blue pants and the women in skirts. The man hoisted them up, or pulled them between his legs; they did twirls and the cancan, hybrid mixes of skating and dancing, vaudeville and go-go. The music was plinky and obnoxious, and practically drowned out by the chugging drone sounds of the vat-shaped mechanism hidden by the awning, which kept the ice beneath them cold. When the music stopped, they bowed, prompting applause.

Over the course of their performance, the sun had returned, as Tristan had said would happen. I looked his way and saw that his eyes were a little wet, and the skin of his face was red with emotion. He also had sugar on his chin from the doughnuts. It glistened, sickly and slick. I wondered what he had been thinking about during the performance, to now appear so affected. The paths in life he had not taken, his medical issues, ghosts, suicide.

Then he turned to me, perfectly aware of my gaze, and said, "Brilliant stuff."

I realized that the performance itself had moved him. I realized also that he and I would connect again, and not as members of a bigger group. I had a new friend.

The three ice-skaters had nowhere to hide during their break, under their awning. They stood on the ice with their backs to us all, smoking their cigarettes, talking among themselves, trusting the cooling mechanism to drown out their chat. It felt improper, even disrespectful, to watch them now, the way we had watched a moment before.

"Filthy face," I said to Tristan.

His expression changed instantly to something self-conscious. He wiped the sugar off his mouth, and it fell to our feet in little clumps. Before long, the music began again, and so did the performance.

9

I didn't make it back to Expo for a few weeks. I spent every weekend working with Michel, repairing televisions, and during the week I had no one to go to the islands with. Though I thought once or twice about heading over alone, I always chickened out, fearing it would make me sad to go without a second person to develop adventures with. Étienne's work at the French Pavilion involved so little downtime that Expo was the last place he wanted to go outside of work hours. When he got home, he only wanted to rest while I made our dinner and drinks, and then to read his paperbacks, some French and some English. *Voyage au bout de la nuit*, *The Autobiography of Malcolm X*, *Silent Spring*. Right before bed, on the bedroom floor, he would do his push-ups and sit-ups, and then in the bathroom, his facial isometrics. He usually closed the bathroom door beforehand, but sometimes he seemed to forget I was home and kept the door open. If I leaned back on the couch, I could see him in there, his unfolded chart of isometrics laid out over the sink, as he made the same ridiculous faces in the mirror, over and over, to keep the muscles of his face pleasingly shaped and to ward off wrinkles.

I took no issue with playing the housekeeper. I made less money and had more spare time. Driving around with Michel a few days a week produced only enough income to prevent me from having to ask Étienne for cash when I went to buy our groceries and booze. After the shopping, I had nothing for the rent.

Most evenings, I spoke with Tristan on the phone. His everyday experiences working at Expo were, to me, a portal to that place; I envied his job and harboured some shame that I had never made my own attempt at finding work there. When our conversations ended, I always retained a rejuvenated feeling.

"Where did you learn that game we played with the celebrity names?" I asked one evening, when we were talking about that first party.

"It's just an old party game. I almost suggested a different one, where we go around the circle and we each share something about our lives we've never told anyone. I used to do that at parties all the time. Everyone loves doing it, if it's a game they *have* to play. What they love is the excuse to confide. I'll bet you've got it picked out now, the thing you would share. I'll bet you could think of it straight away."

He was right, I did have something. "First kiss," I said.

"Tell me the story," he said, and I did, quite easily, though I hadn't previously thought of it as a story. It had just been something that had happened to me.

"Well," I said, "a boy was staying with us alone for some reason. His name was Ray. All I remember is that our dads had been friends from the war. We were the same age, twelve or thirteen, and I didn't really like him much. He complained a lot—the pillow was too soft, the bedroom was too drafty, I hogged the sheets. I probably would have called him a sissy, but I didn't say that to his face."

"There weren't other boys around," said Tristan. "You can't call someone a sissy unless there are other boys, or you feel the cruelty all to yourself."

"Another thing was that he couldn't believe we didn't own a television. One night he really wanted to watch *Ed Sullivan*. He panicked that he'd miss it, and he wouldn't stop going on about it, so I told him, 'I know something better,' and I took him to see the goats nearby."

"Yes," said Tristan solemnly. "Goats are marvellous."

"They are! It was downhill to the neighbour's farm, where the goats were, and we walked fast. Then we ran, stomping our feet. You know how it is when you run down a hill and you can't stop. And when you run really fast beside someone, you end up laughing together. He had been so sulky—and now he was laughing! Hearing him laugh like that was like realizing I was in love with someone, or maybe with something. Even something like a moment. I wanted the feeling that gave him that laughter to last forever for him. I wanted him to think of joy when he thought of me later. A lot later. We sped up even more when we could hear the goats. Do you know how goats sound?"

"Like humans screaming."

"Exactly. It was getting dark, but you could see them, and they came to us, which they like to do, except for two who were actually having sex, one below the other. Ray and I watched them, and even though I knew what they were doing, I said, 'What are they doing?' so we could both pretend we didn't know, because that felt polite. And then, suddenly, he was kissing me. I hadn't seen his face approach, it was dark. There was just suddenly a mouth against mine. It's hard to explain, but I remember thinking for a second that that was what came before kissing, and that what happened next would be the kissing. Then I understood, *that* was the kissing, it was happening already. I hadn't thought of tongues as things that had a taste. I remember hoping that mine tasted good for him. His tongue tasted amazing to me. That night I pretended to fall asleep on the couch, and I stayed there all night, because I didn't know what would happen if we were in the bed together. I had no idea, and I was really scared. The rest of his visit, we pretended nothing had happened. It was easy to pretend this, because we had never shared admiring looks, or kind words, or anything like that. Neither before nor after. And then he was gone, picked up by his dad."

I looked down into my drink, a very neglected Rob Roy. It was mostly meltwater, with a cherry sunk to the bottom.

"So there," I said. "That's the untold story I would tell at a party."

"Thank you," said Tristan sincerely.

We talked about other things now, though it was Tristan who did most of the talking; I spent the conversation thinking quietly about Ray, who I had not remembered for so long. Tristan had helped me unearth the whole thing. I never thought the story would have much utility, but there I was, fascinating somebody with it.

A quiet fell on the conversation, and I almost introduced the idea of wrapping it up and calling again soon. Then Tristan said, "I love sissies," as though we were still discussing Ray.

"Oh," I said.

"As a boy," he added, "I hated sissies, although I surely was one, which I would wager was also true of you. But the only people I could love would have to have had such a past. A boyhood that the strong survive. The strong alone."

ONE EVENING, TRISTAN SUGGESTED THAT HE COME OVER to my place, with his tarot cards and a bottle of whisky. I said yes and gave Étienne an apologetic heads-up, to which he responded with a brisk shrug before looking back down at his book, *The Golden Notebook*. Nervous about the measly state of our apartment, I turned the radio to a music station and put some food out: cold cuts marbled with fat globs, sliced-up carrots and bell peppers with no dip. I fanned these things out on their Melmac plates and placed a wilting carrot leaf across each. When Tristan arrived, we kissed cheeks; Étienne waved hello from the couch.

"Darling decor," said Tristan, proceeding to walk around and inspect every element. I followed, explaining what was mine (almost nothing), what was Étienne's (a few things), and what came with the place when we first began renting it (most of it). Étienne stayed on the couch, a finger in his book keeping his place, uncommitted to socializing. But he committed once Tristan produced a bottle of whisky he had nicked from the British Pavilion. Penderyn. Étienne helped himself to generous amounts. Tristan had only one sip, then left his glass alone. We sat chatting around the milk-crate coffee table, on which sat Tristan's tarot deck, wrapped in purple silk. A song came on the radio that I recognized vaguely, though I couldn't place it immediately. Tristan noticed that I was lost in it.

"I believe this is the Righteous Brothers," he said to me. "The song is called 'He,' and I can barely stand it. So rich and sweet—enough to rot your teeth."

"Of course," I said, remembering that I had heard it on the radio before. "I don't like that last line—how God is sad about how we live but he loves us anyway."

"He probably is, if I'm honest," said Tristan, "but I haven't put much stock in his opinion since my voice was still squeaky. Squeaky like the Righteous Brothers."

Étienne and I chuckled at this, and the song concluded in its crash of strings, cymbals, and male voices. Étienne seemed distracted as the conversation continued, prompting Tristan to ask him, "Cat got your tongue?"

"I like what you have said about God," said Étienne. "It is unusual to meet anyone who is not very devout. Now, with you and many others arriving for Expo, I can remember that there are many in the world who do not have any God at all, and these are happy people, sad people. Every people. There is a world out there—not just the Protestants and Catholics of Montreal. I am happy to remember this."

"And for you?" Tristan asked Étienne, topping up Étienne's whisky and mine, but not his own. "Do you *have any God at all*?"

Étienne smirked. "The more I try to think, the more I do not care. But if he is there, I agree with the song. He is sad, and he should be. Look at Vietnam, look at the Sinai Peninsula, even look at the streets of Detroit or New York. Or Montreal, *bien sûr*—outside of our own window. You go to Expo, you think it is harmony—every country, harmony. Such perfect little lies, I must say. The way we live *would* make God sad. It makes anyone who pays attention sad-sad-sad."

Tristan nodded sacredly at this, though I knew he was only as caught up in current affairs as I was and probably couldn't spell *Sinai* out loud, or find the peninsula on a map. Neither of us gave Étienne much of a reply.

"I'm sorry," Étienne said, "you boys wanted to play cards. Here I go, crying about the world. Yesterday morning at the pavilion, they told to us about *politeness*. I have lived here in Canada for a longer time than the others, but it is not something I understood before they told us this. Now I understand. Here, if you must choose between telling the truth and being polite, it is best to be polite. I am forgetting where I am. Excuse me—I am bad company. Have a good game."

As Étienne poured himself one more finger of Penderyn, I said, "They're not cards you play actually. They're the kind you *read*."

"That's not perfectly true," said Tristan. "The cards do know some parlour games, and it's good to let the spirits have some fun sometimes, instead of putting them to work. Good night," he said to Étienne, who echoed him before lighting himself a cigarette and carrying the ashtray into his bedroom.

Now Tristan and I spoke at a whisper. "I must admit," said Tristan, "I'm not quite as worldly as your friend. It seems rather exhausting, caring so much."

"You're more worldly than me," I said. "I've never even been in an airplane. Visiting Expo is as close as I've come to travelling the world."

"There will be time for all of that one day." He started shuffling the cards. "I have little doubt you'll see everything you want to."

"It was funny to hear Étienne talk about telling the truth," I said, speaking even more quietly. "He actually fibs a fair bit."

"Sometimes when you tell a lie, it's perfectly external—it was inside of you, and now it's been given to somebody else. Other times, though, when you tell a lie to someone else, you tell it to yourself as well, and believe it. He strikes me as a man of character. Of the first kind of lie, not the second. Big difference, pet." He gave me a smile and a raise of the eyebrows, pleased with himself. "Now let's see if I'm half as clever with the cards tonight as I would seem to be with my words."

He shuffled the cards and dealt me a hand, then directed me through a tarot card game that even he found confusing. He had to correct himself about the rules multiple times. If I was taking the game seriously, rather than just enjoying his company, this might have bothered me, but as it stood, we simply laughed a lot together.

Tristan frequently looked out behind me, through the bay window.

"Do you see something?" I eventually asked.

"There's a bird that keeps flying through the street light," he said, "but I don't know of any birds that fly like that at night. Just a little bit of motion, small as a palm, over and over."

"Could be a bat."

"That must be it." He smiled to himself, and said, *"Jamais vu."*

"What?"

"A feeling I just had. With *déjà vu*, what you're doing feels like something you've done before. *Jamais vu* is the opposite of that. I had it when you spoke. A feeling like the moment you're living is something you've never, ever done before, not even *this* time. It's quite pleasant, really. *Déjà vu* often precedes a seizure for me. This feeling, however, causes me no grief. It just arrives and leaves."

I didn't mention to him that, while I had never had this feeling, I found it comprehensible, nor did I mention that I found it comprehensible because of him. Everything he did seemed to me a unique move, the first of its kind—so special that, even after its occurrence, history was missing it. I ran my tongue across the smooth film of whisky on my front teeth. Even though it wasn't very tasty, I poured myself more and drank it down.

THE NEXT EVENING, I WAS HOME ALONE AND MORE BORED than usual, having a fresh sense of Tristan's company and missing it dearly. The air was warm and the night sky a clean blue. While flipping through Étienne's pornography, I realized that I had soured on it. It was no longer enough for me, even if it was enough for Étienne. I finished my vermouth and headed over to the edges of Mount Royal to cruise.

Approaching the hill, I felt expectations pinging in my brain about the body I would soon place against my own, and all its possibilities. I wanted him to act eager and unrushed. Those who rushed felt ashamed of themselves, and ashamed of the man they were with too. I had come to understand this. Unrushed meant unashamed. I wanted him also to stay well-mannered—for instance, to speak a little before we parted ways. At least he could say *goodbye*, and preferably more. I always liked a bit of chit-chat before the scatter, like when your train begins to slow and you turn to your seatmate, with whom you've been quiet, and ask for first time: *Heading home or somewhere new?*

I entered the bushes keenly. Sprinting through the rough, I noticed, off to my left, two men who had paired off already. They formed a big black mound with two voices, shushing itself perilously at the sound of my footfalls. Further in was an unaccompanied man, in a simple white tank top and jeans. One of us said, "Hey," and the other said it back. He looked me up and down in a manner that could have passed for innocent. I surveyed him back, less ambiguous, and led him to a spot deep in the thick. It struck me as familiar—perhaps I had been to this very spot before. But unlike my previous time in that place, there was a bed of inexplicable orange flowers that I could just make out in the moonlight.

Before anyone's hand had even touched the other's belt, or any mouth the other mouth, he said, "I'm Gabe. What's your name?"

Remembering my first cruising partner's advice to never give a real name, I said, "My name is Tristan." I felt an awkward pang—I hadn't meant to take my friend's name, it was only the first name that occurred to me—and then I pushed away all thoughts, because things had started, we were kissing. He lifted my tank top up to my neck, though not over my head, and glided down onto his knees, kissing my chest, my belly, and finally my waistline. I looked ahead into the dark of the woods, and once or twice down at the orange flowers. I thought of the earth below the flowers, and the space around the Earth, and how the things that seem still are actually moving, just as much as the things that are moving evidently, because everything is moving, because we're on the surface of a planet. The roots of the flowers clutched the Earth tight, as though they would otherwise go flying.

"Tristan," Gabe whispered. I put my hands on his head. He had a buzzcut, and when I stroked it one way, I felt the million little filaments return to their natural grain immediately, the same as if nobody had touched them. I focused on the warmth of his mouth, and when he said a second time the name he thought was mine—"Tristan"—I came, and empowered by the sudden sense that I deserved everything I had ever wanted, I knelt, then crouched. I wanted to. His penis was already out, with his palm wrapped around it; I put it in my mouth, and my hands into the flowers, and my chest and erection down against the dark, cool earth. With his free hand on my shoulder, he came into my mouth. His cum tasted like nothing, same as water.

When we got up off the ground, I asked where he was from.

"Israel," he said, zipping up his fly. "I'm with the Expo."

We walked together back toward the main path. Distant street lights gave us better views of each other's faces. I saw now that he was very handsome. "Well," I said, "in Canada, names don't usually matter so much during this kind of thing. Just so you know."

"Names don't matter here?" he asked facetiously, pointing at my chest and his, back and forth. "Sure they do."

It annoyed me that he didn't give the advice credence. But I didn't know exactly how to elaborate. It was just something someone had once told me, same as I told him now.

"In the dark," he said, "I would have put you at about thirty. Now I think younger."

"I'm twenty," I said. The pair of men I had passed previously had dispersed, and only one man remained there. He reclined on his back in the dirt, with dirt also in big smears on his shirt and jeans.

"I like my name," Gabe said to me. "Gabriel was an angel, as you may know already. He did the talking for God. I like my name. I'm not afraid to share it."

131

"Of course I know about Gabriel the angel," I fibbed. We slowed down our pace, now that we were out of the thick. I felt the grit of the earth in my briefs.

"What does the name *Tristan* mean?" he asked.

This caught me up. Everybody knows the meaning of their own name. I could have said anything—*flower, sky*—and he would have believed it, but I couldn't think of a lie. "It's Welsh," I spouted after a telling silence.

In response, he laughed. "When someone asks you a question about yourself, you should answer it decent." This was the last thing he said. Then we weren't walking together anymore, we were just walking beside each other, and he at a quicker pace. In no time he was gone ahead. Then far ahead. I walked alone back home, comforted that I did know that one thing. I knew my way home from the park.

10

On our phone chat the next night, I asked Tristan what his name meant.

"Sorrow," he said, "but nobody's thinking of that when they give the name to their babies. They're thinking of the dragon slayer. There are Tristans galore back home, though I'm pleased that so many here in the new world find the name unconventional."

Then he told me a plan he had hatched. The Supremes would play at Expo the next day, and he had heard a rumour from a co-worker that Diana Ross enjoyed the company of queer men. When the Supremes toured, she was said to make surprise appearances at gay bars after the shows. Not to perform—just to enjoy herself. Tristan asked me to think hard about the queer bars in Montreal, so we could determine how to find her the next night. "Don't think of the most popular place," he said, firm and careful. "Think of the place that Diana Ross's people would most likely direct her to."

"The Peel Pub," I said, having no idea what kind of people her people were. But it felt possible that she would appear at an English-friendly spot, if anywhere at all, and Davey played so much Motown that it felt like a sensible fit. I agreed to this plan, even if it would empty my wallet.

When Tristan and I arrived, both wearing simple tees and tight jeans, we saw that the rumour had spread. The place was busier than I had ever seen it. Management had cottoned on to the rumour too, charging five dollars for entry. But that cost also made the possibility of Diana Ross arriving feel very real, and we paid up smiling.

Our entry disappointed the men and women who were watching the door, as did the entry of every person who wasn't Diana Ross. At the bar, I caught up with Davey, who confirmed that this was a busier night than usual, but not by all that much. "Really, it's Expo," he said. "So many queers, in from all over. It's great, except the ones who don't fucking tip."

By this time, Tristan had disappeared into the crowd. I ordered two Mai Tais, knowing that Tristan loved a sweet drink. I found him standing over a half-full booth.

"Look who I found," he said to me, and gestured to Ye, who sat in the booth with three others.

"Ye! I was so sorry to hear about your pavilion," I said. The Chinese Pavilion had only just reopened after a month out of commission following a fire. I remembered seeing the plume of smoke, all the way from the city, and thinking of Ye once I heard the story on the radio.

"Yes," she said, in a voice that sounded almost annoyed, "but instead of waiting for the pavilion to reopen, I found work at the Bay. I've decided to stay in Montreal." Her English was much, much better than before, after just a couple of months.

"Have you learned French as well as English?" asked Tristan, clearly as impressed as I was.

"Not really, but it is not difficult to find English work here," she said. "Mary doesn't speak French, and she has lived here for most of her life."

She nodded at the person beside her, who wore a baseball cap and a plain blue jersey and who I had thought at first was a man. This person, Mary, looked up at us briefly. She made no offer for us to join them, and neither did Ye, even though there was room for us in the booth. The conversation had evidently ended. Ye turned to Mary and the other women at the table, and they all spoke so quietly that we couldn't much hear.

Tristan and I found a space to stand against the wall. "That was odd," I said to Tristan.

"Did you find?" he replied. He liked to come across as insusceptible to surprises and denied them when they happened. We sucked our straws. Ye suddenly glanced our way, issuing us a dirty look. This was when I put together that she had not stumbled to this bar by accident. She was a homosexual, enjoying the company of other women like her. Like us. Her coldness had to do with our behaviour, the night the three of us walked home. While discussing the Australian man at Habitat, we had kept his maleness obscured, not knowing how she would react. Now it was clear that this had been condescending. Insensitive too. How frustrated she must have been that night, stuck with two men who gave her no credit and who showed no interest in learning more about her, talking instead over her head, in a language she was still new to.

"I think I understand why she's here," I said to Tristan.

"Lesbians," said Tristan. He spoke nonchalantly, putting on like he had known this all along. "I had quite forgotten about lesbians." He chortled.

"We were being silly that night," I said.

"You were simply exercising an abundance of caution," he said, "and I followed your lead like the seasoned co-conspirator I am."

"But I'm sick of all the code talk. *Friends of Dorothy.* I've never met a Dorothy in my life. Nobody names their daughter Dorothy. It's a name for movie characters. And I've never regretted being clear with others about who I am. I just want to answer every question decent."

Tristan nodded along, again feigning omniscience. Then he kissed me on the cheek. "You're right, you know," he said.

"I do know. I am right. Thank you."

The music increased in volume significantly. "You Can't Hurry Love" by the Supremes. Everyone got excited, as though it was perhaps not a recording. Alas, Diana Ross had still not arrived. The fact that Davey had dropped a Supremes record made me suspect that he had received some intelligence on the matter, and that Diana Ross wouldn't come after all. Now he was trying to give the people some of what they wanted.

The dance floor, where many men had stood in circles of conversation, reverted to its purpose. Those who wanted to chat moved away from it, and those who wanted to dance closed in. Tristan was one of the latter group. He put his half-finished drink on a nearby table, then took my empty glass out of my hands and put it down too. He led me into the welcoming chaos of the dance floor. The next song was "A Lover's Concerto." Diana Ross sang, asking how gentle the rain is, and instructed us all to see, beyond the hill, the bright colours of the rainbow.

I felt glad she did not show up. With no celebrity stealing the attention, the night felt more like something that belonged to

Tristan and me. Davey ran out of Supremes records but kept the Motown vibrations going. "Dancing in the Street," "This Old Heart of Mine," "How Sweet It Is to Be Loved by You." Finally, to end the night, the James Brown that Davey loved so much—"It's a Man's Man's Man's World." A slow song, to give us all the sense that it was time to go home, and to make each person feel like doing so was their own idea.

11

In late June, I came home from work to find a note on the table beside the phone:

Call from Tristan
Empress 5:50 – movie – YOU ONLY LIVE TWICE
I cannot make it
Have fun w/ your friend
É

The film began right as Tristan found me and took his seat. The newsreel before the feature mostly focused on the Queen's visit to Ottawa the previous day, and it mentioned that her next stop was Montreal. I clutched Tristan's wrist in intrigue, but he gave me an affectionate eyeroll, from which I understood that he—and, to his mind, everybody else—knew this already. The film itself was a little boring. I spent most of it studying the French subtitles, determining just how far along I had come in my learning. Mostly I had no clue which spoken English word corresponded to which bright yellow French one.

As we left the cinema, I asked Tristan why he wanted to come see this film in particular, when we could have gone to *Barefoot in the Park*, or *Belle de jour*.

"I always make sure to see the new Bond film," he said.

"I really didn't take you as a James Bond fan."

"Oh, I adore it. It's all so otherworldly, serious and ludicrous at once. The villains, the chases. The drama. As though there exists a secret island lair of any sort, anywhere on Earth, let alone one with a walkover bridge, and a pedal you can press to make the bridge disappear, to feed underperforming employees to your piranhas. It's glorious."

We walked through crowded streets.

"The most maddening part might be his hair," said Tristan. "He swims and shags and leaps from rooftops, and the whole time, that perfect part stays perfectly parted."

"I like his haircut," I said.

Tristan reached for my ear and put a lock of my hair between his fingers. "What's stopping you?" he asked. "From a new look, I mean."

I couldn't think of a good answer. I hadn't gone to a barber in months. I couldn't quite muster the spend, and simply hoped that I passed as a man making a late attempt at the shaggy look.

"Let me have a go at it," Tristan said. "We'll get you in top shape tomorrow, and then you'll be fit to see the Queen."

He was serious—he was finally going to accompany me to Expo on a day we both had off. As we headed into a nearby diner for a bite, I could feel a big dumb smile form on my face.

I SET ÉTIENNE'S RADIO ALARM TO GET ME UP EARLY; IN THE morning, the radio blared stories about the Queen's impending arrival. The host interviewed individuals from the Expo office, and they all sounded nervous about something going wrong. Earlier in the Queen's tour, during a leg up north, someone had told Prince Philip to keep his fork because there was pie. This was characterized by the radio host as a humiliating error, and I wondered exactly why. Then I headed to Tristan's place, which I had not been to before.

The furniture was simple and spare. "I'd like to decorate," he said, "but I'm here for such a short while, and in all honesty it's hard to justify bothering." All he had that was truly his was a small pile of pulpy paperbacks on the kitchen table—*Starship Troopers*, *The Long Tomorrow*, *Planet of the Apes*—and a Mona Lisa beaded curtain in the doorway to the kitchen. "Found it at a flea market on day one," he said, running his fingers through her face. "That and the Tiffany lamp in the bathroom, which desperately needed more light."

Indeed, the bathroom had only a tiny window facing a brick wall outside, and no ceiling light. Stray pubes and beard trimmings crowded the base of the toilet. The mirror had a beige patina of grime, so thick that a finger could draw a picture in it. Tristan seemed unembarrassed by the mess and might not have even really noticed. I suspected he had never had to tidy growing up. He dragged a kitchen chair into the bathroom and said, "I suppose that if we're going right to the Expo from here, we don't want trimmings all over your nice clothes."

He paused, as though what he had just said was a command. He looked at me expectantly, and I understood that I was meant to strip down. I began by taking my emerald ring out of my pocket and placing it on the sink, so it wouldn't slip out while my clothes were loose. Tristan picked it up and gave it a close look.

"Asscher cut. Very art deco, which of course is coming back now. It's beautiful."

He tore a square of toilet paper and folded it into quarters, which he placed on the sink, and the ring went on top of it. I took off my T-shirt, jeans, and socks, and sat in the chair in just my briefs. It was perfunctory, like undressing at the doctor's. Tristan made no joke or comment. He was in a professional mindset, surveying my head, finding the angle for the first snip.

"What's so bad about keeping your fork for pie?" I asked once he began.

"I was listening to that too," he said. "Nothing's bad about it, really. But the posh thing to do is to use a different utensil for a new course. Far from a hanging offence, if you ask me. People just get nervous with important people." He held the scissors in his left hand and my head in his right hand, all delicate. He gripped my chin, or sometimes my cheek or forehead, reorienting my head as it suited his work. "And pies are savoury in England. If it's for dessert, you've got a tart."

As he spoke, I forgot that I was naked. I also, somehow, forgot that I was a person. Tristan often gave me an intense look that made me feel like I wasn't one. To his gaze, I was a head of hair, and that was all; his only company, in that bathroom, was the project he worked on.

Before long, the window let in a paltry dose of sunlight. Within that time, we shared an even briefer moment, when the bevelled edges of the mirror above the sink caught the sun's rays, throwing tiny rainbows across my bare shoulders and chest. Noticing one of the rainbow strands, Tristan put his scissors aside and cupped his hand in front of me, taking the rainbow off me, placing it into his palm. He grinned like a child who had caught a bug.

As he stared at the rainbow he had caught, he asked me, "Did you hear the other radio program, afterwards, about the eyeballs of the animal kingdom?"

"No."

"They wanted to know if animals could see colours. So they did all kinds of tests. It turns out, some of them can't—dogs, for instance. But some can see colours that even we can't see. Certain birds. And some of the plainest-looking birds have the most colours to see. To each other, they might look more astounding than we could possibly imagine."

By the time he finished speaking, the rainbow had faded away.

"I love dogs," I said, not knowing what else to say or do. Then the rays of sun faded too, and the Tiffany lamp was once again our only source of helpful light. Shortly thereafter, Tristan was finished, and I was covered in clippings. He advised that I shower, handing me a pink towel with a never-washed smell. The bar of soap in the shower was encrusted with yet more hairs, and as I washed, I thought daringly of how it had felt to sit there, more project than person, my clothes somewhere else. I developed an erection and jerked off economically, not thinking with much detail of Tristan, but of his hand, which could have been any man's hand, on my face, and of how purposefully it had guided my gaze in this direction and that. I scuttled the blob of cum to the drain with my feet and pushed it through the many long red hairs tangled there. In the cabinet, I found pomade, with which I flattened down the new haircut. I put on my shirt and pants, placing the ring back in my pocket and throwing its little toilet paper bed into the bin.

When I went back out to the main space, Tristan had changed into nicer clothes—pinstriped pants, a yellow collared shirt, a bright white knit, and deerskin driving gloves. "Looking fabulous," he said, approaching to adjust my hairline with his gloved fingers. Then he gave me a strange look and backed up.

"Did you have a wank just now?" he asked.

I didn't know how he had determined it. Laughing, I admitted that I had.

"Me as well," he said in a stage whisper. Then he joined me in laughter. "Oh boy," he added, with a bright sigh. In a strange but successful attempt to cut the tension, he gave me a peck on the hairline and turned away immediately. And then we got a move on to the Metro, to go to see the Queen.

But we never caught a glimpse of her. Her presence rendered half the island impenetrably thick with crowds. Rather than fight through them, we opted to spend the day exploring all the unoccupied pavilions on the barren half and buying lunch from a hot dog vendor who normally had one of the longest lines on the island.

To eat, Tristan removed his driving gloves, and I noticed that he had painted his fingernails green while I was showering. The polish also covered the tips of some of his fingers and had caught in the hair of some of his knuckles. At the sight of this, he gasped and held the opening of one of his gloves to his eye. "Polish everywhere," he said, horrified. "I fear I've ruined them."

"Why did you wear them at all?" I asked.

"Well, painting my nails is something I've simply always wanted to do. I did it once before, long ago, using a bottle from my mother's vanity. But I learned too late that you need to remove it with a special polish, and my father's reaction was enough to make me banish the thought of trying again. Then, the first time I was over here, I realized I'd quite like to achieve the look again, and Expo seemed the perfect place to flaunt it. Beautiful, otherworldly, impossible Expo. The polish—and the remover—have sat in my drawer ever since the idea dawned on me, and today finally felt like my opportunity. But I rushed the job while you showered, and look how slowly they dry." He scraped the polish off his knuckles and fingertips with his thumbs, which were not smudged.

"My question was why you wore the gloves," I said. "Not why you wore the polish."

He smiled with a childish jubilance. "Flaunting it here feels easy, but it's the getting here, and the getting home, that's at issue. The spectacle of it, I suppose. Here, I feel—not exactly safe. Perhaps the word is *brave*. I feel braver here—yes."

I understood perfectly and said so. We ate our hot dogs, and I couldn't stop looking at his hands. I thought he looked excellent and knew immediately that the next time I jerked off, I would think of his hands again, their knuckles and polish—hairy knuckles, green polish.

After eating, we made a game of exploring all the pavilions with "Man" in their names, of which there were several. At Man the Creator, we learned how long it would take a man to walk to the moon if a road connected it to the Earth. At Man the Producer, we bought paper cups full of overpriced coffee. At Man the Provider, bridges reached across pits that held livestock. Donkeys, cows, horses. "They could film a Bond piece here," Tristan commented, and I pretended to push a pedal with my foot; he in turn pretended to descend and get eaten alive by the farm animals, and to plead for his life.

He jabbed me and pointed to a handful of goats climbing wooden structures and each other. They had the highest fence. "People love them," he said. He was just making a smarmy comment, but I was caught off guard by the sight of goats, which reminded me of home, and of Ray. When I didn't reply with laughter, but rather with a small, shocked silence, Tristan left me alone with my sudden little wistfulness. This struck me as one of the great kindnesses afforded to me in perhaps my whole life: Tristan leaving me alone with my thoughts.

I looked at the goats for a while, then at other things: the sky, the paths behind and ahead. Tristan and I kept walking, and remained quiet until we entered the next pavilion, Man the Explorer. The building was a gigantic hexagon, and the first thing we walked through was a blown-up model of a human cell. We stared together at a big, beanlike thing.

The silence between us was there for my sake and was mine to break.

"Blood cell?" I guessed.

"Perhaps," said Tristan. "What brings you to this conclusion?"

"It's red."

"Have you ever seen the insides of a living thing? We're red the whole way through."

Unexpectedly, the red bean lit up. Neither of us had pressed a button or anything like that, and we couldn't see anyone else around. The bean had just decided it was time to grow bright, like a street light that knows when it's dark.

"We never finished that game," I said. "About things you've never told anyone before. I told you about Ray, and then we moved on. You still have to tell *me* something. Mine was my first kiss; do you remember your first kiss?"

"I'm not sure," said Tristan, after thinking. "By the time I first kissed someone, I had done so much else. I do remember a bully named Gwyn, whose cock I sucked every week for a full school year. Sometimes twice a week. It began at detention. He was an angry bloke, often fighting with the other fighting types. I was there no doubt for talking back. We got into some scuffle, while we sat at our desks, bored from doing nothing. The teacher couldn't send us to detention, because that's what we were already doing, and so we were sent—with a sponge and a bucket—to give the tiles at the chapel a good scrub. While we were working, he called me a fairy." Imitating Gwyn, Tristan put on a deep and angry voice: "*I'll bet you would love nothing more than to suck my cock, ya little fairy.* The next thing I knew, we were at it. Banish with the left hand, cherish with the right. That was him. *Such* a Capricorn. I told myself, *Next time I can bring my blazer from the classroom, to fold up and put between my knees and the tile floor.* And I did bring it, the next time, and the time after that. We just kept going with the bucket to the chapel, Mondays after last bell. Every teacher probably assumed some other teacher had told us to. A permanent punishment, à la Sisyphus, for two of the most frustrating shitheads of their collective careers. Gwyn with his anger. Me with mine."

The big bean went back to being dark.

"Never kissed," said Tristan. "Never traded roles. Never really spoke. But we kept that chapel sparkling through senior year. I believe he's in Chester now. That's just on the border of Wales and England. Believe he sells shoes."

He looked from the bean to me.

"People come and go, I think," he said. "You never know who it is you'll end up thinking about, deep in the future. Who's making an impact. Who you'll be different later because of. And who won't turn out to matter a single bit."

Others came into the room. Tristan and I went further on, finding neurons and muscles, plasticky mucus, and hair follicles jutting out of the wall. It reminded me of the film *Fantastic Voyage*. All the oversized body parts shared the same unnerving translucency, in various cloudy colours. I thought of how some things are produced naturally by human bodies, like bones and organs, and others are made by human hands, like cars or buildings; it was impossible to think that these objects had either of these origins. They disgusted and intrigued me. Some lit up for us and others did not. Maybe their light bulbs needed replacing, and maybe they were not made to give light.

12

Expo turned into an absolute obsession for the whole city. Michel mentioned that his wife and children went over on both days of every weekend while he worked, and, as he and I completed our house calls, it felt inevitable that our small talk in customers' doorways and living rooms revolved around Expo. Everyone had been there, and everyone had plans to go again. I got over my self-pity and developed the habit of heading there on my own, whenever I had enough spare time, with a sandwich wrapped in paper and a flask filled three quarters with tonic water and one quarter with gin. Even on days when I didn't at first intend to go there, I would often find myself heading in that direction, encouraged by my own lack of imagination, and by the slope of the city.

I walked through the Czech Pavilion, full of beautiful glass artworks, many times. I tasted Brazilian coffee for the first time and sat in benches near the entrances of different African pavilions, to hear the fascinating music clearly, without having to tolerate the lines. I visited the Venezuelan Pavilion, out of a love for the maple-flavoured gumballs they gave out for free at the entrance. Sometimes my brain hurt, and I knew that it was from expansion. From learning so much about the world.

One afternoon, while walking past the many colourful spinning rides of La Ronde, the amusement park on the easternmost section of Expo, I had the thought: *I want to go to Expo.* Of course, I was already there. But I still wanted to go, and my being there didn't extinguish the desire—like when someone wants a cigarette even though he's in the middle of smoking one. Continuing through the crowds, I suddenly recognized the face of a young boy sitting on a bench. I was delighted to realize it was Tomas, my former landlady's grandson.

Excitedly I broke into a sprint as I approached him through the crowd. He recognized me and leapt off the bench to break into a jog as well, almost spilling the paper cup of bright orange shaved ice in one of his hands and waving frantically with the other hand.

"Hey, chief!" I knelt and threw my arms around him. "I want to lift you right up, but I don't want to spill your ice."

"It's not as good as the other one I had," he said.

"You mean from the other island? I totally agree. The snow cones over there are better. Are you here with your mother and *vo-vo*?"

"Just Mom," he said. "Is *this* where you live now?"

I intended to tell him that I lived on the third floor of a house in a long row of houses that all looked alike. But I was distracted by the sight of his mother, Gloria, approaching huffily from the same direction as Tomas had come, almost in a run. She seemed in distress at the sight of her son talking to a stranger. In a panic, she called out for Tomas, who turned and waved to her.

I was eager for her to see that Tomas was with *me*, not a stranger, and was perfectly safe. As she came close, she told Tomas sternly, "Go wait for me at the Spider." Before he could protest, she repeated, *"Go."*

I felt a little upset that she didn't recognize who I was, but I attributed this to my new haircut and to her panic at the thought of her son being snatched by a stranger. As Tomas headed reluctantly in a new direction, I said, "Hello, Gloria! Long time no see."

"Leave my son alone," she said quietly, "and get the fuck away from here. This is a place for children. Get the fuck away from these children."

She knew who I was, and had known from afar, and considered me a greater threat to her son than a stranger. She took short, shaky breaths and did not break eye contact with me.

"If I see you here again," she said, "I will call the police, or I'll kill you myself. Get the fuck away right now, you shit-eating, piece-of-shit freak."

For a moment I could not speak. Once I could, I said to her, "I'm sorry."

She broke eye contact finally and headed in the same direction Tomas had gone. She had learned—from her mother, no doubt—that I was queer and had reached dark conclusions about what I was capable of, or about what I might have already done. I hurried away from La Ronde as quickly as I could without breaking into a run, suddenly sickened by the sight of every child there, at the thought of her thoughts about me. I felt the need to vomit, but when I stopped in front of an open garbage bin and said out loud to myself, "Chunder, chunder, chunder till you're done," I couldn't get anything out or even properly retch. I felt that the only way to ever get rid of this pre-vomit feeling was to return to Gloria and clarify how wrong she was. *I will go and explain myself,* I thought. *I have to do it this second.* I turned around and tried to pick out the ride she had instructed Tomas to go to, the ride called the Spider. But they all had ghastly, spinning limbs, and repulsive colourings, and the same jutting rhythm when they slowed down or sped up; any of them could have been described that way.

I found a bench as far away from La Ronde as I could get without leaving the island entirely. I felt incapable of the long voyage home. I only had the energy to do one very specific thing, something I had previously been too timid to do. I felt as though I had no other recourse. I found the British Pavilion and entered the line. Finally I would visit it, although I had no idea how Tristan would act in my presence while working. But I trusted completely that, by spending time with him, I would feel better, no matter the dynamic.

Once I got to the end of the lineup and entered the pavilion, someone grabbed my wrist immediately. It was Tristan.

"Sir!" he shouted into my face. "I'd be pleased to provide you with a guided tour!"

He looked at me persistently. I understood at once: I was supposed to act like a stranger, and this way we could spend time together. I froze, then gained my composure. I wanted to talk to him about Gloria, but I also trusted completely that this game would be a fantastic distraction. Eventually I said, "Nice to meet you."

"My name is Tristan. Yours?"

"I'm Gabriel," I said, grinning. He made an impressed face, that I had devised an alias so quickly, then walked me through each room, pointing out artifact after artifact from the display:

life-sized dioramas, photo collages, a car painted with the Union Jack. With each element, Tristan shared some accompanying fact in the chipper tone of a rehearsed professional. I asked follow-up questions, maintaining the ruse, and feeling better after the shock of Gloria's confrontation. Whenever the song playing changed, he shared the name. "Eight Days a Week," "Silence Is Golden," "You Don't Have to Say You Love Me." As my personal tour went on, Tristan's enthusiasm drew in strangers. We eventually had a small group formed around us.

We came across a cluster of sculptures that looked like sad, eerie mannequins from a store. "I don't much like those," I said.

"Yes," said Tristan gamely, "how could I have forgotten we have a connoisseur amongst us? For those who joined late— Gabriel here is a student of the arts. Remind me, sir, what is your medium again?"

"Macramé."

"Yes—*macramé*. God's work. Shall we move on?"

More tunes from the British Invasion played, loud enough for Tristan to have to shout. Here and there, he built my phony backstory a little more. "Gabriel, you mentioned earlier being the oldest of eight children? With that being the case, I'm sure you find this depiction of the British family a little scant." He asked too if anyone agreed that my haircut was astounding. "Please remember to share with me your barber's information. Clear genius."

The final room of the pavilion looked very different from the rest. It had a shallow pool of water, and human sculptures that seemed like a serious departure from the mannequins found elsewhere. These humans stood ten times taller than us and had long, daunting limbs. A man from our group guessed that they were by someone named Giacometti, a suggestion at which Tristan laughed kindly. "Little doubt that he was an inspirator here," he said thoughtfully to the man. "Alas, this isn't the Italian Pavilion."

We all stood at the feet of the stretchy men and women, with their hands enormous and welcoming, their privates uncovered and abstracted. We became quieter; the figures set a tone of quietude. All statues keep quiet, of course, but with these ones, somehow, you could tell they were doing it. They reached for each other's faces, took each other's hands, and wrapped their arms around each other's sloping shoulders. They were including each other in what they were doing, and including us too, liplessly shushing us, effortlessly dwarfing us. Never had I occupied a room like this, with two layers of population to it, one below and living, one above and still. I felt like something discovered beneath an upturned stone, an insect or small animal, some member of some frantic rushing colony. It was pleasant and unpleasant, but most of all, it was alarming. I had never thought of myself as a person who was much moved by sculptures, paintings, or art of any kind, but now I felt that I was going to cry.

"How much did that most recent Giacometti go for in New York? I'll bet our artist friend will know," Tristan said, nudging me insistently. "Gabriel?" But I no longer felt like playing around. I wanted to keep studying the giants, to keep receiving the addictive, morose feeling they imparted. It was like the loneliness of standing in a crowd, multiplied by itself, an impossible mixture of company and solitude.

"Thank you for the tour," I said to Tristan soberly, no longer in character.

Hearing my wavery voice, he caught on immediately and snapped out of his character too. "Oh, Jesus, I'm sorry, pet," he said to me. I went for the exit and caught my breath outside by a chunky grey fountain covered in complex textures and colourful components. I found a seat facing the fountain, between a group of women chatting among themselves and a man absorbed in a thin book with the words inside arranged strangely. Poetry, maybe recipes. If I was going to cry, this was an okay place for that. Crowds give a freeing anonymity. I felt my individuality dissolve and the lump in my throat harden.

Tristan came out of the building. He stood over me.

"You're at work," I said. "Go away, we'll talk later."

"I'm on break."

I said nothing. The man with the book got up and left, and Tristan took his place.

"Doesn't take an art student to diagnose this one," he said, pointing at the complicated fountain in front of us. "Absolutely daft. It reminds me of the fortress on the cover of an old science-fiction paperback I read as a boy. When I read the book though, there wasn't any fortress. That made me sad. Someone drew the cover but hadn't read the book."

I looked down at the ground. Ants surrounded a dried-up puddle of something blood-red and sugary, maybe a snow cone that somebody had spilled.

"I'd like to take a guess at what happened in there," said Tristan. "The first time I came into that room, I too was moved, quite deeply. It's powerful stuff to the right soul. My problem is that now I see it ten times a day, and so it has become old hat. But it's good to be in touch with it, like you were. Truly you are among the very great men on this Earth, so open to the world as it goes around the sun."

This validation shoved my emotions up my throat, dislodging the lump there. I cried, and laughed at how silly the crying was. Tristan understood what had happened to me better than I had understood it. He had made me less mysterious to myself. And he respected it, as a development that can take place in a man's heart. "There's more to it," I said, still crying. "I ran into someone today, an old friend. I *thought* she was a friend. But she learned about who I am, and now she hates me. She truly, truly hates me."

"Ah," he said knowingly. "This can happen."

"I wish it couldn't," I said, laughing at the childishness of my argument, laughing though still crying, and still looking down at the ground. "She threatened to kill me. She called me a shit-eating piece of shit."

Tristan chortled. "You're really going to lend a single thought to someone so unimaginative with her insults? Why would a piece of shit eat shit? Really, I wish these bigots would think it through sometimes."

I laughed harder, I felt warmer. Looking up at Tristan, I felt, on my face, the heat of his gaze. It was a simple emotion I had now: relief. Relief that I had met him and that we had become a part of each other's lives. I wanted to tell him about this relief, but I didn't know how I could possibly phrase it. I became aware of my mouth, empty and dry. I wanted to put it to use, even if words were beyond my reach. I wanted to kiss Tristan and to tell him I loved him, and to give him the ring in my pocket, and to watch him put it on.

Registering these desires, I felt gazes additional to his, around us. Had we been alone, a kiss could have taken place very naturally. It would have been the sort of kiss that men shared with women sometimes, by fountains, at train stations, on park benches, at parties. In movies. Joyous and meaningful and long-lasting. But we couldn't kiss, any more than we could climb into the fountain and wash. Sobbing was one thing and kissing quite another. The anonymity afforded by crowds had a limit, and Gloria's assessment of my character had made me feel filthy, and paranoid too.

Even Tristan, whom I considered a truly free spirit, seemed to draw the line at kissing in public, his mouth fumbling awkwardly, having made almost every step that comes before contact with another mouth and having stopped short of that. He mouthed the word *sorry*, his lips shaking with tension. Quickly I gave a face like he had nothing at all to be sorry for. Then I got up, saying in broken talk that his break was likely over soon and that I had to get going.

Turning back as I rushed off, I waved weakly and surprised myself by kissing my hand and blowing. It was a way of acknowledging what had almost happened, an attempt to cut into the tension that had materialized. But the tension persisted into the evening, during which neither man phoned the other's apartment, and into the days that followed.

13

In late July, the president of France was set to visit Montreal. Étienne's work, already busy, called for even more of his energy and attention. His pavilion was to host an event with the president, and the administrators in charge took out their frustrations on the attendants, quizzing them on the spot about every aspect of their job, sending them home if their five o'clock shadows showed, with pay deducted for the day. This began weeks before de Gaulle had even arrived. The humiliations brought the attendants closer together, and Étienne started to go out for drinks with them in the evenings.

Tristan and I remained out of contact for days. We were delaying a conversation that had been due—a conversation about our friendship, and whether indeed it was simply a friendship. My evenings, free of phone calls and visits, provided so few distractions that it dawned on me just how much Tristan had come to mean to me. When I thought of him, I thought of joy. I felt more and more like there was a place I belonged. I just needed to think of a person—of *that* person—as a place.

One morning, I woke up to a rancid and familiar smell. Étienne was going through the kitchen drawers, gathering utensils: mixing bowl, paring knife, wooden spoon, rubber gloves, cheese grater. When he looked to the couch and saw that I was stirring, he said, "I thought we have eggs."

"I used them for mayonnaise," I said.

He crouched down to give the fridge a full examination and pulled from the very back a carton of eggs I didn't know about. "Those must be really, really old," I said, but he shrugged and took an egg anyways, placing it on the table, next to a potato and an open tin of drain cleaner. The cleaner was the source of the acidy odour. I slid my pants on and got off the couch.

He started peeling potatoes. He was rough and inefficient with it, missing whole chunks of skin and losing more meat than he needed to. I took the knife from his hand and took over the job.

"I'll help you," I said. "It's a two-man job."

"Are you hungover?" he asked. "If you are hungover, it is *no.*"

"I'm fine," I said. He went to the bathroom, returning with Vaseline and a comb. I grated the peeled potatoes into the bowl. Étienne added the egg and the drain cleaner. The potatoes dissolved into a sizzling paste, the acidy tinge to the air becoming an almost suffocating fume.

We had last made conk during the early days of our lives as roommates. That evening, we had laughed our way through the whole process, which I found ridiculous and fascinating. Now I had a better sense of what I was doing, as I traced Étienne's hairline with Vaseline, forehead to nape, and piled glops of it onto his ears.

"You're not actually all that kinky," I said. "Why do this already?"

"The boss said, 'Comb your hair.'" Then he pointed at his widow's peak, where a fine bit of fuzz had begun to emerge beneath his otherwise straight and tidy hairline. "He thinks I can *comb* this away."

"President de Gaulle better appreciate the effort," I said jokingly, and began to brush his hair back.

"This will be the last time for me to make conk," he said, staring into the steaming bowl. "Look at this. This is poison."

"Once you told me you would never find work here if you didn't treat your hair."

"Yes, I did say this," he said. When he nodded that he was ready, I dipped my gloved hands into the bowl, then rustled my fingers through his hair delicately. He exhaled through his nose. His face went slack, then tight; his handsomeness disappeared.

"Always I forget the pain," he said, gritting his teeth.

"*Shh,*" I said, carefully navigating the skin around his widow's peak. "It's easier if you don't talk."

"It is true what you say, you know," he said. "If I do not do this, I do not find work here. But after Expo, I will be leaving Montreal, *au revoir.* A friend at the pavilion offered me a job. To go and work in Toulouse. A travel agency."

"I didn't know that kind of work interested you," I said, working as carefully as I could to keep the conk from touching his scalp.

"Maybe it does not, but I want to work. I want to *work.* No more service, no more hosting. The money is—" Instead of finishing the sentence, he waved his hands around, indicating our shabby apartment. "I dropped out of law school because I could not pass. I tried and tried and I could not pass, and I think, *There is nothing for me, oh well.* Now, I think: *There is something. I just do not know it. But maybe I will find it.*"

"I didn't know any of that," I said, and started combing the sludge across his head.

Again, he let out a pained exhale. He said, "Maybe I will save for school again. Save for *something*. I need to do *something*. And, my friend, it is the same for you, you know."

"I do things."

"*Oui, bien sûr*. Diaper truck, dumbwaiter. Now, a different truck. Some days nothing at all. You need a direction."

I didn't answer. I just kept combing.

"I am sorry," he said. "I cannot be polite right now. It hurts."

He took a few breaths, then reached a breaking point, bolting suddenly to the bathroom and getting the cold water going. I came in with him.

"It is okay," he said, "I can be alone."

"I'm the one with the gloves," I said. Both of us were shirtless already; he backed his head up into the flow of water, and I held his head in one hand and rinsed his hair with the other. He sighed with relief as the conk washed out.

"Maybe ask your British friend to tell your fortune," he said, projecting his voice over the flow of the water, more lighthearted in tone than before. "He can find you a direction in his special cards."

"*British friend*," I echoed. "First, he's from Wales. Second, it's becoming something other than a friendship."

I felt my chest tighten: I had not intended to share this with Étienne. Not until whatever it was had firmed up, and maybe not even at that point. But now I did share it, defensively, as an example of a thing I was doing with my life. I was growing close with someone. I turned the water off and kept his dripping head in my hand. "Maybe we'll even live a life together," I said next. "And we'll manage."

"Thank you for your help," Étienne said, getting up, dismissing me firmly, the way adults dismiss children. He towelled off and went about his morning routine. I returned to the kitchen, sitting with a cup of coffee. Only when he was gone for work did I notice a red mark on my shoulder. Somewhere in the mix, I had gotten a blob of conk there, which had caused a welt to form, about the size of a quarter. Before I saw and registered the wound, I couldn't even feel it. Now the pain there was all I could think about.

LATER THAT AFTERNOON I CALLED TRISTAN, FINDING THE silence between us too silly to carry on with. He asked, "Hello?" and I said it was me, and he just launched into things, without addressing our week of dead air.

"Oh my God. I just saw Charles de Gaulle on TV."

"Yes," I said. "I guess he's arriving soon. I had no idea you went in for politics."

"I don't. In fact, I didn't understand a word he said. But his *way*. Mad, daft, and chock full of conviction. What an *orator*. What does Étienne make of him?"

"To Étienne," I said, "he's just a lot of work at the pavilion. For my part, all the small talk at work these days has been about people's plans to watch the motorcade."

"It's all I'm hearing too. Shall we make an appearance? And this time, we'll make sure to actually *see* the person," he said.

But when we saw how empty the Minirail was, we suspected we had gotten things wrong. Consulting a newspaper on the seat beside him, Tristan noted that de Gaulle was only visiting city hall that day, and his visit to Expo was the day following. We had both just assumed Expo was the site of everything important. We laughed, a little frustrated at our own foolishness, as the train thrust us toward an almost empty island. Its crowds were thin, its life gone. According to the newspaper, de Gaulle wasn't arriving at city hall for another three hours. We decided to first grab dinner at Expo and then to make our way there.

"Étienne could have straightened you out about the dates, you know," said Tristan.

"We barely see each other," I said.

We were greeted again by the sight of the Canadian Pavilion's upside-down pyramid as we exited the station. The island was so empty that we could easily stand in the shade, which was usually in demand, while we sorted out what to do, now that we were there. Tristan had the idea that we'd dine at Wienerwald in the Austrian Pavilion, a restaurant that was usually too popular to get a table at. Sure enough, there was no lineup today, and inside, every single table was available. We were led to one of them by a waitress whose blouse, beneath her red-green dress, was immaculately white, and so was the cloth on our nicely set table. Everything looked immaculate, and I felt suddenly glad that I happened to have put on my nice white shirt. Before Tristan and I realized our timing error, I had envisioned a rushed standing dinner, maybe from one of the street vendors, surrounded by a thick, loud crowd. Instead we would have this fancy sit-down meal in an empty establishment. So it would happen now, during dinner, instead of later: our first quiet time together since almost kissing, the discussion during which we would define our situation.

The waitress brought us steins of beer, and after our "Cheers," Tristan chugged more than half of his. I had never seen him drink so much in an entire night, let alone in one moment.

"I guess we should talk now," I said.

Tristan licked his lips and took another few gulps of beer.

"About us, I mean," I said nervously.

"Yes," he said. "*Us*. I can go first—I've been dying to tell you about a recent adventure."

"Okay."

"Stephan was his name," said Tristan, "and conversation was very light. This was at the Peel Pub, maybe three nights ago. He wore all brown, and all the same shade, but I'll tell you, he made the look *work* somehow. We spoke with our hands, we danced to the Doors, and then we *headed* for the doors. It came together so simply. Only in the cab did I deduce that he had barely a word of English in his vocabulary. It had me worried." He lowered his voice: "Of course, when we got to his place, I remembered that you don't end up doing much talking."

He downed another mouthful of beer. He waved to the waitress and gestured for two more beers.

"I'm surprised you went to the Peel Pub," I said. I resisted the urge to add, *Without me.*

"Enough was enough," he said, "and I had to resort to a dip in the pool of local offerings. No friends of Dorothy at the British Pavilion, you know."

He burped indiscreetly and guzzled more beer. I looked down and studied the ornate patterns in the tablecloth. I couldn't look him in the face.

"I met one," I said, flat and impulsive. "A *friend of Dorothy*. In the woods the other night. He works here. The Israeli Pavilion. And he was definitely *one of us*." Now mine was the voice that went low with implication.

Tristan controlled his reaction, nodding knowingly. Then he shushed me as the waitress arrived with fresh steins. Following this, we were quiet, and I noticed for the first time that classical music was playing softly from unseen speakers. Listening to it, we sipped at our beers. When the food arrived, Tristan tucked into his. I didn't touch mine.

"It's going to get cold," he said.

I took one bite. It was cold already; it had arrived cold. I put the fork back down. "Should I ask you what he looked like now?" I said. "His hair colour maybe?"

"Stephan? He was a blond," said Tristan, like this information was boring, and like I was a bore for asking.

"And mine?" I asked. "Do I tell you now the hair colour of mine?"

Tristan laughed with discomfort.

"It was late, and there was no light, but his hair was really short and I think really dark," I said. "I played with it with my thumbs. And if you asked me what his voice was like, I would say low. And if you asked me what his cum was like, I would say water. I would say it tasted like warm water from a warm glass."

He emptied his second beer into his mouth. "You're in a strange mood," he said quietly.

"I'm just talking. You and I talk."

"Not like this."

"Not about other men?"

"Not about the flavours of other men's semen, no." Then he went back to being quiet. He waved to the waitress, making the same gesture as moments ago.

"Not about other men *at all*," I said. "Not recent stuff. We don't talk about that."

"I suppose not," he said, and he put his fork and knife down.

The waitress brought our next beers, and this time Tristan did not cheers. I kept talking, my words running together. I told him that he and I didn't talk about the sex we had with others, definitely not, and that it bothered me that he had now done so. It bothered me in many ways, least among which was that he had actually slept with someone. Worse was the hollow feeling it gave me, to think of him going to the Peel Pub, or anywhere fun, without calling and asking if I wanted to join him. He and I did that for each other, I told him; we involved each other in the fun we went and had. And worst was the disclosure he had just made, and the way he had made it. So casual, as though we had always had a rapport like that, when really the matter of our sexual lives had been danced around, in a grand choreography, as a sort of mutual courtesy. Disclosures like the one he had made, about some man named Stephan, only worked to unbuild the ill-defined thing we had begun building together. And making this disclosure so soon after our almost-kiss at the sci-fi fountain felt to me like an egregious breach.

As I spoke, he just sat, wringing his hands, looking sorry, saying nothing.

I went on, expressing that when we first sat down at this table, I had wanted to tell him about how he made me dislike myself less, and how I loved my reflection in windows now, because my haircut reminded me of how it felt to be the object of his craft, and how I lately folded a handkerchief on which to rest my ring, like the little bed he had formed out of toilet paper, because it made me think of him. And now I wouldn't do that— he had wrecked it, he had wrecked everything. Then I stopped talking for good. I had a familiar, chest-tightening feeling that I had said more than I had intended to. His hands kept pulling at each other, violent and nervous. He looked at me pleadingly. His face was white.

"Say something," I said. "Please speak."

When he finally opened his mouth, he emitted total gibberish. I knew he was making fun of me, all angry and childish, going on and on. He wasn't speaking English, or French, and it didn't sound Welsh either. He spoke a nonsense of its own kind, wholly indecipherable.

Amazed by his capacity to mock me, I froze. He added gestures to his imitation, shrugging his shoulders, flapping his hands. Had I been slouching like that? Had I been pulling at my hands? I knew I could not love him, or even be friends with him, not if his cruelty went as far as this.

He slid out of his chair. He fell onto the floor. He wasn't mocking me. He was having a seizure.

The waitress rushed over; I knelt next to him. His jaw clenched tight, and so did every other muscle of his body. His hands were at his chest, clutching each other, their white knuckles vibrating.

The waitress asked, "What is happening?"

"He's an epileptic," I shouted, and she hurried off for help. I got on the floor and placed my hand on his chest, in case he couldn't see that I was there. He looked at me, then to the side, over and over; he made *s* sounds. I reconfigured him to be on his side, with his head in my lap. Maybe *s* was for "side." He felt stiff as wood.

"Does this hurt?" I said, and he made *n* sounds. I hoped for "no." I focused on rubbing his back, and said, "It's okay," over and over. Rocking him like a baby, I once again noticed the classical music and said, "Listen. Music. Can you hear it? Hey. It's okay. It's okay."

The waitress arrived with a medic who asked me questions about Tristan. If he had seized recently, how long it typically lasted. I didn't have answers.

She directed her attention to Tristan. "Can you hear me?" she asked loudly.

"Yes," he said, easier to understand than before. I noticed that his lap was soaking wet, and his neck had loosened up. In fact, his whole body was no longer stiff. It had ended surprisingly quickly.

"Sir," said the medic, "you tell us when you think you might be able to get up, and we'll take you for help."

"Yes," he said again. He unlocked his hands and brought them to his face, keeping his head in my lap. He hid away like this, taking heaving sniffles. I kept rubbing his back. After a deep breath, he uncovered his face, the skin flush with blood and slick with tears and snot. He looked up at me.

"I pissed myself," he said.

"I know," I said. "Maybe you have clean clothes at your pavilion."

He moved into a sitting position. I put my arms around him, and he squeezed my shoulders with his hands.

"I pissed myself," he said again, softly this time, into my ear.

"I'm sorry I was yelling," I said.

"I'm so *tired*," he said.

"I'll go and get you clothes," I said. It wasn't a conversation; we were just two people speaking out loud in the aftermath of something shocking, barely able to follow each other's words. I kissed his briny cheek. Our mouths met in a purposeful, aggressive kiss, each tongue deep in the other man's mouth. He started to break down again, but I pulled back and shushed him, and told him that everything was fine, and to stand up now. The medic and waitress didn't react. They both just seemed glad that Tristan could stand. The medic took him from me, throwing his arm over her shoulder, asking if he had the strength for the five-minute walk to the medical facility.

"Can we take breaks?" he asked quietly.

"Yes," she replied.

He turned to face me as they walked off. He had his childish face on, the skin marked with well-defined red-and-white blotches, the tears and snot shining stickily around his cheeks and chin.

ARRIVING AT THE BRITISH PAVILION, I EXPLAINED TO A young woman that I was a friend of Tristan's. "He asked me to come get a few of his things." We walked through the almost-empty pavilion, and again I noticed the unsettling gazes of the sad mall-mannequin statues. Then the tall, spindly statues that had moved me to tears. At the entrance to the staff room, the attendant hesitated. With her hand on the doorknob, she turned to me. "You've not come to steal something, have you? You really are a friend of his?"

"Yes, a friend," I said, and I watched her face as she made the decision to believe me.

I dropped off Tristan's uniform at the medical facility and waited outside, smoking cigarettes I'd taken from his change-room shelf. After an hour, he walked out, exhausted and quiet. He thanked me for the clothes, bummed a cigarette, and, on the Metro ride home, he rested his hand on top of mine, between our laps, hidden away. He was a hollowed-out version of himself, lacking stamina and focus. His hand gave mine squeezes, and he asked me to come with him to his place, where he drank a glass of water and took a long, long shower while I sat at his dining table. I noticed a faint yellow stain on the base of my white shirt and gave it a sniff. It was urine—I had gotten some on me and had only now noticed. I unbuttoned and removed the shirt and shoved it in the garbage beneath Tristan's sink. I sat in my tank top and read the first page of a book that was on the table, a paperback called *The Ballad of Beta-2*.

Tristan emerged from the bathroom in a fake-silk white kimono and sat beside me.

"I've been cut loose," he said. I already knew that there had been an expectation for all attendants to disclose any health issues, and that Tristan's plan, if he were to have a seizure at the workplace, had been to lie and say it was his first one. "I forgot," he said.

"Forgot to lie?"

"No. I remembered my plan, but when they took my history, I told them everything about my medical history. *That's* what I forgot—the terror, with seizures. You think you're going to *die*. So I told the whole truth and nothing but, right down to the clementine I had for breakfast, thinking that the woman would be best equipped that way. It was all that felt important. I very much wanted not to die."

At this he mugged his mouth and furrowed his brow, as though he had to really think about his last statement. Then he laughed to himself a little.

"Good to know," he added, speaking as much to himself as to me.

"Then what?"

"They let me rest for a spell," he said, "and when I woke up from my daze, a man from the main office, with a hideous tie, confirmed that I am up a creek. They brought me a glass of water with old lipstick marks on it, and then they showed me the door."

"You can stay for now though?" I asked.

"My visa status is left to the discretion of my pavilion's management. I'll visit first thing tomorrow. Do my best repentant. The visa would carry me to October as planned."

"And with no visa?"

"Two weeks," he said. "Then home."

He filled his glass again at the sink and chugged it down. He moved like an old man, depleted by the journey home and by talking.

"I need to sleep," he said. Then, more quietly: "Would you stay?"

"Of course," I said.

He grabbed my knee and gave it an affectionate shake. Noticing the conk-burn on my exposed shoulder, he brushed the space below it with his thumb, then leaned down to kiss the wound itself. "Looks fresh," he said.

"I helped Étienne with something."

"There's honey in the drawer if it's smarting," he said, then headed right into the bedroom, to collapse onto the bed. Even with the curtains drawn and the sunlight still bright, he fell asleep immediately. I heard his snoring, easy and even. I didn't know if I was meant to stay until he had fallen asleep, or for the entire night. And I was very hungry. There was indeed honey in the drawer, and not much else. In his fridge I found only a clementine, which I ate immediately, and a half-empty carton of eggs. I found gin in a cupboard in the living room and drank it room temperature, reading *The Ballad of Beta-2* until the sunlight disappeared. Then, in the blue-dark bathroom, by the light of Tristan's Tiffany lamp, I squeezed some toothpaste onto my finger and brushed.

In the bedroom, Tristan had fallen into a heavy sleep on top of the covers, still in his kimono. I took off my clothes and entered the bed, sleeping much better than I ever managed to do on the couch at home.

14

I n the morning, I woke first. I used Tristan's phone to call Michel. Speaking very quietly, I told him I couldn't work that day. When I heard Tristan stirring, I started on some fried eggs.

"Don't you have work soon?" he said, entering the kitchen.

"I called in sick. I'll come with you to Expo."

Tristan smiled with bright wet eyes.

I used his shower and his pomade. He lent me a pair of plum-coloured underwear and a snappy baby-blue dress shirt. Emerging from the bathroom, I saw him filling a flask with the gin.

"Is drinking what sets off your seizures?" I asked.

"I'm not sure, and neither have any physicians been. We're medical marvels, us epileptics. But from previous experiences, I do believe that drinking is a trigger, for me at least. I've also gathered from experiences that my fits are kind enough to space themselves out, at least so far. Never more than one visit every couple of months, reliable as the phases of the moon. So. If the news today is good and I can stay here awhile longer, I swear, I'll go to church, I'll marry a nice lady and raise a brood of valedictorians. Lord, hear my prayer." He locked his hands together and fell to his knees and touched his forehead to the linoleum. "And if the news is bad," he said without lifting his head, "we'll just you and I get good and blotto."

WE HAD MISSED DE GAULLE'S SPEECH ENTIRELY. I HADN'T even thought to turn on the radio to hear about it. The newspapers in the Metro station described the scandal of his declaration *"Vive le Québec libre,"* and the cars were more crowded than ever before, because this really was the day that de Gaulle was visiting Expo. With difficulty, I translated the first sentence of the front page for Tristan and shared the gist of the article, or what I thought of as the gist—that de Gaulle had fanned the flames of separatism.

"Separatism between what?" Tristan asked.

"Quebec and the rest of Canada," I said.

"Is Quebec not its own country already?"

This turned heads all around us.

"It's a province," I said. "It's like Wales."

"Wales is a country," he said. "But actually, it's part of the Kingdom too. It's all a bit complicated, and more than a little daft. I suppose these things always are." He gave a self-deprecating smile, then stared off into the window beside us, which only showed the dark of the underground. He was preoccupied. He wanted to know his fate. Walking through the halls of the Metro to switch trains, we passed by a steel drum player who stood beside a giant sign reading VISIT EXPO. I had seen this busker before and had previously stopped to listen and tossed him change. Tristan and I rushed past him. The echoes of the steel drum music were not as pleasant as I remembered. This time I found the music annoying.

While he visited his boss, I waited at the ugly sci-fi fountain, reading *The Ballad of Beta-2*. Tristan emerged after I had read just a few pages, looking sad and smiling through it.

"Two weeks," he said. "Then banished. Simple as that."

"I'm sorry, Tristan."

"Yes, well. While we're here, let me show you one thing. And then we can fuck off from this blasted island forever."

We headed to the Christian Pavilion. In the lineup, we got started on the gin. More than once, he said to me unprompted, "I'm okay," which meant I was unknowingly looking at him with a piteous face. Beyond that, he didn't say much, until we were inside, where a series of photos hung on the walls, depicting happy children and bright flowers. As we descended a spiralling staircase, the photos got weirder. Blurry bodies with nauseatingly undetailed faces and household objects instead of arms and legs. Some people who came to the top of the stairs turned around at the sight of these images. I too was turned off, but Tristan insisted that we continue down the stairs. On the lower floor, a black-and-white projection was playing in a theatre room.

"It's just getting started!" said Tristan. "Oh joy." I could not tell if his *oh joy* was sarcastic or sincere. We scurried in and sat near the back. Many seats were empty, except for a father-son pair and a trio of old ladies.

The title card read THE EIGHTH DAY/LE HUITIÈME JOUR. The film began with grasslands and pan flutes; a beach scene, fireworks, carnivals, noises of explosion and delight—until suddenly, the footage showed a race car crashing into a crowd of spectators. Then the film went back to nice stuff. It went on like this, with seemingly no original footage, just an assortment of pilfered film clips and newsreels, alternating between happy and disturbing, shocking and banal. Holocaust victims lying dead, Hitler delivering a speech, Charlie Chaplin evading cops. The music was bouncy and silly, even when the footage was upsetting.

As monks began to light themselves on fire, the old ladies sitting near us got up and left; I saw that the child was burying his face in his father's jacket. The film stirred in me no emotion except annoyance and embarrassment toward the filmmakers, who had made a painfully bad film. When it ended, Tristan shook his head admiringly.

"This is viewing number *eleven* for me," he said. "I cannot get enough of this piece of garbage."

"Why do you like it?" I asked. I could see him line up a response, and I added, "Don't say some ready-made answer. I didn't find it funny, and I really want to know what you enjoyed about it."

He took a few moments to think. The man and his son had left, nobody new came in, and the film started again. "I suppose," he said, then stopped himself. He had more false starts like this, as the film played another time in front of us. Finally it came to him. Over the sound of zany music and cartoon gunshots, he spoke more slowly than ever before: "I like that it is trying to be one thing, and that it's failing and being something else instead. That other thing—that unintentional thing—it feels like it *belongs to me*. To me and no one else, except perhaps others who are just like me. We, the ones to whom so little belongs in earnest."

"I'm going to miss you," I said. He looked wounded; he had forgotten about his impending departure, and now I had reminded him. He took a swig from our gin flask. I put my hand on his knee, and he put his own hand on top of it. We kissed on the mouth and kept kissing as the film played again on loop. I moved my hand up from his knee to his waist. Then to the buckle of his belt. I wanted his erection in my hand, and the strength of this desire eclipsed everything else.

Then we heard feet on the stairs at the entrance to the theatre, and voices. Tristan sighed. "Not here," he said regretfully. I pulled away, also regretful, and looked at his face and the bright white light across it. Then the film cut to a nighttime scene, and his face was dark and gone.

We came out of the Christian Pavilion, into the light of day. "Should we visit our friends at Wienerwald?" Tristan asked facetiously. "Check out the new carpeting?"

"I'd like some ice cream actually," I said, and we entered a nearby lineup. The poster depicted a luscious soft-serve cone, but when we finally got to the stand, they were just selling Popsicles and charging a whole dollar for each. Having spent so long in line, we felt obligated to buy some, even though they could be purchased at a store, a box of ten for fifty cents. We received an orange and a red, and we each ate half of each. Then, with nothing left to do at Expo, we left.

In the Metro, Tristan gave a sigh. "I had déjà vu before the fit, when you were speaking," he said. "I sat there, thinking, *There he goes again, this angry young man. Yelling as he does, tearing me to shreds.* Then I realized I had never seen you angry. I was scared for two reasons. Scared that my brain had gotten things wrong, so I knew a fit was coming. And scared that you were angry. You're typically so kind and calm."

He drank from his gin, then I did.

"I certainly don't ever want to see you angry again." He spoke with the same rare sincerity that he had employed when telling me why he liked the film.

"You won't," I said.

By the time we arrived at our stop, we had polished off the gin. When we got to his apartment, I lifted his shirt over his head immediately. His long hair fell all over both our faces, and he brushed them clear. His thumb got in my mouth. It tasted like Popsicle. We stumbled through the Mona Lisa beads, into his bedroom. The window there, like the window in the bathroom, faced a brick wall, and its curtains remained undrawn. The brief daily moment of nicely angled sunshine arrived, and in this light, Tristan became a neon shape, seared onto the surfaces of my eyes. When I shut them, he remained there, a form made of impossible colours, embedded on the backlit black-red wall of my eyelids. Wherever his body wasn't bright white, the imprint failed to transfer, its nipples and navel and patch of pubes becoming blank black shards in the greater texture of the human figure.

15

His body always felt cold, even though it was summer. He had been this cold the whole time we'd known each other, but touch had been infrequent between us. Now we made up for lost time, each wearing a pair of Tristan's brightly coloured briefs at most, all day long, excepting for quick excursions outside his apartment for cigarettes, booze, or food. We always wound up in the same formation: me pressing my feet against his bare, interminably cool chest, from the other side of the unmade bed. The position gave us a degree of distance conducive to conversation, which went on for hours at a time. Even bathroom trips didn't stop our rambling; the one who didn't have to go came along and sat against the bathroom door. That was also where I sat when he painted his fingernails green once again, on one of the early days. And whenever our endless conversation reached an unclear juncture—about the future, specifically about *our* future—we would fill the sudden silence with proximity. One of us would reach under the bed for a morsel of Crisco from the can that we kept there and generously lather the other man's asshole, us both going *shh* for some reason, *shh, shh,* and the one who entered the other asking constantly

How's that, and the one being asked saying *Wait* when it hurt and *Christ* or *God* or *Yes* when proceeding was okay. One afternoon, we discovered oily imprints on the covers: stamps of our hands, stomachs, bums, and scrotums. The stains would wash out with difficulty. This did not distress us. The bedding, like the bed, like the bedroom, was soon to disappear from both of our lives.

Only at 7 a.m. every morning did we linger in the kitchen for longer than it took to make and pour coffee, or cook and consume our meals of fried eggs or liver sandwiches. This was the hour at which Michel would possibly call; I had provided him with Tristan's number, to contact me about any shifts. For days, the phone did not ring at all, and when finally it did, it wasn't Michel, but a friend of Tristan's. Tristan spoke as little as he could, in his brightest, most smiley voice, while rolling his eyes at me. The person on the other end of the line wouldn't stop talking.

"I'll see you there, love, but for now I really must go!" he said quickly after a few minutes, and hung up the phone, slumping into his chair. He explained that the call was from an attendant of the British Pavilion, inviting him out for drinks that night.

"Do you want to go?" I asked.

He laughed and shook his head emphatically. "She was clueless about my situation," he said. "She'll find out at drinks with the others, and then she'll be mortified that she called. Another girl from the pavilion, Denise, is engaged. That's what they're celebrating. I might have mentioned Denise—she wanted desperately to stay here in Canada. Apparently, she found herself a husband, so now I suppose she can." After thinking to himself for a while, he added, "To my credit, I once gave Denise a tarot reading that had this very outcome. Well done for me."

"You never did my cards, you know," I said.

"That's because you don't go in for it. I'm not dogmatic about it and I certainly don't care to shove it down your throat."

"Oh," I said. "That's true. I'm sorry about that."

"To each their own," he said, kissing the top of my head as he took the breakfast dishes away and placed them in the sink, on top of the dishes from the days before.

"Would you like to read them now?" I asked.

"Why would I do that?" he said candidly. "You'll only make fun of the findings, I'm sure. And even if you try at politeness, I'll know you're holding back."

"Then don't tell me what you see," I said. And that was what we did. I shuffled and split the deck, and he laid five cards down in the shape of a plus sign, then a sixth crosswise onto the middle card. He studied them privately and said nothing out loud, not even "hmm." One of the cards was the Hierophant, a big man in a big red robe, and the rest of the cards were numeric and forgettable.

At three o'clock that day, we boiled perogies, unsure if it was our lunch or our dinner. We turned the radio on and listened to Dionne Warwick. "Walk on By." We sang along, sharing a delighted look at having found out that we both knew the words, not only to the chorus but to the verses too. Then, when it ended, we heard applause—the version being played was from some live recording, not the version usually on the radio. Warwick's voice had sounded just the same. The applause felt like a curtain getting lifted, revealing all these people we hadn't known were there. I thought suddenly, and disturbingly, of how all those voices hooting and cheering belonged to real people, and that the people would age, but the voices on the record would sound the same, in five years, in fifty years. The day would come on which the last of them would die, and the record would still retain all their cheers, any time somebody played it.

That night, like every night, Tristan and I kept a stubby candle lit beside the bed, to see each other by a quality of light that was special to that time. It gave our bodies drama, like floodlit marble sculptures. We found each other ludicrous and captivating; we operated with eagerness and levity. Then we blew the candle out and fell toward sleep with a luxurious sense of unhurriedness, facing each other, legs braided together. We alternated between conversation and silence. The space between our speaking grew and grew, and whenever the speaking concluded, each man wondered whether sleep had arrived for the other.

At some point, I whispered gently, "What's a hierophant?"

Tristan didn't answer. Perhaps he was asleep. Then I felt him inhale.

"*Hi-rophant*," he said correctively. I had said *hee-rophant*. "So you're a little curious about the cards after all."

"No, I'm really not," I said. "I just don't like when I don't know a word."

"It's a priest," he said.

"Okay. Thanks."

"And," he said next. But nothing followed.

"What is it?" I asked. "And what?"

"I won't tell you what your reading showed," he said, "but there is one thing I could share from it. Because I was already thinking it anyway."

"Okay," I said.

"It's something, I think, about that boy you knew, Ray. With the goats. I think you might think that he made you... the way you are. Queer. But if you ask me, he didn't make you anything. I don't think that's how this works. I think it was already there."

He put his hand on the very middle of my chest, just below the plane of the nipples, where the skin is thinnest and the bones are the most sunk. Another passage of silence took place, during which neither man felt any need to speak to the other. But I did speak, after a while.

"I know that," I said. "But maybe, if he never came along, no other man would have either, and then it could have stayed all inside. And I could have—I don't know—been with girls."

"Would you have preferred that?" he asked with mock defensiveness.

In a sloppy attempt to show how much I enjoyed his company and body, I reached down and weaved my fingers softly into his pubes and scratched gently. "Have I told you much about a man named Honoré?" I asked.

I felt him shake with laughter. "You talk about him all the time," he said.

"Oh," I said. I thought that at most I had mentioned Honoré in passing. I laughed too. "Well, he had one life, and then a whole other one. Girls, and boys."

"Of course. And never the twain shall meet."

Tristan manoeuvred his hand over to the left side of my chest. He pressed against me lightly. He was looking for my heartbeat, just to look for something. Once he found it, his hand went away.

"That approach takes a certain kind of person, I think," said Tristan. "It's certainly not for me, and I don't think it's for you either."

"Maybe not," I said, pronounced as though a rebuttal would follow. But instead, I just clutched him close and allowed the silence to stay. Talking had given me a sense of good exhaustion, and I felt sleep would come very easily now.

"I have heard another theory about it," said Tristan. "I'm sure Honoré knew this one too, so maybe you'll know it. The idea is that it happens to us because of our mothers. They love us too much. Not that this is every man's case, but some, and perhaps yours."

"My mother died when I was really young," I said.

"I know," he said, "but she had time enough to love you, and she could be loving you still, from wherever she is."

I pulled him closer. He said nothing more, and soon I heard his snoring.

THE NEXT MORNING, I FINALLY GOT A CALL FROM MICHEL. When Tristan came out of the shower, I shared the news of the call with him delicately, thinking he'd be upset by a break in our long streak of sole companionship. But he was affable about it, almost surprisingly so. He sat in a towel at the kitchen table, leafing sleepily through an issue of *Esquire*, while I busied myself getting ready.

"You're not sneaking over to Expo instead, are you?" he asked jokingly. "I know you miss it."

"Time with you is better," I said. "I haven't thought about Expo."

As I headed out the door, he spoke again: *"Jamais vu!"*

"Is that so," I asked, pausing in the doorway.

"Just now," he said smiling. "You've never left my sights, not once before. Not even now, as you walk out of here."

I closed the door behind me, already impatient to return to him.

Around rush hour, Michel and I noticed that the streets were less crowded with traffic. Michel speculated that this was because of the Metro, with people commuting in a different way. "It's actually more busy than before in this city," he said. "It's just hidden." To this I said nothing. Visiting home after home to do repairs, I felt anxious, even somehow fraudulent, to be in the company of strangers, of locals, of people who weren't Tristan. When Michel dropped me off at my and Étienne's apartment in Mile End, he told me, "Perk up, kid," and I realized I had been bad company, impatient to get back to the intoxicating world that Tristan and I had constructed together, rank and veiled and poorly lit and temporary. Before returning there, I went into my apartment to get a few clean changes of clothes and full bottles of liquor. As I filled up my backpack, I heard Étienne's bedroom door creak open.

"He is alive," he said. He carried a cigarette in one hand and his ashtray in another.

"Hello," I said. "How did de Gaulle go for you?"

He gave me a cursory kiss on the cheek as a greeting, before pouring himself a cup from the coffee pot and taking a seat. "A great success," he said. "My boss was very happy. Now I feel like it is missing. This is the nature of events: they come, they go. But I had many dreams about it. I mean before. In bed, on the Metro, standing awake: dreams. When the day arrived, I was so prepared that it felt like a place where I had been before. And now I feel..." he said, and whatever it was that he felt, he didn't know the word.

"Say it in French," I said after he spent a moment searching. He gave the notion new consideration, but still shrugged. Whatever he felt, no word in either language could capture it. I reached into his shirt pocket, where he kept his cigarettes, and lit one for myself while continuing to pack my bag.

"I heard that Tristan must leave," said Étienne.

"Yes, soon."

"I am sorry that this has happened. When I heard, I was very sorry."

"That's nice."

"When does he leave?"

I bristled. I didn't like thinking about Tristan's departure. "A week or so," I said.

"Will you live here again, after he is gone?" he asked.

I was frustrated by this question even more, and by thoughts of how Étienne just wanted me around, to cook and clean, and fix him drinks, and listen to him rant about his workday. Already I was having imaginary conversations with Tristan about it and arranging how I would report everything. I would tell Tristan that Étienne had been selfish and unkind.

He got up out of his chair. "I want for you to be *careful*," he said, his voice unexpectedly soft. "When he goes, when it is goodbye, this will not be easy. Crazy kid."

He gave me a pained and friendly look. He hadn't been thinking of dinners or dishes at all. He had been thinking about my welfare. He kissed me again on the cheek before putting out his cigarette and emptying his mug into the sink, having had one sip. And he went back to his room, leaving the ashtray on the table for me.

I felt bad for finding him villainous. I hadn't noticed the sweetness to his words, and the sweetness to his little goodbye peck. I felt bad also for having disappeared from the apartment for a week without even sharing my whereabouts.

"Bye for now," I hollered at his closed door. I also shouted, "I'll be back soon." I wanted to run to Tristan immediately and to put my mouth over his mouth and my arms around his torso, tightly, instead of giving any thought to the little word that now ran through my head over and over, like a phone number I was struggling to memorize and terrified to forget—*careful*. Hesitantly I said one last thing in the direction of Étienne's door: "Thank you." Then I put out my cigarette and left, the backpack clanking against my shoulder.

WHEN I RETURNED TO TRISTAN'S, I NOTICED THE PHONE CORD, which I had laid tidily on the table after speaking with Michel, hung loosely off the side now, filled with awkward tangles. Tristan was in the bathroom, scrubbing the bathtub with Ajax and a rag, by the light of the Tiffany lamp. There were pawprint-like streaks in the side of the tub, demonstrating the shoddiness of the job he was doing.

"Thought I'd put a dent in the tidying," he said upon seeing me. "That deposit seems a far sight from here."

"Deposit?"

"Forty-five dollars I won't get back unless the place is sparkling. Not that Canadian cash will do me much good, but I thought you could use it." He knelt and kept scrubbing. I stripped down to my underwear, same as he was, to climb in and help. I showed him how to scrub more effectively and taught him that even when it looked clean, he wasn't necessarily done; he had to feel for the grime with his fingers. I brushed his hand against a clean patch and then a grimy spot. He went "Aha," delighted. Then he changed completely and sat all apathetic on the lip of the tub.

"We're just getting into it," I said, continuing to scrub.

"There's too much to do." He waved around bleakly at the bathroom, and the whole apartment beyond the door. "I'm overwhelmed."

"We can just do a little every day. The place is tiny. We'll be done in no time."

At this, he once again perked up. "Good thinking," he said, and took the rag from my hand. He winked reassuringly.

"Who called today?" I asked.

He continued scrubbing. "No calls," he said.

"The cord was tangly."

"Ah," he said. "Now that you say that, yes, there was a call. I forgot but now I remember. Nothing important." His technique had regressed already, his scrubbing again ineffective. I knew he was lying, and I thought about going to my backpack and fixing myself a drink from the booze in there. But if I did this without fixing Tristan one too, he'd know I was upset, and I wanted to keep my mood to myself, just as Tristan was keeping something from me.

After a few moments of feeling me watch him, he shared after all. "I'll tell you, pet," he said. "I was going to not tell you at all. I was going to think of an elaborate lie. Alas, my disposition is much like it was with the doctor the other day. I'd rather tell you the truth, in case there's a chance it helps with the pain."

He put both his hands on my knees.

"I booked my flights. I thought I'd do it while you were away. There were two routes that get me to Heathrow, one that leaves tomorrow and one on Sunday."

When he said *tomorrow*, I felt my body seize.

"The Sunday flight is within forty-eight hours of my visa expiry, and apparently it's criminal to put it off so late. I could end up in real trouble. So I booked for tomorrow. I had to. Departure at eight o'clock in the morning. That's all."

"Oh," I said. We had talked now and then about how he needed to make that booking, but it was a nicely distant, abstract notion. Now it was real, and sooner than expected by five days. I slumped into the tub and lay awkwardly across his lap. The smell of cleaner swirled around my head. We did nothing for a long time, and then I heard him take a snotty breath in. Knowing he was crying, I let myself do the same.

The evening passed like this, in the tub. As we shifted to accommodate the body parts that fell asleep or got crampy, we exchanged looks of exhaustion, even of resentment. His face often resembled that of a sad child, tormented by an incredible unfairness. Sometimes one of us wept, and in such moments, the other man kept it together, rubbing the back or belly or chest of the weeping one. A bit of kissing took place during this prolonged time, and a bit of chatter too. We shared random thoughts as they occurred to us. We agreed that I'd keep the apartment myself until the end of the lease a week later. I'd spend the week cleaning and would pocket the returned deposit.

Eventually we exited the tub. In a drawer, he found his bright red passport for Expo. We flipped through it together, studying all the stickers and stamps from all the pavilions he had visited. "I can't imagine I'll need this," he said, "but of course, I'll take it home. Months from now, its weight in my hand will bring me right back here."

I kept a few of his things for myself, like a pair of thick brown socks and a toque I liked the colour of. He also left *The Ballad of Beta-2* for me to finish, but I had to promise to read the whole thing.

"That way we can talk about it," he said, and then he stopped himself from saying more. We had not yet addressed the idea of staying in touch.

"Maybe we could write letters," I said, once the silence was too noticeable to easily bear.

"To be honest, that sounds dreadful," he said, clutching me. "That instead of this."

"Don't think that way," I said. "I want to know at least that you're still alive, and for you to know that about me."

He considered this. "Yes, I could do a thing like that."

"Okay," I said.

He took a heaving breath and said, "If only you were a girl, or if I was—then you could simply put a ring on my finger and we could wed, and I would be able to stay forever."

I went to the bathroom, picked my pants up off the floor, and reached into the pocket. I took out the ring and did as Tristan said, slipping it onto his finger. The moment of shimmering sunlight came and went, and when Tristan held his hand up into it, the green of the stone changed from something deep to something light, like the grass of a field. Then Tristan gave the ring back. We decided to skip dinner and just head into the bed. There, we kept up the same routine as we had struck in the bathtub, alternating between administrative exchanges, chaste kisses, crying fits, and a silence laced with the potential to break. Brief passages of sleep took place as well, sometimes individually and sometimes simultaneously. These different states had in common the act of touch, with each body covering as much of the other's surface area as was sustainable.

At some point we were both awake, and each aware of the other man's wakefulness.

"How are you feeling?" I whispered then.

"Boneless," he replied.

In the morning I stirred and could sense him in the room, getting ready for departure. I knew he was trying to keep me from waking to avoid that last goodbye. I wanted to skip it too, so I kept my eyes shut and my breathing even. He went into the bathroom for a while, and though I couldn't hear what he was doing, I noticed a strong chemical smell. Nail polish remover. Then I heard the front door open and close. The apartment fell silent again.

Part Three

I REMEMBER LIGHTS

XX

Shortly after I used the toilet, a lineup formed for it. I stood in the crowd in the middle of the cell and watched the line move along, and eventually noticed a courtesy taking shape: the man whose turn it was would sometimes ask the man behind him, *Shit or piss?* If the man only needed to urinate, and same for the man who was asking, then they'd stand together in front of the bowl, side by side, to help the lineup move along more quickly.

Some stood around in a group, near the toilet, talking to each other with a frantic energy; the man with painted black nails led the conversation. For a moment, I joined the circle, but I found it impossible to focus on any talking. How could these men have any kind of proper conversation, knowing we could not exit the room we were in, even if we tried? I remembered my idea of counting everyone, as a way to pass the time until we were freed. This was more manageable than talking, though I kept losing track or forgetting the number in my head, and never made it past ten. Some men, because of their tiredness or drunkenness, were able to fall asleep sitting up on the benches. This too I found impossible to even imagine, though I sometimes caught myself nodding off and jolting back awake.

I was roused when a man broke the quiet by yelling toward the barred door, "If you're going to keep us, you need to feed us!"

Others chimed in, speaking French and English. "Yes! We must eat!"

"You can't let us starve."

"It's our human right!"

This kept up for a long time. The cops on the other side of the bars just stared off. While some men shouted complaints, others covered their heads with their jackets, leaning against their neighbours on the benches, or against the wall. One man, sitting in the corner, yelled suddenly, "Shut up! Stop whining!"

"But they're treating us like dogs," replied one of the protesting men.

I suddenly thought of Dorothy; I wondered how I would have managed her last walk of the night, if I had gotten John home with me. Would I have asked John to come along for the stroll, which I did with some men, or would I have trusted him to stay at my place alone while I completed a short trip around the block, which I did with others? Or would I have asked him, in some discreet and improvised way, to leave? I did that sometimes too. But with John, I couldn't imagine this. I believed we would have shared the bed, all night, and I even envisioned us walking Dorothy together in the morning. With such thoughts—thoughts of that other evening, made of better circumstances, the evening that didn't transpire—I passed the time for a good while.

Someone came into the cell who hadn't been there before. He was not a cop, but a fellow found-in, wearing a sharp red dress shirt with large sweat stains beneath the arms, and the top three buttons undone beneath his beard.

The man with nail polish, who earlier had been recruiting individuals not to plead guilty, asked the new arrival, "Where are you coming from?"

"There is a second cell, and that's where I was before. I asked to make a phone call. Now they put me here."

"Why did they let you do that?"

Another man asked, "What else can you do? Can you get us food?"

He didn't answer these questions. He just gave everyone talking to him an uncaring look, similar to that of the cops. His inquisitors gave up on him and started again to yell through the bars about their right to be fed. It dawned on me, incrementally, first that the new arrival was someone I knew, and then that he was Honoré, exhausted and downtrodden to the point of unrecognizability. It was unusual for us to acknowledge each other's existence in common spaces, let alone to talk, but the special environment of the cell changed our unwritten rules. And he had broken these rules already, earlier in the evening, just outside the bar, when he had asked me, "Do you see?"

At the sight of me, he sighed. I approached him.

"Honoré," I said. "Did you notice a man in a reddish jumpsuit in the other cell?"

He pulled a pack of cigarettes out of his pocket, and one cigarette out of the pack. A few men in our vicinity turned to face him. Immediately, Honoré said to them, "Last one," holding the pack upside-down and shaking it in front of their faces. He crouched to strike a match against the floor, then sprang back up and blew his smoke in the direction of the bars.

"Anglo, young guy, brown hair," I said. "His name is John."

"They did not make any man wear a jumpsuit. It's like this one. We kept our clothes."

"It was his own jumpsuit, not a prison outfit. Stylish."

"I remember no jumpsuits."

He drew from his cigarette with every breath and tapped it with every draw, even when there was no ash to fall. Like me, he wanted time to pass as quickly as possible.

"I haven't talked to anyone all night," I said. "I've been panicking sometimes. But talking to you is easy. Can you stay here with me, for just a few minutes?"

With his foot, Honoré swiped away the ash on the floor, then crouched down again and stayed down, taking a seat, leaning against the bars. He motioned for me to join him, and once I did, he put his hand on my knee.

"Nothing to panic for," he said. I looked down at the hand on my knee, a wedding band on its ring finger. It had been there for a few years. I had never asked about it. "They don't know what they're doing. They arrested more of us than they have room for. Where I was before, it wasn't even a cell. Just a holding room, with ten of us in there. Not to mention"—he checked his watch— "it's Saturday morning now. All the work they have to do, it will move slow. But they will get it done. Whatever they need to do. And then we will be freed." He exhaled smoke through his nostrils.

"Will you plead guilty?" I asked.

"Me, I've worked hard. I've gotten as good as I can. As *clean* as I can. Anyone who looks at my situation and thinks, *He must try harder*—such a person does not understand that I have tried. This is trying the hardest, right here."

He gestured generally, at the cell that we occupied.

"Maybe even *you* don't understand everything," he said. "But I know I am not guilty, not of anything. None of us is. You are not guilty either. So stop panicking. You are innocent."

"Once, you called me innocent and I hated you for it."

"That was a different *innocent*," he said.

The way he said the word this time made me think of Dorothy again. I began to cry.

Honoré said impatiently, "Come on. Please. Don't do this. I will leave you on the floor alone."

"My dog is all alone right now."

"Ah. I'm sorry about this. I forget his name."

"Her name. Dorothy."

"Hmm. What a stupid name."

Above our heads, the men formed a chant: "*On a faim,* feed us now!"

I pointed at Honoré's ring. "What's *her* name?" I asked.

He gave me a tempering look and pressed his cigarette against the floor on his other side. He had smoked it right down to the filter. "Odette," he said blithely.

"Is that who you called?"

He laughed. "No. I called my shrink. This is why they allowed the call—I said I had a medical emergency, I showed them the phone number in the phone book. *Doctor.* The cops don't need to know what kind. One of them even dialled the number for me. I will see him in the evening. My shrink."

"Are you worried about what Odette will think?"

"There are many nights I do not come home. With a little dog, I would be more worried. I suggest you try to sleep, little one."

We heard the men above our heads cheer suddenly and turned to look between the bars to see the source of the excitement. Two officers had approached the cell, each with a colourful box under his arm. When they reached the cell, they pulled out Popsicles, wrapped in paper. Laughter and groaning came from the men above our heads. Honoré and I stood up, and we joined in the laughing.

"Ice cream time," said a man behind me.

"We've been very well-behaved," said another sardonically. "We deserve some treats."

Through the bars, the officers handed out Popsicles, which were passed down until everyone got one.

"What a fucking insult," said the nail polish–wearing man, who had not been laughing. "They're only doing this so they can say they didn't let us starve. This is less than the bare minimum."

"Eat," said the man standing beside him, and the nail polish man took a breath and unwrapped his Popsicle.

"What colour?" Honoré asked, showing me that his was orange.

I unwrapped mine. Purple.

"Trade?" he asked, and we swapped. He nodded, to say thank you as well as goodbye, then headed further into the cell, to eat his Popsicle in solitude. I had already begun on mine and couldn't think of the last time I had tasted that taste, nectary and plasticky and compelling and wet. Alone again, I felt my panic come back. I fought it off by sucking on the bare Popsicle stick, past the point when it ran out of sugariness, until the only flavour was wood.

16

A transit strike took place through all of September, which decreased business at Expo, and with it, Étienne's workload. He spent his new-found time preparing for his return to France, getting his affairs in order ahead of his new travel agency job. One morning, he wrote letters to potential landlords in Toulouse; another, he came home with dry cleaning and kept the clothes in their bags, saying he'd only unbag them once it was time to pack and leave. His method of departure contrasted greatly with Tristan's: that single afternoon of unfocused cleaning, that last-minute packing job. Tristan had made no effort to find work ahead of his return home, and I didn't know where he was now—London, or Cardiff, or elsewhere entirely. I received no word from him, and had no way to send the first letter.

By now it was autumn, with the rotting crabapples and the ice-cold wind and the patches of orange all over Mount Royal. After a long summer of sun and exposure, my longer sleeves and added layers felt maddeningly noticeable. They weighed, they itched, they slowed my movement down.

The orange-coloured trees went red, then lost their leaves entirely. The mailman only ever brought flyers. The transit strike ended, but Étienne quit early anyway, to fly to Toulouse at the start of October, weeks before Expo concluded. On his last morning in Montreal, he came home with two lobsters in a wooden box. I spent the afternoon preparing lobster thermidor, boiling and bifurcating the lobsters, mixing the meat with wine and cream, shoving it back into the bodies and broiling them. During dinner, we toasted our vermouths to Étienne's new work, his new life.

The next morning, I found a blazer of his I had always liked, hanging on the doorknob of the bedroom that was now mine. I donned the blazer and found forty bucks in the pocket—the last of Étienne's Canadian cash, left for me. I flopped onto the bed, the pillows of which still smelled of his conk, rancid and appealing. This smell would fade away in time. Now that I could have the bed to myself, my own smell would take over—the smell that followed me everywhere and was to me the same as no smell whatsoever.

That night the apartment was too quiet to tolerate. I went to the Peel Pub, which was much less busy than it had been during the height of the summer.

Davey asked if I was doing okay. "You look blue."

"I don't know. Expo's almost over. That's sad."

He laughed. "I can't think of a single reason to miss it. I only just visited recently, and I couldn't think of why I had gone. The buildings *look* plastic from far away, and walking around over there, I saw they actually *are* plastic. They'll fall apart and rot into even more of an eyesore. It's a floating garbage dump."

I didn't reply to this, and Davey kept himself busy slicing lemons and limes. I took the paperback out of my back pocket. *The Ballad of Beta-2.* I was about halfway through, and when I finished the chapter, I turned the page to find that the next page's text was upside-down. I flipped the book over and realized that, on the back, what I had thought was an advertisement for a book or movie called *Alpha Yes, Terra No!* was actually a whole different story, by an entirely different author. If you flipped the book over, you could start the other story; it was a two-in-one. I had expected the first story to keep going—there were so many unread pages in my right hand. Instead, I had read every word, and there was no story left.

I VISITED EXPO ONE MORE TIME, ON ITS LAST DAY. I WENT to the Christian Pavilion and descended the stairs surrounded by human bodies and modern technology thrown grotesquely together. I sat through a few consecutive screenings of *The Eighth Day*, drinking rum from a flask, trying to find the things Tristan had found in the film—humour, brilliance, appeal. I watched the gunfire and the cannon fire. I watched Hitler rant in fast motion to the sound of chipmunk-voiced Italian opera. I watched indifferent soldiers march past corpses left in snow, and a blooming dandelion fade into the mushroom of a nuclear bomb. The film got less disgusting and disturbing with each viewing, but no new emotions came to replace the disgust. There were just fewer and fewer emotions, until I felt nothing, not even the clothes on my skin, not even the stale air in my nostrils and throat. I was the only person in the theatre, but I thought to myself: *How sad that this film is playing for an absolutely empty room.*

Exiting the pavilion and entering the dark of the night, I heard a very loud explosion. My shadow flashed on the ground beside me, nested momentarily in sharp neon green. It was fireworks.

Crowds rushed out of all the pavilions to watch them. I joined in the current of strangers and headed to the middle of the island, where the view of the fireworks was least obstructed. At the sound of each explosion, everyone erupted in jubilance. Some of the explosions were so bright I could have read a book by their light. Some started dense and became willow-like, lingering for so long that I wondered if they were really still there, or if they were just the glowing impressions that eyes retain sometimes. They all left smoke behind.

The fireworks show moved through peaks of activity and valleys of quiet night-darkness. I felt that the humans responsible were trying to tell a story. The narrative was vague, being told, as it was, exclusively through the medium of explosions. But its aim was to impart victory. To celebrate Expo, to celebrate the beauty of its buildings, to celebrate the perfection of the summer we'd all had. I thought briefly about the fireworks show at the opening of Expo, and the Russian woman who thought it was the sound of terrorist attacks. But these explosions were harmless, free of victims, free of malice. Their job was to celebrate many things, including that no *real* explosions or terrorist attacks had happened. Nothing had ruined this perfect party.

I looked away from the explosions, at the people around me. Green and blue hues landed on their greasy faces like fingerpaint. Everyone's mouth was either smiling or wide open. Smoke from the explosions piled onto itself, taking over the whole island. The wind was weak, so the smoke stagnated above all our heads. Slowly, it descended into our faces, stinking and stinging. When the show started, everyone had been cheering and clapping their hands. Now everyone was coughing and using their hands to cover their nostrils and mouths, or to fan the smoke away.

17

A strange feeling came over me after Expo ended, and it was suddenly the only feeling I could really experience. If Michel had asked, on one of our drives, how I was feeling, I might have tried calling it anxiety, gloom, or relentlessness—but these words all felt insufficient, and Michel didn't ask. One evening, on a cold walk through my old neighbourhood of Little Portugal, I found a way to describe it to myself that almost felt accurate: *fear of time.* Time seemed to be closing in on me, or to finally be taking advantage of the power it had always had. I could move from place to place during work, house to house, room to room; I could step outside for fresh air. But no matter what, in terms of time, I had to go forward, and so did everyone else. I had to age, children had to grow up, old people had to contract illnesses and die. For months, I talked half-heartedly to TV repair customers about the news and the weather. The whole time, I would constantly stare at the second hand of whatever clock was in view. On every clock, the process felt both too fast and too slow to be real. I acted my way through the day, playing the role of a healthy human being. Then I got home and lay on my bed, sometimes with a comic book open on my chest, but never finding the energy to read it. It felt as though the world itself was cause for calamity, its limits, its way of decaying, and getting dusty and filthy. How its buildings looked a little unfashionable already and would only look worse as more trends came and went; how books sometimes fell behind shelves in bookstores and libraries and homes, dusty books that nobody would ever read again.

When I searched for a source of this anxiety, my only real clue was a thought I would have sometimes, the anguish of which was sharper than the anguish brought on by any other thoughts. It was when I thought about Expo, over there, on its islands. No footfalls on its concrete, no laughter in its hallways or lobbies, never again to be populous, never again to be a fun place. The wind blew through it, the sunlight dulled the vibrancy of its bright plastic casings. Though there was talk on the radio of reopening Expo the following summer due to popular demand, the commentators clarified that certain countries would not participate, that certain buildings would be shuttered, and that some buildings had already been damaged by the winter weather and would likely get demolished in the spring. There was something so sad about a place from which all the attention was gone. I couldn't think about it for too long or I would become suddenly conscious of my breath, and even the deepest inhales would feel too shallow.

ONE MORNING, I RECEIVED A LETTER AND RECOGNIZED THE handwriting on the envelope right away. Tristan had finally written to me. I read the letter, then hid it beneath the couch cushion, even though I no longer had a roommate who might come across the things that were mine.

A few days later, I got another piece of mail: a bulletin outlining a new job opportunity had been provided to all the TV repair company's employees. The job was in a town called Brandon, in Manitoba, and came with an apartment, and the successful candidate's train ride there would be covered too.

"Did you get that bulletin?" I asked Michel on our next drive together.

"Yes," he said, "and I thought of you actually."

"You think I should apply?"

"*Bien sûr*. It is perfect for you. No family, nothing to keep you here. And you will make more money. A place to start over *through-through-through*. If you don't take this, I think you are perhaps a lost cause."

To prove to Michel that I wasn't one of those, I agreed to his idea of arranging a meeting between me and our boss, at which the job became mine if I wanted it. Surprised by how easily I had earned it, I decided that a big change like this was the best way to conquer my anxiety, my fear of time. A few weeks later, with two suitcases given to me by Michel and filled with all my things, I began my voyage to Brandon.

First I took a train to Ottawa. As I disembarked with my luggage, one of the attendants stopped me and said, "Transferring, correct?"

"To Brandon."

She took both suitcases, said she would stow them for me, and told me which platform to go to for my second train.

"Do I have time for a coffee?" I asked. She looked at her watch and nodded reluctantly.

On the other end of the train station, I found a small counter selling coffee, with tables and chairs. I ordered, took a seat with a clear view of my next platform, and opened the book I was carrying in my hand, *Valley of the Dolls*, which had sat open and unread in my lap during the three-hour ride from Montreal. I still couldn't focus on the book; men and women were rushing all around me, darting between the station entrance and the ticket booths, between the lounges and the platforms. They all gave off such a sense of importance, moving in straight lines with blank looks on their faces. I wondered if I gave off such a sense, sitting with my book and coffee—the sense that I was a man who had something very important to do that day. I knew this wasn't actually the case; relocating to a small town to repair televisions for a living felt like an incredibly futile gesture. It felt, in fact, like the most boring thing a person could do with his life. But I liked that my story was hidden away. For all these people knew, my life had meaning and intrigue, just like theirs.

Drinking my coffee, watching my platform, I indulged in this feeling of fascination and hoped it would stay with me indefinitely, though I knew it would fade as soon as I got on the train. Then I'd fall asleep, waking up at my destination.

I had almost finished my coffee; I noticed grounds at the bottom of the mug. For a bookmark, I was using Tristan's letter. I unfolded and read it, as I had done many times in the preceding days.

Hello pet. A little word for you, from me, at long last.

I had trouble sleeping last night. It was a night wherein I experienced many dreams in succession. In the first, I was riding the Metro alone. I looked out the window and saw that I was up high in a marvellous pink sky. One of those cleaning people came onto the car. It was you. I asked if you fancied a trip to the cinema.

You said you couldn't, as you were waiting for a call. Down in your mop bucket, there was a telephone. It was slimy like a barn animal just born. I asked whom you expected to call, and you pretended not to hear me. But I knew that the answer was your mother, and now I felt very silly and foolish, to think for a moment that it could be anyone else. Other dreams followed—~~reg~~ Regency balls, a sudden test I haven't studied for, tawdry matters really— but you came back again before I woke for good. Now we were eating at some restaurant that could have been any. I told you about the first dream, with the telephone in the mop bucket, and how I found the dream funny. You sniped back—"That's all well and good, but what would have been even better would have been a <u>letter</u>! Couldn't you have written to me, to tell me you had dreamed of me?"—and I felt agony at the oversight. Then I woke up, relieved that I could write you after all. So, that is what I've done. Just as you instructed . . .

Now it's later in the day. I can't just send that note alone, not without telling you a little about where I am and all that. So: I'm caretaking a youth hostel up north, not too far from a town called Durham. Before this I was in Cornwall, in a different stately home from this one. Wales before that—Betws-y-Coed, which I would love to hear you make an attempt at pronouncing. (In case it will bother you later—Betws rhymes with lettuce and the rest you'd guess correctly.) Somewhere in there, I had a weekend in Birmingham. Always in these empty, harrowing houses. Usually with a ghost or two for company (laugh all you want). It began with a temporary gig, keeping one old place in good shape. Keeping lights on and movements in the windows, so the hermits who might happen upon the place don't get any ideas. I cleaned the sludge from the gutters and waxed the window shutters. I even gave the bathtubs a good scrub like you taught me, feeling for dirt, not just looking for it. All that was enough to impress them, it seems. Now I'm in the system—they call me a 'floater'—and I go where they send me and help on the minding-and-cleaning front. Not bad work, really. Simple stuff, and I rather like the travelling around.

It's later yet now. I'm by the fire with my nightcap. Reading over what I've written, there's an amusing truth I've stumbled onto, which is that I am of course a hermit myself, if you think about it. Lucky that nobody sees it that way. The chap from headquarters told me on the phone once that being unattached was a fantastic asset. Indeed it can feel, at times, like living at the edge of the world. It might as well be Mars—and the nights are just as cold as that, down in my dungeon. I go to bed beneath a pile of fleeces thick as the dictionary. On the worst nights, I find myself wishing I hadn't left you that smart little toque with the bobble, though I'm ~~boyed~~ buoyed by the thought of you sporting it on Metro rides.

I've certainly been granted plenty of time to reflect. I don't think I could have ~~done what I~~ taken part in what we did, without knowing, the whole time, just how limited our time was. That's the sorry truth. I'm a bit of a self-saboteur—remember how horrid I was at Wienerwald? That was me, in top form, destroying the thing that was working, or trying to. The reality is, you and I only became possible once I was able to define the whole thing by its ~~tragedy~~ brevity. I was punishing myself for no reason. Maybe we both were. I haven't really found a way to stop the thoughts about you. That first kiss at the Christian Pavilion, I revisit often. I know it was not our first kiss, but the first one where I wasn't covered in my own piss, so can we keep it in the books this way? I remember feeling that you weren't doing <u>anything</u> else. Just kissing. I was your whole universe, and the moment was eternal. You *didn't have any plans and you weren't going anywhere. Just kissing me. It was overwhelming.*

Now I have run out of passages of our time together to suddenly remember, which makes me think that that's it: I've remembered them all, and they're done now. A limited resource. You'll notice this latest page is all wrinkled and that's because I threw it in the bin. Then I thought better of it. It makes me glad that you are anywhere at all, if not nearby. Very glad indeed to know this about you. Does it make you glad to think the same? That I am out there, somewhere, as opposed to not being anywhere? Now that I have asked it, I find I cannot wait to watch the postman collect this tomorrow, and to hear back from you after that. I need to know.

How rude to write an entire letter with so few real questions. Rest assured I want to know your any and all. Love and warm, warm thoughts (aspirational thinking). xoxo. T.

Putting the letter back in my book, I noticed that my train had arrived at its platform, and I wondered what emotions I would feel if I stayed seated where I was, nursing the last of my coffee—the final, grainy slurp—and watching the train depart, without me in it. Would there be panic, or relief? Some blissful mix? They called for passengers, and soon they called again. The train was a brisk walk away from my chair, and the crowd between us thin and navigable. I wondered if a man would poke out of one of the doors and call, "All aboard," as in movies, and if a large plume of smoke would fill the surrounding space as the train pulled away impossibly slowly. Then, someone did call, "All aboard," though it was a woman, not a man. The same woman who had helped with my luggage.

A place to start over through-through-through. Michel had said this, about Brandon. *Through-through-through* doesn't mean anything; he meant *through and through*, as in, completely. Specifically, that I could live in Brandon without anyone knowing that I had ever been a homosexual, that I had ever shared my life and heart and time and bed with men. I knew this was his thinking, and that it was a form of kindness. In Brandon I could get to work on a cleaner and more customary life, and from this effort, happiness would spring.

I tipped the last of the coffee into my mouth and sucked on the grounds as though they were candy. I made a quick list of the things on my person: a book, a letter, a wallet, my emerald ring. In my jacket pocket, sunglasses with the lenses a little scratched up. I was wearing one of my favourite pairs of underwear and one of my newest pairs of socks, free of holes, still bright white.

The movies were right: there was indeed smoke as the train pulled away, though not much, and its departure from the platform was quicker than I had expected. It was surprising to me, and funny too, for such a large vehicle to suddenly prove so swift and determined in its actions. It absconded with my clothes, my toiletries, my plans for the day, my plans for the days to follow—with almost my every possession. But I knew that wasn't the right way to see it. I was the one absconding. At the counter where I had bought my coffee, I asked if they served anything stiffer.

"Chateau Laurier's across the street," the man said. "Looks like a castle, but it's a hotel. Best bet for something like that at this hour."

The moment I entered the hotel lobby, a series of ideas came to me all at once, accompanied by an intoxicating sense of urgency. At the front desk, I booked a room, and at the concierge's counter, I filled out a request form, using a tiny pencil with no eraser, tied to the desk with a piece of grey string: *Nearest jeweller. Nearest travel agency. How to send telegram. Much obliged.* I wrote my room number too.

Several hours later, I sat in my room upstairs, listening to the radio, with even fewer items on my person than there had been right before that Brandon-bound train pulled away. When the phone rang, I picked up immediately.

"Hello, Tristan."

"Goodness, pet," said the voice on the other end. "What a treat to receive word from you, and now to hear your voice."

Before I told him that I had sold my emerald ring, or that I had bought a flight to London, I asked him to wait. I went to the desk at the end of the bed and opened the bottle of vermouth I had bought in a convenience store on Sparks Street, right after seeing the jeweller. It was a little pricey, but I had found the calligraphy on the label very beautiful and had more cash in my wallet than I had ever had before. I poured a finger into the tumbler that had come with the room and took a first sip, then lifted the phone to my mouth to speak again.

18

At the train station of a town called Penrith, Tristan and I hugged for a long, long time. I had visualized this moment many times during the days preceding it. I felt incredibly glad to see him, and in his arms I began crying. I felt his body shudder too. When we pulled away from each other, he wore his child-like face, smooth and bright red, simple and glad. He took my backpack off my back, expressing surprise that it was so small. Once we were in his car, a baby-blue Volkswagen, he grabbed my hand and gave the ends of my fingers a long kiss. His hair was short now, like the Beatles in *Help!*—a mushroom mop top.

"I feel stronger this way," he said, noticing me notice it. "Like the opposite of the story of Samson. You, on the other hand, look like death."

I checked the passenger mirror and agreed. My hair felt greasy, and I had bags under my eyes. He put his hand on the gearshift, and I put my hand on his hand. The sky looked both cloudy and bright; I had no instinctive notion of what time it was and would have believed the sun was setting or that it had just risen.

The scenery we drove through became sparser and greener as the drive went on. I knew we were heading toward a hostel called Barrow House, where Tristan had a few days left in his contract. Now, in the car, he told me that he knew his next destination, a hostel called Frog Firle. Unlike most other hostels, Frog Firle operated through the winter. Tristan would head down there soon, and I'd go with him.

"It isn't meant to get so cold down there," he said. "Ramblers pass through every season, all year long. It's in the south—right now, if you didn't know, we're in the north."

"I knew that much. About only that much."

"You'll see the whole of England on the drive," he said, shooting me an encouraging wink before turning back to the road ahead. "And we'll have to find you work once we get there. Maybe even at the hostel itself. It's great work really—you can take real pride, and you're tired when it's over. But we'll have to wait and see what we can sort out for you. That's part of the fun, isn't it."

We arrived at an enormous mansion. Tristan explained that the hostel featured eighty beds, spread out in ten large rooms, all of which would stay empty until tourist season began again after the winter. He led me up wide staircases, down long halls flanked with rows of tall wooden doors. The last staircase was thin and winding, and led to the servants' quarters. The ceilings hung too low to stand straight, and on the one window, a large crack spread across the glass. He had leaned records against the window—Dusty Springfield, Diana Ross, the Ronettes—and he had also placed some turquoise scarves over the lamps on the two nightstands. His tarot cards, wrapped in their purple silk and placed in an ornate metal bowl, took pride of place on a bookshelf in the wall, flanked by science-fiction paperbacks.

"You've made this place your own," I said. "More than your place in Montreal."

"I just feel more at home here, even though the whole idea is that I go somewhere else in a few days. And then another place after that, and possibly another and another."

He took a few decorative pillows off the bed and put them on the floor.

"*We* go somewhere else," he said, and kissed my neck. "Not just me."

I didn't bother to unpack, though I did check in my bag for the red candy tin that contained all the money I had, converted to pounds. Then Tristan and I lay together on the tiny bed, in our clothes and above the covers. It was a tight fit, and if we weren't careful, either man could have slipped off, so we tucked our limbs below each other's bodies for counterweight.

"What's that sound?" asked Tristan, resting his head on my chest.

I listened for noise and heard nothing. Even beyond the cracked window, I heard no wind, no animals, no traffic. "There's no sound," I said. Then Tristan poked my stomach, and I realized it was grumbling. I wasn't especially hungry. It was just something my stomach did sometimes when I lay down. To me it was a ubiquitous sound.

"How did I never notice this about you before?" said Tristan.

I fell asleep before I could point out that Montreal was never silent.

AFTER AN UNKNOWN AMOUNT OF TIME SPENT ASLEEP, I woke up with even less of an idea of the time of day. It was pitch black, and I could not remember the layout of the room, or what was in it, aside from the bed. Tristan was not there. No walls were within reach, only empty black space. I stumbled around for a light switch, stepping very carefully, in case there was a stair or piece of furniture. I found a doorknob and opened it, and carefully headed down the staircase. I walked a series of totally dark hallways, feeling for turns. I knew I wouldn't be able to find my way back to the servants' quarters, and that my only hope now was to plow forward until I found Tristan, wherever he was.

I couldn't remember the name of the town I was in, and I couldn't remember the date. The big black gap I was occupying could have been any place in the world. Or it could have been a place that was apart from the world, like the centre of the moon. Pitch black, unknown, over there. It was a loneliness so vast that I took pride in it. It was mine and nobody else's, and anything could come from it. Eventually, I noticed a bit of lamplight coming from the crack below a door, like a long bright insect or reptile, resting in the corner, preserving its energy. I opened the door and found Tristan lying in a very wide room, in a double bed surrounded by undressed bunk beds, with a lamp on beside him. He had a book in his hands; at the sound of my entry, he laid it down on his stomach. "You were snoring," he said, and grinned, and made room for me.

I cuddled up beside him. "Let's never be apart," I said. He began to brush his hand through my hair. The cover of his book read *Dune* in chunky, fancy handwriting. The picture behind the text was of a sandy mountain, with two small figures climbing or descending it.

IN THE MORNING, WE HEADED BACK TO THE SERVANTS' quarters, where Tristan handed me a big, rickety cane. "Let's take a hike," he said, taking for himself a long and sturdy umbrella with a good, curved handle. We headed down a series of staircases, all different widths. We heard the clattering of metal dishes.

"That'll be Kitty in the mess," Tristan said as we headed toward the noise. "She comes and checks in on the place. A lot of these properties have the one local who won't stop lending a hand, even after the hostel association provides workers like me. On your best behaviour, pet. We must be very nice to her. You'll probably think her a tad eccentric, but she's harmless, all told, and quite sweet in her way."

Kitty sat at a large table, applying polish to a pot. The radio was playing a folksy version of "He's Got the Whole World in His Hands." She wore her hair in a loose grey bun. "You must be the Canadian," she said in an accent I found billowy. Then she asked for my help with the scrubbing. "You look quite strong and strapping, fit for the task at hand."

Cajoled by Tristan, she told us a little about Barrow House. She said a bachelor had built it almost two hundred years before. "All these rooms," she said, "and just one man. Can you think of it?" Then her story tapered off, and I noticed she was staring into the pot I was scrubbing, like it was a fire in a fireplace.

"Town today," she said suddenly to Tristan. "Not hiking. Town."

"Town it is," said Tristan, looking up from the cigarette he was rolling. He took my cane, and his cane-like umbrella, and stowed them away in an armoire.

As we headed outside, I asked Tristan why we were changing plans.

"Because Kitty said so," he said, lighting the cigarette he had rolled for himself. "She's got *the gift*—she knows things. People come to see her in town, when they can't find something valuable. She's always right. So we'll head to town and have a merry time."

I rolled my eyes at this. He stuck his tongue out and made a funny face.

Looking in front of us, I saw how truly beautiful the world beyond Barrow House was. I couldn't believe I hadn't noticed on the drive in that, just beyond the front lawn, lay a gigantic shining lake, and past it, dull-coloured mountains, their tips lost in the blue-white fog. Tristan told me the lake's name: Derwentwater. He pointed out an island and said it was unattached to the ground below. It moved about as slowly as the rate at which fingernails grow. In this way, the island, and indeed the lake, was always changing. "But to really get a sense of its progress," Tristan said, "I suppose you'd have to visit once, and then return years later to look again. But it would take maybe fifty years for the progress to be visible. By then you'd be a different person."

In a store in town, I found a pair of slippers just like the pair that had been in my luggage and had taken the train to Manitoba without me. Later, Tristan found a ten-pound note in a bathroom stall and spent it immediately on a smart wool vest he wore out of the store. Sitting on the patio of a quaint café, we watched a man propose to a woman at a nearby fountain. She said yes, and we were the first to notice the event; Tristan delighted in getting the public applause started. I allowed my skepticism about Kitty's supposed powers to fade. Even if I wasn't exactly a believer, I looked forward to reporting to Kitty just how nice our day in town was, and how right she had been to direct us there.

We ate lunch in a pub, and dinner later in the same pub; we walked back to the hostel as the sun came down. Before heading all the way up, we went to the guest room where we had slept the night before, the room in which I had found Tristan reading by lamplight. He wanted to fetch his book before we settled into his bedroom. When we came to the room, we saw that the bed was cleanly made. "When did you tidy up in here?" I asked.

"I didn't," Tristan replied.

"Then who did?"

"It must have been Kitty the busybody." Then something dawned on him. "We left tissues," he said quietly. Almost to himself.

It was true: we had made love after I found him there, and had wiped up our cum with Kleenexes and left them on the floor next to the bed, thinking we'd clean them up later. Kitty had beat us to it unexpectedly.

I said, "She'll think it was me. All alone. Not such a big deal."

"She knows that's my book," he replied quietly, pointing at *Dune*, which had been placed neatly on the desk at the end of the bed. His eyes darted around, frantic with calculation. "I've talked about the book. She'll know I was here too. She'll know we were here *together*."

I had only once before seen him as nervous as this: at Wiener-wald, moments before his seizure. I eased him down onto the foot of the bed, where we sat together.

"Will you be okay?" I asked.

Understanding that it was a question about his epilepsy, Tristan nodded.

"Since she's psychic," I said, half-joking, "maybe she knew already."

He didn't laugh. Instead, he shot me a critical look, like I wasn't taking the matter seriously enough. A long silence ensued between us, during which I rubbed his back.

"She could get me fired," he said eventually.

After a few moments, he calmed down a little, and we headed up to the servants' quarters. I moved slowly, behind him, surprised by the sound and depth of his breaths.

THE NEXT MORNING, TRISTAN SUGGESTED WE DO THE HIKing we had postponed the previous day, and retrieved the cane and umbrella from the armoire. We followed a muddy path to a hill called Red Pike. The hike itself was muddy too. The whole way up, I kept a steady pace, while Tristan alternated between cautious crawls and sudden bursts of speed, so that we passed each other many times while ascending. We didn't talk much and hadn't done so since finding the cleaned-up room. Tristan had surprised me with his fear of being found out, and I didn't know how to express my surprise, or even whether it was surprise. At some point on our hike, while I studied a rock that was curiously much smoother than the many rocks around it, the better word occurred to me suddenly. He had not surprised me—he had *disappointed* me, appearing so ashamed, he with whom I had once had conversations about free love, brave sissies, and decent answers to every question, no matter the ramifications. For his part, whatever he was feeling he kept to himself.

Eventually, we reached the top of Red Pike, where we smoked cigarettes, drank a bottle of red wine, and peed it out. I admired the view, hazy and grey, and watched a ferry take its time slicing through Derwentwater. From there, the lake appeared full of dark, shoving ink. Smoke issued from the chimneys of the sparse and distant cottages. I felt a slight and inexpressible love for all the people in all the houses, holding all their hands out to all the fires they had put together to keep warm. Heading to the other side of the summit, we came across a pile of rocks in the shape of a man, which I considered charmingly unusual.

"The cairn," Tristan said. "The highest point of the summit."

For a late lunch, we headed to the same pub we had visited the day before, though this time our meal was less enjoyable. Less jovial. The new quiet between us felt incidental when we were moving, but it was harder to ignore as we sat facing each other, in a not-too-busy pub.

"More hiking, I think," said Tristan as we paid up.

He decided we'd tackle Cat Bells next. We saw other hikers there, but, unlike at Red Pike, we encountered them only on their way down. One of them told us, "Best to turn around, boys," as he passed. The evening had begun falling, the light had begun fading, a faint fog was developing in the air—and we were less than halfway up.

"So, should we turn around?" I asked Tristan.

"I hiked here the other day," he said. "I know the way to the cairn. We'll be up and down like a shot."

I had never thought about what happened when it got too dark to continue a hike. I supposed we would have to try to rest until the sun was back. We would lie on the ground and cuddle for warmth—except that I'd be in no mood to cuddle, because it would be Tristan's fault that we were stuck. As we continued, Tristan seemed to doubt his sense of direction. At every pause, I said we should turn around, but he insisted that we continue, with more and more irritation in his voice. We kept heading up, in silence, properly mad at each other. I wanted to be safe; he wanted to be trusted.

"Is that you two?" we heard a voice yell, somewhere far below. We turned around and saw a flashlight beam. It was Kitty, at the foot of the hill, illuminating a slim dirt path downward that we hadn't noticed. We weren't nearly as high up as I had thought, and we still had a long way to go before the summit.

"Of course," said Tristan quietly, grinning. Now he couldn't insist that we continue. If Kitty thought it was a good idea for us to turn around, then it was.

We headed down, and Kitty waited, shining the light so we could find our way. We walked to the car park together. Tristan told her we were likely to leave the next day, or the day after that. Since we probably wouldn't see her again before departing for Frog Firle, we began saying our goodbyes.

"Take care," she said to me as we stood at the Volkswagen.

"Will do," I said.

"Of him, I mean," she added. "Take care of this one. He is a special soul."

I nodded.

"Enjoy this time," she said, speaking to both of us now, and sighing. There was a change to the scale of the things she was addressing. These were her last words to us and she wanted to give them gravity. "You're still untethered. Both of you. It's beautiful. All these memories, these hikes and weekends— someday, when you've both moved along in life, with jobs and wives and children, this will be the faintest trace. Maybe you won't even remember it. Enjoy it now, boys. Enjoy all of this."

As Tristan drove us back to Barrow House, he and I maintained our previous quiet. I was fixated on Kitty's comment about the notion of faint traces, of forgetting. Of wives and children. I didn't like the idea that all this would disappear from my memory. Tristan and I weren't just enjoying ourselves, I thought. We were building something, putting our lives together. And Kitty knew this about us. Now I could picture her discussing us with the town women who came to her for palm readings or tarot sessions, or whatever she did to delude them. I saw them laughing about it over coffee, framing us as nothing more than roommates—two boys, both working, neither married, just getting started, and how silly, even how charming: they share a bed at night. They think they are in love.

"What did you think of her *wives* comment?" I asked Tristan.

"Such generosity. It was her way of saying, it's fine, it's nothing. This," he said, lifting his hand off the gearshift to point between himself and me over and over. He was grinning with relief. "Nothing to report to the higher-ups. I'm off the hook."

"But this isn't nothing. I don't want a wife. I didn't think you did either."

"Of course not, pet." He patted my knee briefly and kept his hand there. "But I can't lose my job. We don't all have red candy tins full of money in our rucksacks."

I pushed the lighter into its socket beside the radio dial, to heat it up.

"It's just a job," I said. "At Expo, you didn't care too much about your job."

His hand returned to the gearshift. "This job is different. I really enjoy it. And work at the British Pavilion had an expiry date."

I lit a cigarette, took the first puff, and handed it to him. Then I lit one for myself.

"Once," I said, "I told you that I wanted to answer every question decent, *every* question, and you told me I was right. I think about that a lot, when I need to feel strong."

He rolled his window down and held his cigarette to it. He let the wind take it away. "That wasn't to be dramatic," he said. "I hadn't asked for a cigarette. I never wanted one. I took it without thinking about what I wanted."

"Do you mind that I'm smoking one?"

"Do as you like. You're a grown man." After a long silence, he added, "I like this job."

I didn't reply. As I finished my cigarette, I stared into the road, into the tiny clouds that the Volkswagen's headlights formed in the evening fog.

X X

I dreamt of a long staircase leading out of a crowded room. It wasn't apparent, or important, whether the stairs went up or down. What mattered was that they went away from the room. I walked the stairs alone; nobody else had noticed them. Chalices and crosses sat in recessed shelves on either side of me. After a long walk I arrived at a cinema, and I knew to take a seat. The film would not begin until I did. It was a new Bond film, and it began how they all began, with colourfully lit women falling and rising, and words projected over them. I didn't try to read the words. After the credits, Bond appeared, fleeing from a villain's lair, with stolen information in his possession. I knew it wasn't a document or futuristic device that he had. It was just a name, the unknown name of some important person. He had found the name and read it, and now he knew it and had to get back to his superiors. But as he fled, Bond was apprehended by a henchman, who brought him to the lead villain. Typically, with Bond in his clutches, a villain would now devise some complicated method for ending his life. Strapping him to a table, with a slow-moving laser beam that inches forward; imprisoning him in an engine room with no evident way out. Bond always found a way out, and film after film, he got his precious information to the right place. But in this film, the villain took no such approach. He simply pulled a gun out of his pocket and shot Bond dead, and that was the end of the movie.

I woke up on the floor of the cell, with the syrupy taste of Popsicles still in my mouth. I couldn't remember lying down and giving sleep a try, and I couldn't understand how proper rest had possibly taken place there, for myself or for anyone. Popsicle sticks littered the floor around me and stuck to the bottoms of some men's shoes. I noticed that the men were all moving in the same direction. The cell door was open, and everyone was being ushered through. They moved sluggishly, without any jubilance regarding new-found freedom; for all they knew, we were being led only to another place of imprisonment. I too felt no jubilance; I too trusted nothing.

The cell was almost empty by the time I got off the floor, though one man was in the back corner, lying down as I had been. Also like me, he wore a suit. I approached him and asked, "Do you need help?"

When he rolled to face me, I saw that the whites of his eyes were filled with red veins, and he had Popsicle-purple vomit all down his dress shirt. More vomit was congealing on the floor beneath his chest.

"We get to go now," I told him.

"Is she here?" he asked, dazed.

"Who?"

"My mother. Is she here? Does she know?"

"I don't know," I said. "I don't know anything."

He moved especially slowly, holding himself up with his hand on my shoulder, coming down from drugs or drink or both. On his feet, he still did not want to leave.

"What if she's learned?" he asked. This wasn't a helpless, unfocused question. He recognized who I was—a near stranger, a prisoner like him—but still tried his luck by asking.

"We'll be out very soon," I said, and tried to smile brightly for him. We were the last two men in the cell, and I worried that the police would lock the cell again if we didn't move along and enter the single-file lineup outside. "She's not here," I said. "Your mother is not here, and she doesn't know where you are."

At this he took a breath and moved with me toward the door.

19

It took two days of driving to get to Frog Firle. I waited in the car outside while Tristan introduced himself and saw about the living situation. Out of boredom, I got started on his copy of *Dune*. When my eyes needed a rest from reading, I looked up at the brick hostel. Haggard roof, unkempt hedges. I thought of Tristan in there, meeting his new employers, acting all muted and on good behaviour, same as he had in Kitty's presence. That different Tristan. Then I thought maybe that was the real version of Tristan, while the version I knew before was actually the different one. Once I came to this understanding, the book, already difficult to get into, became impossible to read. I got out and stood beside the car, smoking and pacing. After a while, I went into the roadside woods to pee, and when I came back, Tristan was approaching the car.

"We'll have to live off-site," he said. "There's no room on staff for you, and I can't exactly take you in as a roommate, with other staff members perpetually present. It's a smaller spot than Barrow House by a fair bit. They recommended a letting agent to me."

In the woods behind me, I suddenly heard ribbiting. It caught Tristan's attention too. "Frogs?" I asked. "Like the hostel name?"

"Nightjars," said Tristan. "I've heard this sound on a record of bird calls I found at one of the other hostels. Pretty unmistakable. And not at all common. They're a bashful bird."

The constant, sludgy drone went on. I couldn't tell where it was coming from. I looked up at the tops of the trees.

"You won't find them," said Tristan, with a touch of arrogance. "They don't want you seeing them, and they won't let it happen. Make do with the sound. It's special enough just hearing it."

WE RENTED A SMALL APARTMENT, ABOVE A RESTAURANT called Seven Sisters Café, in a town nearby called Seaford. We had two fireplaces, one in the living room and one in the bedroom, and luxuriously high ceilings. We found strips of a peach-coloured fabric in the apartment's attic and nailed them to the wall above the windows; there were no curtains, and this way we didn't have to buy any. On our first morning at the apartment, we discovered that, from one particular spot in the bedroom, the jutting white chalk cliffs that gave the café below us its name were visible out the window.

"How are there seven of them?" I asked. "Is each cliff a sister?"

"It's just a name," said Tristan, "and probably everybody recollects the origin differently. I'm sure the locals won't all have one straight story."

If we kept the window open, we could hear the ocean swirling in the distance. Tristan worked a split shift at Frog Firle every day, coming home for lunch and heading back to help with the dinner before a late return home. I spent one week looking for work and found some at a tobacco stand on the town's high street. I worked alone, in a little booth between a flower shop and a bakery. In the booth, I had about as much room to move as I had had at the Reine Elizabeth, making cocktails. I mostly sold cigarettes, but there was a little shelf of candies too. The owner told me on my first day that the markup for the candy was much greater than the markup for the cigarettes, and that I was expected to cajole every customer into buying something sweet. She gave me a tiny notebook and asked me to record every candy sale. The Terry's Chocolate Oranges had the best markup of all; for those, I could give myself two check marks. "If you're after more than a couple shifts a week," she said, "you would do well to fill the book with checks."

During my first shift, people didn't understand me when I told them how much to pay, because of my Canadian accent. I had to train myself to invert my voice at the end, saying, "Sixty pence?" instead of "Sixty pence." And almost nobody bought sweets. When the shift ended, I asked my boss for a key to the scissor gate in case I needed to leave the stand and use the bathroom during a shift.

"Shouldn't be necessary," she said. "You might want to get into the habit of taking your coffee in the evening, after the day."

"What if it's an emergency?" I asked.

"Ideally nothing like that will happen."

On the days I worked, Tristan stayed at Frog Firle with a packed lunch. Sometimes at the tobacco stand, I bought a few chocolate oranges myself, just to meet my quota. In no time, Tristan and I got tired of eating them. They were often all we had in the kitchen cupboard aside from a few condiments and sugar and tea.

On days I did not work, I cut coupons or cleaned, and usually I had the radio on. The music stations played the Beatles, the Who, Herman's Hermits. But I never listened to those stations for long. When music played, I only felt self-conscious; my activities, domestic and solitary, didn't merit any accompaniment like that. Instead, I preferred the news.

I thought of writing Étienne a letter. Unsurely and unendingly, my mind churned through potential language for the part of the letter where I would address my own situation.

I'm in England with Tristan
I'm in England with Tristan and it's very beautiful here
I'm in England and it's beautiful
I found work in England near a big cliff called the Seven Sisters
I'm in England selling cigarettes and chocolate oranges
I live in England for now and I sell chocolate oranges all day,
or at least I try
A little town called Seaford is home now
A little town called Seaford is where I'm staying, for the moment
Tristan works at a hostel and I

I couldn't settle on a phrasing I liked, so the letter remained unwritten. I nonetheless considered Étienne my closest friend beyond Tristan, and since I always felt like I was about to go and write the letter just as soon as I knew how to start it, Étienne did not feel so far away. Tristan, meanwhile, had quickly made friends at the hostel, as was his way. While I worked alone in my stand, he was part of a proper team at Frog Firle. They were all men, and they all got on with each other. He would come home smiling, reporting their stories. Sometimes he was light with booziness, having stayed for a drink after cleanup.

In the mornings, we usually looked out the window, at the chalk cliffs, while drinking our instant coffee. We talked about taking a walk over there and climbing up to the tops of the cliffs. Tristan had a co-worker who walked the whole cliff every morning. But he and I never seemed to find the time between our jobs and tasks, and when we really did have the time, we couldn't find the energy.

WINTER HIT QUICKLY AND IN EARNEST AT THE START OF December. It stayed dark later in the morning; we stopped looking at the chalk cliffs during our morning coffees, because they weren't there to look at. Only a purplish dark. By the time any sun came, Tristan had left for work in his Volkswagen. Customers on the high street remarked that they couldn't remember the last time snow lingered on the road for more than a day. They said this to each other, never really to me. Snow meant fewer customers, which meant fewer chocolate orange sales.

The high ceilings of the apartment made the place difficult to heat. Tristan and I wore our toques to bed, and in the mornings we saw our breath. Rather than making a new fire in the bedroom when it was time to go to sleep, we would keep it going in the living room, and then, at bedtime, Tristan would carry the fire into our bedroom fireplace, log by log, using a big metal shovel we had found in a closet. The carpet in the hallways had black marks in no time, from the soot and the sparks.

One evening, we pulled the Crisco container out from under the bed and found that the oil had frozen solid. First we laughed a little, then we scraped at the surface with our fingernails, dislodging little flecks, which we rubbed between our hands to melt and apply to Tristan's erection. In this drawn-out process, he went soft, and so did I. Eventually we put our pyjamas back on, and our toques. We slipped beneath our pile of blankets. Beneath these layers, we kissed indecisively, grasping loosely at each other's soft penises with greasy hands, until we both fell asleep.

Instead of a Christmas tree, Tristan got a poinsettia from the florist beside my stand, on one of his occasional evening walks. We couldn't justify buying gifts and decided that the poinsettia itself was like a gift, from the both of us to each other. Within a day, its leaves browned and began to fall off, and it wasn't absorbing any water. The short walk from the florist to the apartment had been enough cold to kill it. To Tristan, the plant's death was a supernatural omen. "This is nothing good," he said, making a stony face. He asked me to throw it out. "Street bin," he added, "not our bin." I took a deep breath, went outside, and did as he requested.

When I came back in, he had the tarot cards out on the table. I had noticed that he preferred to consult his cards when I was not around, but I was usually home whenever he was, and I supposed he had been holding out for a moment alone that just wasn't coming. I went and heated up our dinner of rice and beans.

While we ate, he told me a new idea that he had.

"Avon," he said. "Door-to-door cosmetics sales. For my evenings off. It's great fun, really. I did it when I first got to Cardiff and, you know, I made a *mint*. Women love when it's a boy. Imagine the impact of *two* boys."

"Did the cards tell you this?"

"They don't spell words out, like Scrabble tiles or something. They don't even have ideas. It's more like consulting a friend. I'm just looking for ways for us to stay afloat, pet."

"Sounds good," I said. I ate slowly; the rice and beans had no real flavour, aside from salt and pepper.

We drove around town on one of Tristan's nights off and didn't come home until we got rid of one hundred Avon catalogues. When we went around again to collect completed order forms the next evening, the total orders barely covered the cost of the gas we used up doing all the driving. Our final trip a week later, to deliver the products and collect the payments, was by far the quickest one. About half the customers who had placed orders didn't answer the door, even though we saw that their lights were on or we heard their televisions. They had changed their minds, they didn't want the products. This meant we had to send back almost all the little lotions and perfumes.

Sitting by the fire, leafing through the paperwork, I put it together that, if we counted gas and postage, we had actually *lost* money on this endeavour. Tristan asked what I found so funny, which was how I realized I had begun laughing.

"I was thinking about the emerald ring," I said. "When I sold it, I had no idea I'd be broke again so quickly."

He sighed and said nothing for a long time. "Living at the hostel would reduce every expense a great deal," he said.

I was shocked. "I didn't know you thought like that," I said. "In any case, that's not possible. I'm here too, and we can't live there together."

"I know," he said, suddenly very different, warm instead of cold. He kissed my forehead and headed for the door, saying he fancied a short walk.

The sea and the wind were loud that night. Even with the windows firmly closed I heard them. Tristan was gone much longer than usual, and the whole time the wind grew stronger. While packing up the cosmetics to send back to Avon, I sprayed the back of my hand with one of the perfumes. I had meant to take the smallest squirt, but it came out in a huge gush and covered the whole forearm of my sweater with a sickly citrus smell. Even after scrubbing the sweater, and the skin of my arm, the smell stuck around. The wind outside got louder. When Tristan finally returned, I was reading in bed.

"That couldn't have been a very nice walk," I said.

"I drove," he said. "Quick drink with the lads."

"Oh. I could have come."

"Once we figure out how that would work exactly," he said, "I'd love nothing more." He lay beside me, faced away.

THE NEXT DAY AT WORK, TRISTAN HEARD SOMEONE AT THE hostel mention that many of the trees at Friston Forest had lost their branches in the previous day's tumult. It was an old forest, full of standing dead trees. We drove there in the evening and filled the trunk with the damp wood. After this, we always pulled over when we saw loose wood on any hard shoulders. Having adopted this scavenger habit, we soon found a black crib that someone had left in a parking lot and took it for our woodpile. "Who paints a crib black?" I asked Tristan, because sometimes there were British customs I wasn't wise to. He shrugged. In the fireplace, instead of burning, the wood from the crib hissed and sparked, like charcoal. I figured it was just the paint, but it gave Tristan his stony, fearful look, just as the poinsettia had done. He asked me to take the crib out of the fire and all the way outside, far away from the door. He didn't even want to touch it himself—that was the strength of his superstition about this black crib that wouldn't burn.

"I will not," I said firmly, and then I laughed at the thought. "You're afraid of the silliest things. Ghosts, cribs, dead flowers."

"I'll do it," he said, in a hush, like there was no time for an argument, like the important thing was for the crib to go. He scooped it up with the shovel and went out, leaving the door open behind him, even though I knew he'd be gone for a while and that he wouldn't even come back up to return the shovel before going and joining work friends for a drink. I got up and closed the door myself, thinking of the shovel on the floor of his Volkswagen, so far away from its usual place.

When he came home, I pretended to be asleep in the lamp-light of the bedroom. I heard his snores begin and saw, in the corner of my eye, a mark on the carpet in the hallway, bright and white. A spill, I figured at first. When I looked again, I noticed that it was a square of moonlight, tiny and localized. It was coming from between the curtains, just for a moment, and landing on the ground very far from the door, all alone over there. I fell asleep feeling like the little square was company of some kind, in a dreamy nonsense way. I stirred again, later in the night, and looked to find it, but it was gone. The Earth had already moved too much for it to still exist.

20

On Christmas Eve day, Tristan told me to put one of his nice dress shirts on and to come in the car. "I want to take you somewhere," he said in a friendly voice. We drove in the direction of Frog Firle.

I knew already that the hostel was closed for a few days for the holidays. As we walked the cobbled steps to the front door, I got it in my head that a get-together was happening, a party with Tristan's co-workers. The idea of meeting new people and having some proper conversations with individuals aside from Tristan and tobacco-stand customers excited me. I felt especially excited to get to know the people Tristan knew so well already. When he opened the door, and I saw the hostel's interior for the first time, I saw also that no people were there. Instead, candles were laid out, which Tristan began to light, one by one. At one of the dining tables in the mess, there were little menus that he had typed up himself and had even run through a laminator.

"Romantic night away," he whispered proudly once the last of the candles had been lit. "Merry Christmas, pet."

Though I was wrong about the kind of evening it would be, I found this gesture very thoughtful. Tristan gave me a tour of all the rooms. It felt warm in there, warmer than home and warmer than the tobacco stand. We had a delicious dinner of rabbit stew, defrosted from the chest freezer, served with egg noodles. We paired the meal with a rich, dark port. After dinner, Tristan asked me to stand in a certain spot in the dining room, next to the table. "Colder than the rest of the room?" he asked slyly.

"Hard to tell," I said.

"It's something I noticed instantly one day," he said, "and soon after, I learned that this was the room where a maid died. Well, probably a maid, or maybe a guest—nobody's sure. You know the way stories shift around. Over one hundred years ago, during an important dinner. A poisoning. That's all the information that's survived."

I kissed him on the shoulder and conceded that the air could well have been colder in that spot. I found a bottle of applejack in a cabinet and made us cocktails, Jack Roses, using lemons from the stockroom and honey instead of grenadine. They tasted fine.

I looked out the window to find the moon and couldn't. "I don't want to go home," I said. "It's so *warm* here, so cold outside. Cold at home too."

Tristan considered this. Then he took a pack of bedclothes from the front desk cupboard and led me to the master bedroom, where we dressed the bed and cozied up. Tristan revealed that he had brought the Crisco tin, and seeing each other's nude bodies for the first time since the cold snap had begun, we made love.

In the night, we awoke to a strange sound, a constant reptilian drone coming from outside. I listened more closely; the sound was something we had heard before.

"The nightjars," whispered Tristan.

"Shouldn't they have migrated?" I asked.

"Yes," he said. "I suppose some of them simply don't."

We fell back asleep in the warmth of that room and slept easily through the endless growling. I even found it lullaby-like.

IN THE LATE MORNING, AS WE STAYED IN BED CUDDLING AND slowly awakening, we heard someone enter the foyer. Caught off guard, we pulled away from each other immediately. Tristan quietly told me to stay, got fully dressed, and went to see who it was. I could hear their conversation easily through the cracks and gaps of the door and the walls. It was one of the other attendants of Frog Firle, a work friend of Tristan's. He and Tristan expressed surprise at the sight of each other, in a friendly way.

"Thought I might set those mousetraps," said the man. "That and the kitchen inventory. Maybe the stockpile inventory as well."

"Some Christmas," said Tristan, in a voice that was unfamiliar to me, mannish and muted.

"I'd rather be here than home today," said the co-worker. "You know, I knew by the sight of the candles it was either you or Murphy. The bachelors. Nobody already married is laying it on this thick. You can consider that a warning," he laughed.

Tristan laughed along, and the laugh was unfamiliar too.

"Master bedroom?"

"Yeah," said Tristan.

"You just let her rest," said the man. "I'll stay out of your way when you get going."

Tristan came back to the room, holding my shoes. "We're a bit trapped," he said quietly, forcing a grin.

"You brought my shoes because they're men's shoes," I said. "You didn't want him seeing them."

Instantly Tristan put a hand out to quiet me down. "You *mustn't* speak loudly," he whispered. "Speak quietly, please."

We stayed in the room as Tristan's co-worker did his various tasks. Our stomachs were empty, and I had to pee, but Tristan insisted we wait for an opportune time to leave. Bored and frustrated, I took a book off the shelf, *Stranger in a Strange Land*. It was a book I had seen everywhere, in storefronts and in strangers' laps, first in Montreal and then in England. I read the first chapter. It was too thick to finish in one sitting, and I knew Tristan wouldn't like it if I took it from the hostel. I skimmed through the rest of it, just to know where the story went and how it ended. I came upon a passage that seemed familiar:

> *Mike doesn't have technique, but when Mike kisses you he isn't doing anything else. You're his whole universe, and the moment is eternal because he doesn't have any plans and isn't going anywhere. Just kissing you. It's overwhelming.*

"Read this part," I said, handing the book to Tristan.

He took it, and read it, and gave me a quizzical look.

"You wrote this in the letter you sent me," I said.

"I did?"

"I read it over and over. I remember this whole part. You didn't even really change it."

He read the passage again. "Everyone does that with letters."

"I didn't know *you* did that."

"Well, there you have it," he said.

I took the book from him and carried on skimming it, though now I couldn't process the words. "Why didn't you just correct him out there?" I asked, without looking up from the book. "Your co-worker. Say you have a man in here."

Tristan laughed incredulously and replied in a harsh whisper: "I want just *desperately* to know who it was that put you under the impression that life might be as easy as that for men like us."

"I don't know." If I could have yelled, I would have. "Men ask me that and I don't know what to say. Nobody put me under any impression. It's something I just arrived confident of."

"Well, that was stupid." He flashed me a look of childish contempt, then withdrew it and looked instead at the door. "I'm sorry but I'm not willing to lose my job." He laughed to himself. Several moments later, he laughed again, shaking his head. I put the book back on the shelf and said nothing.

By the sound of it, his co-worker was now in the stockroom in the basement. We shared a look about this, threw our shoes on, and made our getaway.

Outside, the sky was bright, and the mud was thick and crackled. Before getting in the car, Tristan and I both headed into the woods. We stood side by side, searing with our pee the crunchy bits of ice lying on the firm dirt. I studied the branches around us and spotted a nightjar, the same colour and texture as the tree bark behind her. I had looked them up in a book at the library in Seaford. She had a little fledgling by her side, its colour just a bit lighter. In fact, that was the only way I was able to spot them. By the lighter colouring of the fledging. The two birds stood, mother teaching child to hold still. They didn't even shiver. I wondered if she knew that she looked just like the tree, or if she only knew that holding still somehow resulted in fewer predators, fewer brushes with harm. Maybe she had no idea about what happened to the birds that moved in the daylight, the ones that failed to blend in with their surroundings, and she only knew the importance of stillness. Tristan didn't notice the two of them, and I didn't point them out to him.

XX

"Remember, everyone," yelled the man with polished nails from the back of the line, "not guilty, not guilty, not guilty." He repeated himself in French, then in English again. When we all passed by a window, I saw that the sky was bright, that it was morning.

The lineup stopped moving, and we were told by officers to wait against the wall of the hall. Along the opposite wall stood a long table with cotton swabs and boxes of plastic gloves. A very tall, solid man arrived, wearing a lab coat and holding a lit cigar between his teeth. Its smoke was thick and noxious. He put on one plastic glove and took the cigar into his ungloved hand. He approached my end of the lineup and said to the man beside me, the one with purple vomit stains on his shirt, "Drop your pants."

"What?" He didn't say this out of incredulity. He truly hadn't comprehended the request.

"Your pants," said the cigar man, giving the other man's belt buckle a small smack with the back of his gloved hand. "You need to take a test."

"What are you doing?" asked one of the men behind me. I saw that others were paying attention to what was happening, and they chimed in.

"You can't ask that of him."

"This is a violation."

A group of cops came close to those who were protesting. One yelled, "You can go back in the cell or you can leave here. If you want to leave, you need to receive a test for venereal disease. This is because of the nature of your crime."

"What crime? There is no crime!" shouted one of the men.

In his loudest voice, the cop reiterated, "Cell or test! You choose!"

I looked over to the man being asked to drop his pants; now he was crying, facing the wall. "It's okay," I said to him. I looked in the other direction, at the other prisoners. Like me they were stunned by what was being asked of him.

"Pants," said the cigar man, and right when I thought the crying man perhaps still had no understanding of what was going on, he reached for his belt and pulled down his suit pants, then his boxers as well. The cigar man reached between his legs and did something to make the man wince. At this some of the men yelled more.

This prompted the onlooking cops to yell back: "This is because of your crime!" "We have to do this, we have to!" One of the cops laid his hand on the gun in his holster.

I kept looking at the man's face, resisting any urge to look down at what was taking place. He looked back at me, or at least in my direction; his eyes had a glaze, as though he saw nothing at all.

"Just enjoy," said the cigar man. He pulled away his hand, which held a white cloth; he leaned back to face the cops who were further down the hall. "He's crying!" he called to them. He laughed and shook his head. "Makes no sense to me. Maybe you'll like *this* more." He grabbed the man's hips and spun him around, and gripped the man's penis. "Is this what you like?"

The man gave a greater wince than before, with an angry, throaty edge to it.

"Is he still crying?" the cigar man asked, his hands still in the man's crotch. I realized he was facing me; I was the one he was asking. "Give me a break," he said. He pulled his hands away and put the samples on the long table behind him.

Without receiving any instruction, the man pulled his pants back up. A different cop waved for him to head down another hall; he stumbled in that direction, with a new faint limp and a sense of hurry, also new.

"Now you," the cigar man said to me, without changing his glove for another one. I gave no thought to resisting his orders; to do so was as inconceivable as punching him in the face and running down the hall. I dropped my pants and briefs and faced the wall, and immediately felt a cold, dry finger press against my anus.

"Much better than the first guy," he said in an encouraging voice. "You must be the real deal. You fucking love this."

"Please," I said. I could hold back almost every word—*stop, don't, shut up, hurry*—but not the word *please*.

"Oh, you love this." He jammed his finger deeper, in a squirming, scraping motion. Then he pulled out quickly, and before he could touch my waist, I turned around willingly. He slid his cigar into his mouth, and took my penis in one hand, squeezing the tip to open the urethra. With the other hand, he shoved a cotton swab in. The pain was searing, like something inserted deeply into a fresh wound. I yelped, which prompted other men further down the line to once again protest. When the swab was removed, the pain remained there. He threw my samples onto the table behind him, next to the previous man's. There didn't seem to be a method of organization to the keeping of the samples; my name had not been requested. He moved on to the next man. I was evidently free to pull my pants back up and move on.

Down the hall, I found the first man sitting on a bench, outside of a double door. I took the spot beside him. I wanted to say something comforting to him, but I couldn't find the right words, and he was clearly in no mood to talk. In fact, when he looked over at me briefly, I saw in his face a sharp disdain. I wanted to ask if he hated me, but I didn't actually need to ask. I knew that he did. And, giving it more thought, I knew I hated him back, perhaps because of what I had seen him go through, and perhaps because he knew I had gone through it too. But the hate seemed to radiate further than that. Hate for him and for others like him, including myself. Hate for all the found-ins, drinking our beers, caught unawares in our vulnerable dark hovel, fated for abduction, starvation, and humiliation, and oblivious to that fate. I sat silent, wanting to do nothing but sleep—to disappear into a deep black state, away from this place, away from my body. But a sharp pain in the tip of my penis prevented me from entering any state of rest. Other men came in slowly, complaining to each other that the cops had gone too far. A lineup formed at a pay phone near the double doorway. I was not among the men who lined up, or the men who conferred with each other. Neither was the man sitting beside me.

When the double doors opened, one man was chosen by the cop there, seemingly randomly, and was brought in to see the judge. Some men pressed their ears to the door to hear the sentencing. "Not guilty," said one of them. "He is saying he is not guilty."

The doors opened again soon, and the man left without stopping to speak to any others. Then another man was brought through, and another. Some continued eavesdropping, while others like myself just sat with closed eyes.

Eventually one of the cops nudged my shoulder and said, "You go next."

I sat across from the judge, who was dressed in an ill-fitting suit and didn't look up from his paperwork as he spoke to me. He asked me if I understood the nature of the charges against me, and to describe the appearance of my wallet, which he fished out of a box by his feet.

"Sign your name here now," he said, shoving a form over to me.

"Not guilty," I said. "I want to plead not guilty." I didn't feel especially brave about the sudden decision; I would have pled guilty and simply paid a fine, if I had been able to turn my thoughts away from the men on the other side of the door, with their ears up against it. But I didn't want any of them to give me a dirty look as I walked out.

The judge sighed and gave me a different form to sign. "You must return in eight days," he said.

"Why?"

"Earlier you received a test, and for proper results you must receive this test a second time."

"The test?" A fast, strong wave of nausea moved through my body, and I again became aware of the pain in my penis.

"You have been charged for a crime. Venereal disease testing is part of your obligation."

"I don't want to take another test."

He kept his eyes on the paperwork, as though I had said nothing. Rather than repeating myself, I simply left.

In the lobby of the station, a window faced the street. I could see that, in front of the main entrance, in the bright daylight, a large group of men and women stood with signs and shirts featuring rainbows and slogans espousing the liberation movement. *Gay is* OK. *Pas de psycho. We will not hide our love away.* I did not want to exit that way and receive looks from this group—looks of pity, looks of love. I found myself frozen in place.

On the other side of the station, I saw Honoré. Noticing the crowd as I had, he'd tracked down a cop and asked something quickly, prompting the cop to point toward a side exit. Honoré headed that way quickly. He scanned the room and met my eyes. He did not nod or wave hello before turning away again. He hurried out the side entrance, away from the gays, away from the possibility of press photographers. As I stood frozen, I saw some men heading in that direction, while others went through the front door. Each of the latter men earned cheers from the growing crowd, and some even joined that crowd. My brain couldn't convince my body to move. It couldn't decide which door to pass through.

21

In early February, Tristan called home from the hostel with some news. "The higher-ups re-evaluated a bunch of the hostel locations," he said with a rush in his voice. "Guest count, seasonality, all that. Something to do with the annual budget. Anyway, Frog Firle is going down to a staff of one."

I was looking out the window. It was still morning, and I could see the chalk cliffs, off-white and unreflective. I felt relief at this news. If Tristan was losing his job, and I was barely earning anything with mine, then I had a legitimate excuse to take what little money I still had and buy a plane ticket back to Canada. The end of our life-sharing experiment could be blamed on circumstances instead of personal failings; giving up was now the reasonable approach.

"I'm so sorry to hear that," I said to Tristan. Then I heard him laugh.

"I'm not done, pet. They want *me* to stay here, as the sole occupant, at least for a time. And I can recruit unpaid volunteers all I like and give them room and board. It can be just us. You'll have a room of your own, we'll have some real privacy, *and* we won't have to fret about rent."

I knew I had to try to sound excited. "That's amazing," I said. Then I felt at least some of the excitement that I had just tried to convey. I decided that I was willing to give this a try. I felt proud of Tristan too for having received a promotion so quickly, at the job in which he took so much pride.

That night we filled the car and left our last week of rent money on the kitchen counter; the next morning, we drove to Frog Firle. I had a shift at the tobacco stand that day, but I didn't bother to let my boss know that I wouldn't be there for it, or that I was leaving town. Driving away from Seaford, I felt like we would never have a reason to visit it again. At the thought of never returning, I felt unburdened, just as I had felt as we drove away from the Lake District. I wondered if I'd feel this way about every place I ever left behind—if such a feeling was part of being an adult, part of being alive.

INDEED, EVERYTHING GOT EASIER, PRACTICALLY INSTANTLY. When we were hungry, we ate food from the mess. When we were cold, we brought wood in from the cords in the back. We worked split shifts, mornings and evenings. In our afternoons off, we napped in bright patches of sun. Though I had a small room that was ostensibly my own, I always slept in Tristan's room, right next to mine. If we weren't particularly tired, instead of napping we went for drives around East Sussex, just to see sights. Bodiam Castle, surrounded by a low, flat field that once had been its moat; the ruins of a priory in a charming town called Lewes; the chalk cliffs of Beachy Head, which were much higher and more dramatic than the Seven Sisters, and where we found a grave-like plaque that read:

MIGHTIER
THAN THE THUNDERS
OF MANY WATERS,
MIGHTIER
THAN THE WAVES
OF THE SEA,
THE LORD ON HIGH
IS MIGHTY!

PSALM 93:4

God is always greater
than all of our troubles.

"It's discouragement for the suicides," said Tristan, trying to light a cigarette for himself and failing because of the strength of the wind.

One afternoon Tristan mentioned an old television stored at the back of the basement. It had broken over a year before our arrival, and no one from the previous staff had known how to fix it. We lugged it up the stairs, and I removed the case to examine the inside. The tube was too loose. "You have to screw it in even further than what feels right," I said.

"You're a godsend," said Tristan, as the television played the opening sequence for *The Avengers*.

"Why would someone have loosened it in the first place?" I asked, and Tristan shrugged mysteriously. I knew he was attributing the issue to a presence, a ghost, a spirit. The dead maid or mistress, or whoever else. This was not the first time he'd done this. If we finished an afternoon of chores but then found one or two tasks not yet done—a curtain that hadn't been closed, a table that hadn't been cleared of crumbs—he would neither accept nor assign the blame. He'd shrug, as he just had, implying that the house had a will of its own.

Onscreen, Diana Rigg fired a gun to blast the top off a bottle of champagne. She and Patrick Macnee poured themselves coupes and raised a toast. Tristan and I mimed a toast too and drank from our imaginary glasses.

ALTHOUGH OUR OLD STATE OF MUTUAL KINDNESS WAS restored, something was nonetheless gone. When we napped, we didn't touch. It was too warm beneath the sheets, and touching would have been uncomfortable. When we watched a show called *Morecambe and Wise* on the television, all the sexual innuendo made us silent and still, and aware of the silence and stillness. We had stopped having sex and had not seen each other nude since Christmas Eve. On that night, Frog Firle had been a sneaky getaway spot—now it was just our home. Our ability to want each other had not withstood the turmoil of Seaford. It was like the poinsettia that had died; it didn't matter how quick the walk was, dead-cold air was dead-cold air. There were no hard feelings between us, but there was no affection either.

One afternoon, we drove to the city of Brighton, which had cafés and a boardwalk, and a bookstore that sold records too. I bought a hardcover that looked interesting. *World Without Stars.* Then Tristan and I sat down on the pebbly beach, looking at Brighton Palace Pier, a formidable structure suspended over the water on rickety-looking pillars. The pier made me think of all the buildings of Expo—unusual, and derelict, and hovering over water with a strong sense of belonging. I shared this thought with Tristan, but he wasn't listening closely.

"Sorry, pet," he said. "I need to talk to you about something important."

"Oh."

"The hostel association has found a married couple who can run Frog Firle permanently. It might have taken longer than this to find a solution, but it looks like they've figured it out quickly. And they've offered me a different spot, in Penzance. That's south-south-south. On the coast and very far from the nearest town."

Two dogs, with their walkers, encountered each other on the beach before us. They sniffed each other's rears, then moved along with purpose.

"Now, you and I could rent a spot off-site, like we did in Seaford, but you would have an even harder time finding work down there. And it wouldn't be too long before they send me to the next hostel, and the next. We've got it good right now. But this whole floater approach won't work with two. Not in the long term. We gave it the best go."

I nodded.

"I can say no to Penzance. We could find a way to make this work. But I like to be honest with you, and I'm going to be honest now. When they offered me Frog Firle, a hostel of my own, I felt a new joy. As though I were at the very start of something. And not just any something. The *biggest* thing: my whole life. My whole life in its most proper and welcoming and welcome form. I really want to keep this job. It feels good to want to keep something."

I nodded more; I understood without effort. But I found it easiest to be absolutely silent. I was still silent on the drive home, clutching my new book, and on the walk in. I went up to the room we shared and fell asleep moments after falling into the bed, napping for the rest of the afternoon. When I woke up, I felt refreshed. The clothes folded in the corner, the sun pouring into the room, my new book on the nightstand—everything felt like it was exactly where it should be, and heading in the best direction. I would be fine, and Tristan would be fine too, each man in his respective corner of the world.

THAT NIGHT WAS INCREDIBLY WINDY, ALTHOUGH THE FORE-casts had called for calm weather. Blowing through the woods outside the hostel, the wind sounded like a rampage of breath. I had gone to bed first and was curled up with my new book. I wasn't really reading. I was thinking about where I would fly to. When Frog Firle was handed off to its new managers, I could return to Canada or potentially go somewhere new. I could even visit Étienne in France if I wanted. I still didn't know quite how to characterize my time in England, to him or anyone, but the task of figuring out the right words no longer felt stressful. It was a story, like any story. I would just tell it, start to finish, to whomever asked.

I heard Tristan's steps coming up the staircase. He had given the main floor the once-over, as the last man to bed always did, making sure the entrance doors had been locked and the common-area windows fully shut. He came into the bedroom slowly, with a stonier look than I had ever seen on his face. He said, "Put your clothes on. I need you to come downstairs now. There's a ghost; I need your help."

I had an impulse not to indulge him with something like this. But I wanted to keep up the kindness we had been practising with each other in the past weeks. Instead of telling him he was being ridiculous, I got out of bed and dressed. We had not held hands for a long time, but as we headed down the stairs, he squeezed my hand tight. I imagined the ghost would be nothing but a sharp change in temperature somewhere, attributable to an open window, or maybe a white coat on a coat rack, left by one of the guests, seen through the half-dark of the evening. But once we entered the lobby, I saw a real figure.

It was an old woman. Her white face was overtaken by wrinkles and, in that way, almost featureless. She had white hair in an old-fashioned bob, and her nightgown was the same shade of white. The legs beneath the gown had blue veins showing along the bare white skin. She hadn't registered our arrival. She was instead surveying her surroundings with a frightened expression.

When we stopped walking, Tristan's hand clenched mine harder than ever. We stood beside each other; we kept our hands held.

"Hello," I said.

The woman turned to me slowly, as though moving through water. I told her my name and asked for hers. She didn't answer.

"Are you staying here? Are you lost?"

She didn't answer my questions. She just looked past us, through us, with a concerned look on her face.

"Did you come through there?" I pointed at the front door. I had been at the reception desk all afternoon, and I could remember every guest I had checked in; she wasn't one of them.

With a small, shaky voice, she eventually spoke: "I don't know where I am."

She started crying. Her tears were white too, like watery milk. I didn't know what to do next. We couldn't go back upstairs with her standing there in the lobby, but I didn't know where to direct her, or how to make her go away.

"Come this way," I said, and led her to one of the empty guest rooms. I grabbed a pack of bedclothes. Tristan seemed less frightened now that he knew someone else could see her too. He helped me make the bed.

"Where am I?" she asked.

"Frog Firle," Tristan said. "A hostel in East Sussex. Are you from around here? Are you from East Sussex?"

"Sussex," she said, still looking very worried. Her eyes continued to tear up, and she began to whimper. The lamplight of the bedroom was much brighter than the lamplight of the lobby; the intricate lace of her nightgown showed now, and the light seemed to break through her skin. Much like her tears, her skin was translucent, not to such an extent that I could see the things behind her, but enough so that my gut told me not to touch her, as any man's gut will tell him on the matter of delicate things. A hand, I figured, might pass through her.

Once we had finished making the bed, Tristan asked her more innocuous questions, and she continued not to know the answers.

"I'm tired," said the woman, unprompted.

"Are you?" I asked. "We've made this nice bed for you. Will you sleep here?"

"Yes, I will," she said.

"Well, that's perfect." I slipped the pillows into their cases, feeling certain she was not going to harm us. She was a lost thing, free of intention or motive, desperate for answers and comfort.

I felt certain that Tristan had been right. We had a ghost in the hostel, undoing chores, opening doors, and now sitting on the bed in front of us. I had made a bed for a ghost: this was the easiest explanation, the only explanation.

I wondered how the bed would look in the morning. Would she still be in it? Perhaps just her gown, or perhaps the bed would be perfectly made, as though nobody had been in it at all. In fact, the bedding might be back on the top of the pile of packs, folded and crisp. Tristan and I would then understand that the ghost, or some greater operator, was rewriting things now, passing off this brief interaction as a dream. And we would have no evidence, no way of convincing others of what had happened. But we wouldn't have the will to try to convince anyone. Nor the need. It would be a private knowledge, ours to hold dear. Just as the ghost's existence and harmlessness had become clear, another thing had also been clarified: that Tristan and I needed to stay in each other's lives. We needed to be there for each other, not only to discuss the ghost, but to discuss the world and its verified inconceivability. Tristan hadn't needed the proof, but I had, and now we had an incredible truth to covet together, for the rest of our lives.

Then something happened that made me more frightened than I had perhaps ever been. The ghost began to scream, emitting a sound both intense and distant, as though it was made from the air inside her skull as well as the air outside the room. It got louder and louder. Her lips weren't moving. Her screeching wasn't coming from her throat the way a living human's would. As it intensified, I looked at Tristan, who now was shaking with terror. Thinking he might have a fit, I came close to him and covered his body with my arms, so he wouldn't fall to the ground. I pressed my face right to his. I went *"Shh,"* not knowing what else to do. "*Shh, shh.*" This was the end, or some kind of end. In that very brief moment, I told myself that it was good that Tristan and I were together for it.

The bedroom door, half-closed behind the old woman's back, flew open all the way. On the other side of the door stood a sweaty-faced woman wearing pyjamas. She was winded, breathing heavily; she was mortal, human, normal. I recognized her face. I had checked her in that afternoon. The screaming hadn't been coming from the ghost, but from her, on the other side of the door. I realized it was a word she had been screaming: *Mum*. She had been running through the halls, shouting, *Mum, Mum, Mum*. She was looking for her mother, and now she had found her. Everything suddenly gained the promise of explanation; everything that happened in the world was plausible after all.

The woman took her mother into her arms and sat beside her on the half-made bed. She explained that she had brought her mother there during the afternoon, while Tristan and I were away. She had tucked her mother into bed without indicating the extra guest. She'd hoped to avoid paying more, though she would pay it now, with emphatic apologies. Her mother had opened the unlocked bedroom door, possibly thinking it led to the bathroom. Then she forgot where she was and which room she had come from.

"She won't be getting any more trips," she said. "Not even one-nighters like this. I'm sorry, boys. I've been kidding myself." Then she walked her mother back to bed.

The terror had left a metallic-feeling residue in my bloodstream. Now I could feel my body flushing it away.

Tristan and I headed back up. As we slid into our bed, we discussed with some humour how we had both been convinced that something supernatural had happened. "Anyone can become a believer," joked Tristan, patting my knee.

As easy as it was to laugh, an incredible exhaustion overtook us. I turned out the lamp and we shimmied toward each other, and held each other before sleep, for the first time in months. Tristan was stiff and clammy, but when I pulled myself away, he asked me quietly not to go. Eventually he fell asleep, and then I did, very deeply. We woke up in the morning with our bodies apart.

X X

ooking through the police station window, I suddenly
remembered Dorothy, my dog, alone in my apartment. My
concern for her—and my guilt at forgetting about her—felt
more pressing than the question of one door or another. The
front door was closer. I rushed through it. The bright of the sun
made me squint, but I soon caught sight of John in the crowd of
protesters. Over his jumpsuit, he wore a jean jacket that was too
big for him.

"John," I called, and he waved me over, opening his arms to
hug me. As we embraced, strangers patted my back and shared
platitudes in English and French: "Welcome," "It's over," "You're
safe now," "I'm sorry for what you have faced."

John put both his hands on my shoulders and echoed the
strangers around us: "Stay with us." Above our heads, clouds
formed quickly, already taking the daylight away.

I spent a long time looking into his eyes. "I wanted you all
night," I said, and he laughed. Others around us laughed too, but
I hadn't meant it in a funny way, nor for that matter in a sexual
way. What I meant was that I had thought of him throughout
the ordeal, and that his absence from my cell had worried me.

But it also kept me occupied, sometimes at least, and for that I felt gratitude toward him.

"I was in a holding room," he said, his hand still on my shoulders. "They ran out of space in the main cell, by the time my paddy wagon had arrived. They had no idea what they were doing, and we're going to fight back and win."

I put my hands over John's, with my arms forming an X across my chest, and I pressed his hands down into the bones of my shoulders. John, already smiling, smiled more broadly.

"Safe," he said. He kissed my ear. "You found me and you're safe."

"I found you, and I'm safe."

"Stay."

I remembered more about him, now that he was a person and not a ghost. That he liked movies, especially *Star Wars* and *James Bond*. That he liked cold water over his head, in a hot place, and that he lived in Ottawa.

"Don't you have to go home?" I asked.

"I'm staying here," he said proudly. "At least for a while."

"What about your job?"

"Oh, come on. If I lose it, I'll get another one."

I realized I hadn't given my own job a single thought the whole night.

"This is what matters," he said. "Stay with us here."

Others overheard his suggestion and nodded at me encouragingly. "We hope you'll join us," said a man I recognized from the cell, the one with chipped nail polish on his fingers.

Near him, a different man handed out sheets of white cardboard and Sharpie markers. "We need more signs made," he said.

John's face lit up as he took the cardboard and marker. "What should I write?" he asked me.

I didn't know what to say.

"Don't write *Gay is not evil*," said someone behind me. "I'm writing that."

"*Gay is ok*," said John.

"No!" yelled someone else. "Mine says that already. *Gay is ok*."

"What else is there?" asked John.

"*Gay is great*," said the nail polish man. At this everyone laughed, including me. It was a ridiculous sentiment. None of us, I thought, would make such a claim in earnest. But then I thought differently, when I noticed that the nail polish man was not laughing. John uncapped his Sharpie and placed the lid in his mouth. He put his hands on my hips and turned me around gently, then pressed the cardboard against my back and wrote. "Gay is great!" he shouted when he finished, holding the sign up high. The men around us laughed and began to chant these words. *Gay is great*.

I chanted too, but not for long. "I have to go," I said quietly to John. "My dog."

He gasped, said, "That poor little dachshund," and hugged me again. Then he gave me a long, passionate kiss on the lips. The men around us cheered. I thought quickly of his body wearing only a towel, in the heat of the sauna the previous evening. It was unclear whether he was kissing me out of affection or making a statement on the steps of the station, kissing a man who could have been any. It made my penis stiffen a little, which increased my awareness of the stinging soreness at the tip of it. When we pulled away from each other, the *Gay is great* chants picked back up.

"There's going to be an enormous crowd today," he said. "I just know it. We have a lot of people in our corner. We're going to fight, and we're going to win."

I thought about how young he was, and I knew it would upset him to say so. Looking properly into his face—shiny from sweat and dark-eyed from no rest, same as mine—I knew he would not go back to Ottawa, not even for his things. He lived in Montreal now; this city was his home. Without confirming whether I'd return, I said goodbye to him, parted from the crowd, and headed to the Metro station.

On the ride home, it was difficult not to fall asleep. I feared I'd miss my stop. Staying awake would have been easier if I'd had my book, which might still have rested open-faced on the floor of the bar. I thought about heading to Truxx later that day, to collect the book or at least ask if they still had it. *The Death of the Heart*. French title: *Broken Hearts*. Étienne and I had recommended many books to each other, in the letters we wrote. This was not his first time getting the English title wrong—not the first time that a book had very different titles in the two languages. In my next letter to Étienne, I would ask if he knew why some books had this characteristic and others didn't.

At the thought of writing to him, I felt a heavy dread. I would have to mention the previous night; he was the person with whom I shared the most private details of my life, and this event was such a detail now. But I didn't want to write any of it down. Heading up the stairs of my Metro stop, I preferred the idea of relating to Étienne any other moment, perhaps even *this* moment, an innocuous scrap of a day in my life. Passing me by, commuters wiped rain off their shoulders—a woman in a plastic jacket longer than her skirt, a man closing an umbrella, whom I recognized as my favourite clerk from the depanneur closest to my home. He recognized me back, and I saw concern in his face. I knew that I looked awful, and that I needed sleep.

When I exited the station, rain was falling heavily. I wanted to tell Étienne this too: that sometimes the rain surprised you, and it was unpleasant, but you accepted the unpleasantness because the sense of surprise was so novel. Jogging to my home, I caught a glimpse of Mount Royal between tall buildings. I knew it was just a gigantic landform, framed by pieces of construction, but my mind was all jumbled, and it received the image as a free-floating rectangle, with clean-cut sides and a top that was frayed and slanting. The rectangle was green, yellow, orange, and red. I would describe it to Étienne. Perhaps my next letter would be very short, conveying just the one thought.

I stopped for traffic at the intersection where John and I had stood when he took my hand. The bathhouse we had come from was a few streets away, though it felt like it belonged in a different city, or some less important world. Nothing was more important than where I was and what I was doing right now. I got to my building and ran up the stairs to my unit. When I opened the door, I immediately registered the smells of excrement and pee. Dorothy, who had been curled up a few feet in front of the door, sprang over and jumped up my legs, barking and squirming. She took brief breaks to run in little circles before resuming with her greeting. When I crouched down, she licked the rainwater off my face and neck; I laughed really hard, which made her even more excited.

I saw the pile of shoes that she, nervous and lonely, had built in the hallway. She could never understand where I had been or why I had been gone for so long. Still laughing, I began to cry as well, and Dorothy eagerly licked the tears off my face. I thanked her, again and again. It was all I could think to say.

"Hey, girl. Thank you. Thank you. It's okay. It's okay."

Outside my window, the intense rain had stopped already; over Mount Royal, a thick and unmistakable rainbow had appeared. It made me think of the men outside the police station, and the rainbows on their signs and shirts. I imagined all of them seeing it too and taking it as a sign. I encouraged Dorothy to look at it—"Up there, girl, look, up there"—and I kept doing this even after I remembered that dogs could not see colour. To her eyes, it would have appeared only as a soft grey bar in the sky.

"Can you see? Hey. It's okay, girl. Look there. It's okay. Settle down. It's okay."

ACKNOWLEDGEMENTS

GRANTS FROM THE CANADA COUNCIL FOR THE ARTS AND Ontario Arts Council supported the writing of this book. Earlier versions of some excerpts initially appeared in the *Ex-Puritan* and *Open Book*.

For providing first-hand details about the Truxx raid and sur-rounding events, thank you to Paul Keenan, Jeff Richstone, Mark Wilson. The documentary *Truxx* (1978, dir. Harry Sutherland) was also extremely helpful. Thank you to Glenn Nuotio and Thomas Waugh for helping me to track it down. Thank you to Ross Higgins, whose thesis *A Sense of Belonging: Pre-liberation Space, Symbolics, and Leadership in Gay Montreal* (1997, McGill University Department of Anthropology) was another valuable resource. Thank you to the organizers of the Habitat 67 guided tours. For different forms of insight, thank you to Thomas Dearnley-Davison, Rita Donovan, Geneviève Lajeunesse, and Guillaume Morissette. Thank you to my amazing agent, Marilyn Biderman, and Meg Storey, a brilliant editor. Thank you to Jay and Hazel and the whole Book*hug team. Thank you to poets. Some in particular: John, Jenny, David, Brecken, Katherine, Catriona, and my In/Words family. Thank you to Stephanie and Illya. Thank you to Melody Tacit. Last thanks to Scott.

BEN LADOUCEUR is the author of *Otter*, winner of the Gerald Lampert Memorial Prize, finalist for a Lambda Literary Award, and a *National Post* best book of the year, and *Mad Long Emotion*, winner of the Archibald Lampman Award. He is a recipient of the Writers' Trust of Canada's Dayne Ogilvie Prize for LGBTQ2S+ Emerging Writers and the National Magazine Award for Poetry. His short fiction has been featured in the *Journey Prize Stories* anthology and awarded the Thomas Morton Prize. He lives in Ottawa.

COLOPHON

Manufactured as the first edition of
I Remember Lights
by Book*hug Press in the spring of 2025

Edited for the press by Meg Storey
Copy-edited by Stuart Ross
Proofread by Laurie Siblock
Type + design by Ingrid Paulson
Cover images (l to r): Laurent Bélanger, Expo67: Pavilions of
Ontario, Canada, Western Provinces, seen from the pavilion of
France, CC-BY-SA-3.0; CA2MI, Expo67: USA Pavilion, geodesic
sphere design by Buckminster Fuller, with minirail running through it,
CC BY-SA 4.0; photo of man: ©iStockPhoto.com/Vladimir Melnik

Printed in Canada

bookhugpress.ca